W̶ ̶ ̶ ̶ ̶ ̶ the Ivy Grows

S.Quinn & J.Lerman

S.Quinn
UK

Copyright © by S.Quinn

All rights reserved. No part of this publication may be reproduced, stored in a retrieval system, or transmitted in any form or by any means, electronic, mechanical, photocopying, recording or otherwise, without prior permission of the author.

First Edition 2012

Designed by: The Ghostwriting Company
Manufactured in the UK.

For my readers

1

I hear a voice.

'No. NO! Not this time.'

It's Marc. Shouting.

My eyes flick open, and I feel Marc's arms tighten around me. We're in bed, facing each other, my naked body pressed against his bare chest. It's dawn, and I see pink light glowing through the bedroom window.

Marc's eyes are screwed tightly shut, and he looks in pain.

'Marc?' I say.

'Get away from her!' he shouts, and his arms grip me tighter.

I stare at Marc's closed eyelids as they flicker over his beautiful blue eyes.

Marc's pale face glows in the breaking dawn. He's suffering, and I can't stand it.

'What's wrong?' I whisper. 'Marc? Are you okay?'

Marc bolts upright, pulling me up with him. He looks bewildered. Confused – a little boy on the verge of tears.

I stroke hair from his forehead. 'Are you having a bad dream?'

He opens his mouth and closes it again, then pulls me against his chest.

'It was nothing,' he murmurs, but his voice is tense. 'Just ... a dream about something that happened a long time ago. I'm sorry I woke you.'

'It's okay.' I slip my arms around his neck. 'The sun's coming up. I would have been awake in a few minutes anyway.'

Marc lowers me onto the bed, and I see his chest is

moving quickly, the little white scars on his skin stretching with every breath. I put my palm to his heart. His skin feels too hot.

'Your dream ... it sounded bad.'

'It's over now.' He falls beside me onto the pillow and runs a finger over my lips. Then he kisses me.

I'm about to speak – to ask him more about his dream. But he kisses me harder, and I'm lost in a world of senses. His smell, his mouth, his tongue.

He pulls back and his hands find mine. He looks down at our touching fingers.

'Do you remember last night?' I ask.

A smile pulls at Marc's lips. 'You think I'd forget?'

'Maybe.'

'As if I would.'

'It made me happy. To see you ... lose yourself in me.'

Marc's smile spreads, until I see his beautiful white teeth. 'Oh, did it indeed?' He wraps his arms around me, and I feel his large hands slide around my back.

'It did.' I smile into his chest. 'Very, very happy.'

'Well. I aim to please, Miss Rose.' His brown hair is flopping messily over his forehead, and he looks puppy dog cute, with brown stubble creeping over his jaw line.

'Was it ... special for you?' I ask.

Marc strokes my long hair behind my ears. I know it's gone all frizzy in my sleep and wish I had a mirror. Actually, I don't. If I can't see it, I can pretend it's all smooth and shiny like Lucy Liu.

He picks up my hand and places my fingers to his lips, running them back and forth.

'Special isn't a good enough word.'

I feel myself grinning. 'What is a good enough word?'

Marc shrugs and rolls back so he's looking at the ceiling. 'Language was never my strong suit. I prefer action.'

I prop myself up on my elbow and watch his profile. It's so perfect. He's a different sort of good looking from every angle. From the side, with a little brown fuzz on his cheeks and messed up hair over his forehead, he looks like a boy band member. But as he turns to face me, I can see his full jaw, and he looks sharp and powerfully and *oooh.*

'Action?' I challenge, the grin practically reaching my ears.

He pulls me on top of him, and my hair falls forward over my shoulders onto his chest. I can feel he's hard against my stomach and find myself taking in a deep breath. His size still takes me by surprise.

'Actions speak louder than words.' Marc runs his hands down to my backside, and then lifts me onto him – all of him.

I feel his hardness and size between my legs. He's not inside me yet, but he's placed me exactly in the right spot so he's pushing against me, letting me know he can slip in at any moment.

He holds me like that, teasing me. But I have no patience where Marc is concerned, especially not today. I move my hips so I'm at the right angle to slip him inside, and try to ease myself down.

But Marc won't let me. He holds my hips tight.

'So eager, Miss Rose. Anticipation can be pleasurable too.'

I glare at him. He knows this is torture. 'For you, maybe.'

We watch each other, and he looks totally relaxed. In control. I think back to last night and hope, *hope* it wasn't a one off.

That it's the start of more closeness between us.

I want to have an effect on him. And damn it, I will.

I slide my hand between his legs, gently feeling and massaging.

He sucks in his breath, then lets it out. 'Are you trying to test me, Miss Rose?'

I nod, pleased to feel his hands loosen a little on my hips. This is my chance. I peel his hands away and ease myself down.

I let out a long moan as he sinks deeper and deeper in me, and to my delight, a faint *'Christ'* tumbles from Marc's lips.

I look into his eyes, knowing my own have gone all soft and wanton. Having him inside me like this, filling me up, feels so, so good.

His eyes have gone a little out of focus, and I see him swallow.

'You did say actions are better than words.' The words stumble out of my mouth as the rest of him slides inside me. It's becoming hard to speak.

'I did, didn't I?' Marc raises a devilish eyebrow. He's definitely back in control, now.

'Yes,' I murmur, feeling my thighs touch his hips.

I hear something outside – raised voices – and tense up. The voices are a long way away. Perhaps outside the college gates. But something about them doesn't feel right.

2

'What was that?'

'Photographers, probably,' Marc answers.

I stare at him. 'You're kidding.'

Marc shakes his head. 'No. I knew they'd be here this morning.'

'But how did they know *you'd* be here?'

Marc laughs then. 'They don't. They're here for you.'

'For me?'

'Sophia, if you're serious about us being together, this is what life will be like. Photographers are going to be camped out, wanting their piece of you. I hate it, but that's what you're signing up for. You can still change your mind.'

'No.' I shake my head. 'I know what I want.'

The voices get a little louder, and I feel sickness in my stomach. 'I'm scared, though. Did you ever get scared? In the early days?'

Marc puts his arms around me and pulls me to his chest. I feel him move inside me.

'Ooh!'

He puts his nose against my neck and inhales.

'God, you smell good. I never used to be scared. But I'm scared now.'

I pull myself up, feeling him rearrange inside me again, and look at him. 'You are?'

'Of course I am. I have something to lose now.' He takes a piece of my hair and winds it around his hand, letting it slip over his palm. 'I'm scared of losing you.'

I frown. 'Of losing me?'

Marc lets my hair slide free and runs his fingers back

and forth over my hips. 'My world isn't the real world, Sophia. And I think once you realise that, you might want your old life back. I wouldn't blame you. And then, of course, there's me. Once you find out more about me, you might run a mile.'

'I won't,' I say, shaking my head. 'Last night was the start of us. The real start of us. And now I have you, I won't give you up.'

'Oh, *really*?' Marc grins, then rolls me onto the bed so he's on top of me. I suck in my breath.

'You won't give me up?' He's still inside me, and I feel a pleasant ache as my body rearranges itself around him.

'I couldn't if I wanted to. You're like an addiction. A bad habit.'

'A bad habit?'

We're both smiling now.

'A *very* bad habit.'

'You can't say you weren't warned.' Marc's grip tightens around my backside. 'But now there's nowhere to run. I have you exactly where I want you.'

'I wouldn't want to be anywhere else.'

A look of sadness flashes in his eyes. 'Be careful what you wish for.'

I lift my head. 'Meaning?'

'Meaning ... there might be sides to me that you won't like.'

'I'm pretty sure I've already seen those.'

'No.' Marc shakes his head. 'There's more.'

'More?' I keep my tone light, trying not to let whatever dark thoughts are troubling Marc to overtake him. 'Marc, we all have things in us that we don't want others to see. But intimacy, a relationship – that means sharing everything. Light and dark. I have my dark sides, too.'

I think of how jealous I feel sometimes. And how

insecure I am about why Marc wants to be with me.

'Oh, I've seen your dark side, Miss Rose.' The smile is back on Marc's face, and I'm relieved.

'Oh, *really*? And what exactly have you seen, Mr Blackwell?'

'You're far too trusting,' says Marc.

'I'd hardly call that a dark side.'

He begins to move back and forth, slowly but with a firmness that takes my breath away.

'*Oh*,' I murmur as he moves faster.

He picks my legs up and wraps them around his back, moving hard and fast now.

After last night, we feel different together. Still hot. Still sexy. But ... closer. His body feels meshed with mine. A part of me.

I take his face in my hands and look right into his clear blue eyes.

'Will you come again?' I whisper, feeling him thrust deeper and deeper. Pleasure begins to build up. 'Oh *God*, Marc... will you?'

'Not yet,' he says, his eyes closing. 'Not until you do.'

He lets out a long breath, and his hands grip my backside, then he pulls himself inside me, deeper, deeper, deeper.

The pleasure is so intense, it's almost painful. I writhe under him, pinned down by his weight. He's not letting me move, not letting me get away from the pleasure. He nearly has me, all of me, and he knows it. A few more thrusts and I'll be his. But I don't want to do this alone. I want him to be with me, all the way. Just like last night.

'Wait,' I breathe. 'I don't want to do this yet. Not without you.'

He rolls onto his back, taking me with him.

'Let me see you,' he says and lifts me away from his chest.

'Oh God, Marc,' I murmur, moving back and forth. I can't help myself. I can't think straight. I can't stop myself moving. 'Marc. Oh Marc.' I feel waves of warmth moving up my legs. They hit my stomach all at once, and I fall forward onto his chest.

Marc's hands tighten on my hips, not letting me escape as warmth spreads over my whole body.

'Oh,' I moan, feeling pleasure everywhere. But it comes with a sadness. He didn't come. Have I lost him again?

'Marc -'

He silences me by pressing his lips against mine, then rocking me back and forth. Once, twice, three times and then ...

He groans and his eyes tighten, teeth gripped together. Every part of his body relaxes, and he sinks down into the bed, his eyes half closed.

'Did you ...?' I ask.

Marc nods, gently.

I bury myself in his chest, snuggling against him, feeling his scars and his chest hair, smiling as I feel his arms come around me.

'I love you,' Marc whispers. 'Ready to face the world?'

3

I'd been trying not to think about what's waiting for us outside the college.

Wrapped up in Marc's arms, cocooned in my bedroom, we're safe. But out there ... I know paparazzi will be waiting for us. Waiting for me, more precisely.

They're going to get quite the story this morning. A Marc Blackwell bonus.

I think about the picture they took of Marc and me at my dad's house. God knows what story they'll tell with it in the morning papers. Innocent girl seduced by wicked older man? Or slutty student seduces her Hollywood hunk teacher?

'Are you sure you're ready for this?' Marc asks, serious now. I was enjoying his playful side and wish, *wish* we could just be a normal couple. But ... we're not. Not in any way.

'Nearly.' I'm enjoying my cheek against his warm chest and want a few more minutes of him – his bare skin, his beautiful smell and his strong arms.

We lay like that for a moment, until I force myself to move.

'Let's do it,' I say, tearing myself away from him.

'You're sure? Because Sophia, I could get out of here without being seen. You can still call this off. I didn't want any of this for you. Believe me. I still don't.'

'But I want you,' I say. 'And all this comes with you. It's part of you.'

Marc props himself on his elbow, and I get a nice view of his long, toned arm. 'Let's have breakfast, then go give them their pictures.'

I shake my head. 'I'm too nervous to eat.'

'You should eat something.'

'Honestly, I couldn't. I just want to get this over with.'

Marc sighs. 'Fine. If you insist.'

I slip away from him and go to my wardrobe. I put on clean underwear, and my hand hovers over a navy trouser suit Jen made me buy for auditions. I should look smart. Capable. Adult. Not too young.

I feel Marc behind me, and he reaches over my shoulder to pluck out my favourite pair of skinny jeans.

'Wear what's you,' he says. 'Be yourself today. They should know who you really are. They'll love the real you, just like I do.'

I turn to him and look up into his blue eyes, so clear and light today, like diamonds reflecting the sky. 'Marc. Why do you love me? I mean ... that's what they'll all be thinking, won't they? Why would someone like you fall in love with someone like me?'

He smiles, and my heart melts. 'Because you're you.'

'Meaning?'

'You don't see it, do you?'

'See what?'

'What it is that makes people love you.'

'People don't love me,' I laugh. 'At least, no more than anyone else. I don't see what makes *you* love me. I'm just ordinary. Just an ordinary girl from an ordinary place.'

'You're certainly *not* ordinary,' says Marc. 'I've never met anyone like you in my life. If you'd been anyone else, this situation would never have happened.' He sighs. 'Christ, what a mess.'

I feel a pain in my chest. 'A mess? Is that how you see us?'

Marc lifts his head, and I see pain in his eyes. 'Not you. Me.'

'You're not a mess. You're perfect.'

Marc laughs. 'And that's why I love you, Sophia. Because everything to you is good.' He puts his arms around me. 'Get dressed, now. Your public is waiting.'

4

We walk out of the accommodation tower, hand-in-hand, dazzled by the bright sunlight. I'm wearing my most comfortable clothes – a black sweater that I've had since forever, jeans and Converse. The real me.

Of course, I'm also wearing the navy cashmere coat Marc bought me that fits like a glove and gives me a far better figure than I have. A little bit of Marc can't hurt today.

Marc is wearing what he wore last night – a black t-shirt, cargo pants and grey trainers. He's showered, and his hair is a little damp.

No coat, of course. Typical Marc. He's not noticing the cold at all, and it certainly *is* cold today. He looks every bit the action hero, and I marvel at the fact this man, this handsome Hollywood actor, is holding my hand. We're together. It feels crazy to even think those words. But they're true.

The grounds are quiet and empty, and there's a feeling of total stillness as we crunch along the gravel path. I guess it must come from all those sleeping students, metres away from us in their warm beds. Lucky them. All they have to worry about is breakfast and today's lectures.

It's a beautiful, cold crisp day, and the icy white blue sky reminds me of the day Marc found me in the woods. A sliver of fuzzy sun shines above us, but it's definitely autumn now. Almost winter. The air is cold and mist is coming from our mouths.

What will become of my life at college once we tell the world?

'Marc.' I squeeze his hand and pull him to a stop.

'What will happen, once we tell everyone? Will I ever come back here?'

Marc smiles. 'Of course you will. It's all arranged.'

'What ... how?'

Marc takes both my hands in his. 'I planned everything.' He raises an eyebrow. 'In the highly unlikely event that you'd decide to throw away your privacy and your safety to be with a man like me.'

I smile. 'You must have known what an easy choice it would be for me.' I raise an eyebrow back.

'I have other plans in place, too.'

'Other plans?'

'In case you change your mind.'

'Change my mind?' I swallow. Does he not have any clue how I feel about him? 'I won't change my mind.'

Marc shakes his head and his brow furrows. 'Don't speak too soon.'

'Marc, I -'

Marc squeezes my hands. 'I won't be teaching you anymore. At least, not in the classroom.'

'No, Marc. You promised. You can't leave. The other students -'

'Sophia. You should know by now, I would never break a promise to you. I'll still be teaching the other students. But you and I will have private tuition. You won't be attending my classes anymore. I don't think it would be appropriate, do you?'

I think about that. It seems like an ideal solution, so ... what's my problem?

I suck in a breath. 'Things like this, can we talk them over first?'

'You don't like what I've planned?'

'I don't like not being *asked*.'

Marc pulls me too his chest, and black cotton rubs my cheek.

'Oh, Sophia, Sophia. I promise I will do my very best to stop being a controlling monster. For you, anything is possible.' His tone is light, but I can tell he's serious.

'It's okay,' I whisper, taking his hands.

'Come on.' He squeezes my fingers. 'I want to find out what's waiting out there. The sooner I know what we're dealing with, the better.'

We hold hands, walking along the path. As we turn a corner, I see the college gates up ahead, and my heart catches in my throat.

There, behind the wrought-iron, is a black swarm of photographers, jostling and fighting each other to get close to the bars.

Some have climbed up the gates and are pushing their cameras over the metal spikes. Others are pushing against the black railings, their jackets squashed, arms and legs spilling through.

Oh my god.

There's a flash. Then another. Then dozens, snap, snap, snap, like a pan of popcorn.

I put my hand to my eyes.

'Marc -'

'Stay close to me.' His voice is cold. Angry. 'We have good security here. They won't get over the gate. Just stand close to me. God, I wish you didn't want to do this. I wish we could fly away to my island, and you'd never have to deal with all this rubbish.'

'We have to do this.' I swallow, hard. 'I don't want to live in the shadows.'

Marc raises an eyebrow. 'You can have a lot of fun in the shadows.'

I smile. 'Maybe. But I like the light. Nothing grows without sunlight.'

We walk forward, and my knees feel weak. There are so many photographers. And they seem so ... violent.

Grasping. Uncaring. All they want is a piece of us. They don't care that we're human beings.

'Where did they all come from?' I whisper, noticing one of the photographers is wearing a suit. The way he stands makes him look important – like a lawyer or businessman. Where the other photographers fight for a spot, he stands coolly at the front, and no one tries to jostle him out of the way.

He has a long face, neatly clipped black sideburns and choppy black hair, styled fashionably. Something about his grey eyes makes me think of a detective – there's a cleverness about him that scares me.

I think I've seen him somewhere before, and then it hits me. Giles Getty. From *The Daily News* newspaper.

5

Marc sees Getty too, and his face darkens. 'Some of them came straight from the gutter,' he says, glaring. He grips my hand tighter. 'Christ. Someone must have known ...'

'Known?'

'That we'd both be here today. This wasn't supposed to be ... *Christ*. This is close enough.' He pulls me to a stop. 'If he's here ... this is a bad idea.'

'Who?'

'Getty.'

The cameras are still flashing, and there are white spots floating in front of my eyes.

'What's so bad about him?'

'I've known Giles Getty a long time,' Marc growls. 'An old enemy, you might say. He's dangerous. Especially where women are concerned.'

Marc leads me away from the gate. 'We'll do a press interview later. For now, I need to get you somewhere safe.'

He pulls me back towards the college. We weave in and out of buildings and along gravel paths until we're standing outside Queen's Theatre.

'Where are we going?' I ask, stumbling over gravel. 'The back gate is over there.'

'There's another way out,' says Marc, taking a bunch of keys from his cargo pants. 'In here.'

He unlocks the theatre's huge wooden doors and pulls me inside the building.

It's cold and dark in the theatre, and everything goes pitch black when Marc slams the doors closed. I hear the key crunch in the lock.

I can still feel Marc's hand in mine and hear his breathing – quick and shallow.

'Marc? What's happening?'

'Just keep hold of my hand. It's okay. Don't be frightened.'

I hadn't realised it, but I *am* frightened. My heart is thumping hard in my chest and my mouth is dry.

The way Marc reacted to Getty ... something's going on. Something bad.

'Why did Giles Getty bother you so much?' I ask as Marc leads me through the theatre. In the darkness, with Marc holding my hand, my heart begins to slow.

'Let's just say I know more about him than most,' says Marc. 'Everyone knows he doesn't play fair. Or nice. He'll stop at nothing to get his story, and he doesn't care who gets hurt along the way. But there's more ... he's already ruined my sister's life.'

'Your sister?'

Marc doesn't answer.

'Marc?'

'Sophia, Getty isn't a man I want to talk about. Especially when I'm with you.'

I swallow. 'You know your way through here,' I say, stumbling over a raised floor tile. 'Even in the dark. Do you do this often?' I hope he can hear the smile in my voice.

'Yes.' Even though I can't see him, I know he's smiling back. 'As a matter of fact, I was in the dark for years until I met you. Totally in the dark.'

'And now?'

'Things are different.' He runs his thumb back and forth over my palm.

I can feel the bulk of the stage beside us and know we're heading backstage. We come to a stop, and I hear the clunk of metal and the rattle of keys.

6

'A secret passage?' I whisper.

'You could call it that. This door leads to a space underground.'

'Is this how you got in last night?'

'Perhaps. But I can't reveal all my secrets.'

There's a flicker of orange light, and I blink as it stings my eyes. I see a long, stone staircase in front of us, and the smell of mould hits me.

Cold air floats up from the staircase.

I turn to see Marc, his handsome face shadowed in orange, and marvel at how I'm standing here beside him. It still doesn't feel real, being with Marc. The curve of his cheekbones and the lines on either side of his mouth. His thick eyebrows and those eyes, blue as a summer sky, watching me.

He's really all here. In real life. With me. This is no movie.

He sees me looking, and smiles.

'Don't worry. There are no monsters down there.'

'Oh no?' I smile back.

He raises an eyebrow. 'Are you calling me a monster, Miss Rose?' He places my hand on a cold, wooden handrail and helps me to the first step.

'Well. You seem to have a secret cave. That's a little bit monstrous, don't you think?'

'I did warn you that I wasn't like other men.'

'That's for sure.'

Marc closes and locks the door behind us. 'Hold on to me.'

He takes my hand and leads me down the staircase. Soon, we reach a big, flat concrete space at the bottom.

In a far, dark corner is a black Aston Martin with tinted windows.

'Yours, I take it?' I say as we walk towards it.

'Very astute of you, Miss Rose. How did you guess?'

I know Marc is teasing me, but I can't resist saying, 'It's black. Like everything you own.'

'Everything I own? You're mistaken there, Sophia. I own a lot of red things too.'

'What happened to the Ford Mustang?'

'This car is faster.'

'Isn't an Aston Martin James Bond's car?' I ask as Marc takes out a key fob and clicks it. The car locks flick up with a space age noise I've never heard before.

'James Bond has lots of cars.'

'You turned down the role of James Bond, didn't you?' I ask as Marc opens the passenger door for me.

Marc nods.

'Why?'

'The character didn't suit me.'

'But you have his car.'

'It's not his car. It's my car. James Bond has the DB5 and the V8. This is a bespoke Rapide S. It's one of a kind.'

'I stand corrected. But Marc, you're an actor.' I slide onto the leather seat. 'You can play any part. How can you say a character doesn't suit you? You could easily play James Bond.'

Marc jumps into the driver's seat and snaps his door closed. 'When it comes to national icons, I'm careful. I don't want to ruin them for people.'

'Ruin?'

The playful look leaves Marc's face. 'Think about it, Sophia. Think about what I'm in to.'

'You mean ...' I'm not quite sure how to phrase the words. 'Needing to be in charge?'

In response, Marc starts the car, and I close my door.

I stare out of the window at the bleak, dark underground space. I feel weird about what Marc just said. *The things I'm in to*. It's true. His tastes are unusual. But I sort of thought that, now we're a couple, he'd be open to more ways of making love. That we'd be more equal.

'Marc -'

'Let's change the subject.' Marc puts the car in drive and spins the wheel. We drive towards blackness, but then a long line of white light appears, growing wider and wider until I see a road and the tall townhouses of central London.

We zoom out onto the road, and I grip the seat. The car turns corners at speed. 'How did you learn to drive like this?' I ask, my voice a squeak.

'Filming *Lightning Bolt*,' says Marc. 'The stunt guy vanished, so I learned how to drive racing cars. I nearly totalled two cars, but we shot all the scenes we needed. Fear of death is a great way to learn quickly.'

He looks totally relaxed and at ease behind the wheel, one hand casually gesturing as he talks.

I, on the other hand, am extremely tense. To look at Marc and me, you'd think we were in two different vehicles. I hate going fast.

'So where are we going?' I say.

'Not far. Somewhere with good security. And somewhere we can do a press interview.'

'And that would be?'

'The Carlo Hotel.'

'The *Carlo*?'

Marc smiles. 'You've heard of it, then?'

I burst out laughing. 'Who hasn't?' I look down at my clothes. 'But Marc ... you're joking. I mean, look at how I'm dressed.'

Marc gives a tiny shake of his head. 'It doesn't matter.'

'Doesn't matter?'

He doesn't answer, but I'm pretty sure I know what he means. It doesn't matter, *because you're with me*.

I swallow. I'm not all that keen on fancy places. Or perhaps, fancy places aren't all that keen on me. I always develop two left feet whenever I'm taken anywhere special. Two left feet and stains all over my clothes. And that's just the Essex restaurants Jen likes to go to. I've never in my whole life been anywhere like the Carlo.

'Why can't we go to your townhouse?' I say. 'It's safe there, isn't it?'

'We can't,' Marc says, far too quickly. 'Not today.'

He glances at me, I guess sensing that I feel a little confused by that remark.

'I have a visitor right now.'

'A visitor?'

'Correct.'

'Who?'

'No one you know. She needs somewhere to stay right now. That's all. She won't be there long.'

'*She?*'

'It's not for long. You don't know her. It's nothing for you to worry about.'

'Who is she? Someone you dated?' I hear the ugly jealousy in the words.

'No one you need to worry about.'

I can tell by Marc's expression that this conversation is over, but I feel sick. I chew at a thumbnail and try to shake away the bad thoughts floating into my brain. Who is this woman staying at his house, and why the hell didn't he mention it before?

Don't get paranoid.

We drive onto Piccadilly, taking a left turn, then a right.

Marc is so effortlessly in control. Calm. Collected. The anger from before has totally vanished, and he's back in charge. But I don't want him so in charge. Right now, I feel like we're slipping apart again.

Marc pulls the car to a stop at an intersection and watches the traffic. A big red London bus lumbers past, followed by black cab after black cab.

'Marc, are you sure about this?' I say.

'Sure?'

'About ... me.'

He turns to me. Jealousy or no jealousy, I can hardly move when he looks at me like that – like he's hungry for me. His eyes are drinking me in. 'Of course I'm sure.'

'But Marc ... the two of us ... you're famous. Hugely famous. And this woman at your house ...'

'Forget about that. You're getting upset over nothing. And I wish I wasn't famous, believe me. I'd trade it all in tomorrow if I could.'

'But you're an amazing actor. And I'm just ...' I let my hands fall open.

'You're *just* beautiful and good and open and intoxicating, and exactly what I want,' says Marc, holding me with his stare. 'Am I what you want?'

'You know you are.'

'Then we're perfect for each other.'

The traffic clears, and Marc pulls the car out of the intersection. We coast along the road for a few metres, and I see the blue and gold awnings of the Carlo Hotel up ahead.

Marc pulls the car to a stop, and a doorman wearing a gold-trimmed top hat rushes to open my door.

A Union flag hangs from the entrance way, and I see blue pansies and ivy growing in troughs along the hotel steps.

'Ivy,' I say, smiling.

I see Marc's jaw ripple with amusement. 'I'd love to say I had it planted especially for you, but I didn't think that far ahead.'

I climb out the car, feeling hugely self conscious, and wrap my coat tightly around me. I wish the coat went all the way to the floor, so the doorman couldn't see my jeans and Converse.

Marc hops out of the car, bounds around to the pavement and takes my hand. He tosses the car keys to the doorman and leads me up the steps into the hotel.

'You're nervous,' he says as my fingers shake against his. 'Don't be. There's nothing to be nervous about here.'

'Easy for you to say.'

We push through a revolving glass door, which squashes us closely together, and then spill out into a bright, light reception area of cream and gold.

I stop and stare, my nerves and jealousy temporarily forgotten. The lobby. It's so beautiful. I can hardly take it all in.

It's like the whole room has been carved out of cream marble then painted with strokes of gold.

There are glass doors and mirrors, all accented with

gold, and a gorgeous red rug is spread over the gleaming white floor.

A huge vase of crisp white roses stands in the centre of the lobby.

Marc strides to the reception desk, and I hear my Converse squeak on white floor tiles as I follow him.

There are guests milling about the lobby, and I blush as they turn to stare at us. Actually, they're staring at Marc. I'm an afterthought. When they see me, their expressions tell me they're not impressed.

'Everyone's staring,' I whisper, my throat feeling tight.

'Aren't you used to people staring at you?' Marc whispers back, leaning towards me so our cheeks are almost touching.

I shake my head.

'Then you're not very observant.'

8

The woman behind the reception desk gives Marc a dazzling smile. She doesn't even glance at me. Is she being discreet, or am I not worth her attention?

'Mr Blackwell. Welcome back. How may I help you?'

'Good morning, Caroline. The King Charles Suite – is it free?'

'Yes, Mr Blackwell.' The woman nods. 'Shall I have someone show you up?'

'That won't be necessary. But I'll be phoning down with a list of items that we'd like brought up to the suite.'

'Certainly.' The woman nods, clacks her computer keyboard, then hands Marc a key on a heavy fob. 'Well. You know the way.' She beams at him.

'I do. Thank you.' He gives her a short smile, and she gazes at him, totally star struck.

Marc leads me back across the lobby, past the roses, and I can't help saying, 'Wow,' as we pass them.

The roses are frilly, like a petticoat, and perfectly coloured. It's like someone has cut them out of white silk, and my fingertips itch to stroke them.

A man in a grey suit with white gloves flopped over his shoulder smiles at me.

'White O'Hara roses,' he says. 'French. Everything here is based on French style.'

I smile back and find myself looking around again. Everywhere there is something to see – cherubs carved out of gold, delicate coving and antique furniture. 'It's so beautiful. You must love working here.'

'I do.'

I feel Marc's eyes on me and see he's smiling.

'I'm glad you like it,' he whispers, squeezing my hand.

I give a nervous smile back. 'Who wouldn't?'

'You'd be surprised.'

'The usual suite, Mr Blackwell?' the grey-suited man asks.

Marc nods.

There are glass double doors beside the man, and he opens one for us. 'Allow me.'

'Thank you,' Marc and I say together.

We enter a long, wide space with lounge chairs dotted around. A suited man plays *Unforgettable* on a grand piano, and I hear the rustle of newspapers and the chink of bone china teacups.

The roses forgotten, I feel out of place again, like a little girl snooping in her mother's wardrobe. I'm not good enough for this place. Certainly not without Marc. I grip his hand tighter and try to ignore the looks we're getting.

'Please don't be nervous, Sophia,' says Marc as we walk down the long space. 'You'll feel at home soon. I promise.'

'I'm not sure about that,' I say. 'You seem to know the place pretty well.'

'I used to stay here whenever I came to London,' says Marc. 'Before I bought my townhouse. I love the history here. Most of the furniture and carpets are antique. They were here when the Carlo was first built.'

The fluttering in my stomach softens a little, and a smile sneaks onto my face. 'I love that you're interested in history.'

'History gives us stories, and stories give us movies. I'm *deeply* interested in history.'

We walk on, and Marc weaves me around a corridor,

and then into an elevator.

'Wow again.' The inside of the elevator looks like a shelf of books. I reach out and brush the book spines with my fingers and find they're made of resin.

Marc pushes a button and the doors slide closed.

He takes my fingers between his hands and kisses the tips. 'So curious.'

We look at each other, and suddenly his eyes tell me how much he wants me.

The lift begins to rise, and my stomach drops to my feet. The elevator is cool and silent, and I can hear Marc's breathing. He's looking at me like *that* again. Like he's a hunter, and I'm his prey.

Suddenly, Marc lifts my arms high above my head, then presses my hands against the wall of the lift.

Oh.

He's leaning over me, and I feel his strength. This is getting dangerous.

Marc leans down and kisses my neck, softly and slowly, working his way around.

This is getting *really* dangerous.

'What I wouldn't do,' he whispers into my skin, 'to have you tied up in here, waiting for me to fuck you every time the elevator came to my floor.'

'What about the other guests?' I murmur.

His hands tighten around my fingers. 'If the other guests came anywhere near the elevator, they'd have me to deal with.'

He runs his fingertips down my upper arms, and I feel a silent '*oh*' shaping on my lips. Then his fingers slide back up to my wrists and grip them tightly.

'Sophia, Sophia, Sophia,' Marc breathes. 'I'd fuck you right now in this lift. You do know that, don't you? You do know who you've got yourself involved with?'

The lift is still rising, but I can feel it slowing down.

I feel the hardness of his fingers against my wrists. He starts tightening, releasing, tightening, releasing in a slow rhythm, watching me, fully aware of what he's doing. Of the effect just that little bit of movement is having on me.

I look right back at him, determined to have an effect on him. Determined not to melt under his gaze and let him take total charge of me.

'Don't fight me, Miss Rose. This is the natural order of things. I take charge, and you obey.'

He presses his body against mine, still tightening and releasing.

'What if I don't obey you?' I murmur.

I feel his hardness against my hip, and suddenly he shifts his hands so only one of them is holding me. His free hand lifts my thigh and pulls it up around him.

'As you know, I have ways of dealing with disobedience.'

He looks into my eyes with a fierceness that makes my stomach turn over and over.

The elevator doors slide open with a 'ping'.

9

I turn in shock, looking to see if any horrified guests are watching. But there's no one.

Marc's eyes are still fixed on me, his lips open. I can see he's breathing hard, trying to stay in control.

We're looking at each other, not moving, not speaking, but our bodies tell the whole story. I'm aching for him, and I know he's aching for me too.

Marc breaks the stare first.

'Our floor, Miss Rose.' He releases me from his grip, and I let my arms fall to the sides. My wrists are tingling in a good way, and I'm desperate for Marc to touch me again.

Did he lose control just then? I mean, we were in a public elevator. Hardly the most discreet place, especially since we haven't even given our press interview yet.

'Marc ... would you have? Just then? If the doors hadn't opened?'

Marc raises an eyebrow. 'You mean, would I have fucked you?'

I nod, blushing.

'I would have tried.'

'I'm glad I can have that effect on you. That I can make you forget where we are.'

'I didn't forget where we were,' says Marc. 'I asked that no staff accompany us to the suite. That means privacy. I knew there'd be no staff or guests on our floor. This is a private suite.'

Oh. Right. I feel disappointed.

We step out of the lift, and I feel soft carpet under my feet.

Straight ahead is a white door, and Marc takes the key from his pocket and slides it into the lock.

'After you.' He steps back to let me into the hotel room. Except it's not a room. It's a small apartment. A *suite* - isn't that what Marc called it?

There's a hallway, and as my feet guide me forward, I find bedrooms and bathrooms and a comfortable living room with a fireplace and sofas.

It's not as fancy as downstairs, but it's still lovely. Calm. Liveable luxury. Warm and comfortable, but with touches of grandeur like oil paintings, swooping curtains and antique furniture. When I see the view from the windows over Green Park, I'm disorientated.

'We're much higher up than I thought,' I murmur. 'I guess I lost track of time in the lift. It's so quiet up here.'

Even though I can see buses and taxis racing along Piccadilly, I can't hear a sound. The whole space is totally still and peaceful. I see two layers of glass in the window frames, and realise why.

'Enjoying the view?' says Marc, and I turn to see him behind me. I feel the heat of him against my neck.

A 'bleep bleep' makes me jump, and Marc steps back and whips his mobile phone from his pocket.

Typical Marc. No customised ring tone.

He snaps the phone to his ear. 'Blackwell ... Yes ... So soon? Fine. No, soon is good.' He drops the phone back into his pocket and turns to me. 'Well, Miss Rose. Is the suite to your liking?'

I love it up here, but ... this isn't my world. I don't know what to do here. How to be. Where to sit, even.

'It's beautiful, but ... this hotel isn't something I'm used to. It might take me some time to feel comfortable.'

'Time is what we don't have. That was my PR team. Our journalist has arrived.'

10

'A journalist? Already?'

Marc nods. 'The interview will take place here. In this room.' He gestures to the living area, and I take a look at the fireplace and antique cushioned chairs. I notice bottles of mineral water on a round, wooden table. I guess it's as good a place as any to have an interview. I don't know what I was expecting – some press conference room with a long table and lots of jostling reporters shouting at me for a comment.

I look at Marc, wondering what he's thinking. His eyes have clouded over, and he looks softer and cuter than usual in his black t-shirt and cargo trousers. His hair is as floppy as ever, and he's not clean shaven.

Those curved lips of his look less red than usual though and are pulled tight together as he surveys the room.

I feel his hand around mine and suddenly feel very small and young.

'Just be yourself,' says Marc. 'And she'll love you.'

'She?'

'I invited the nicest journalist I know. Arabella from *Gossip* magazine. We've given her an exclusive, and in exchange, my team will be able to vet the article before it goes to press.'

'Vet?'

'Make sure it contains everything you'd want it to contain. And nothing you wouldn't. I couldn't care less what they write about me, but I do care what they write about you.'

'That doesn't sound very ... ethical,' I say. 'Aren't journalists supposed to be able to write what they want?'

Marc smiles. 'Ah, Sophia. So much to learn.'

'But I want them to be honest,' I say. 'I want them to write what they truly think.'

Marc shakes his head. 'The job of newspapers is to tell a good story. If we don't tell our story, then they'll tell their own. Honesty doesn't come into it.'

'But if she's a nice person, then what's the problem?' I ask.

'Even nice journalists have editors who want to spice up stories. This is a safety measure. Believe me – it's a good idea.'

'No.' My voice sounds firmer than I expect.

'No?' Marc raises an eyebrow.

'Please, Marc. I want her to write what she wants. I'd feel awful if I knew your team had a hand in the final story. It just feels ... icky.'

Marc grins then, his big, broad Hollywood grin.

'Icky? Why Miss Rose, I never realised you were so articulate.'

I smile back. 'Extremely articulate.'

Marc puts his arms around me.

'Okay,' he whispers into my hair. 'If you feel so strongly about it, I'll talk to my PR team. See if we can't come up with a middle ground. I can't have you completely unprotected and at their mercy. But ... maybe we can reach a compromise.'

'Marc,' I say. 'What sort of questions will she ask?'

'She understands that you're young and haven't been part of this world before. But ... she's going to want a story. She'll push, I have no doubt about that. Don't worry. I'll be there the whole time. I'll step in if I sense you're getting uncomfortable.'

'Thank you.' I let out a long breath, feeling a little sick. Until now, Marc and I have been in a cocoon. A bubble. All we've known is each other, but now we're in the real world, trying to hash out a real relationship. And something tells me it won't be easy.

Marc pulls me back from him so he can see my face. 'You know, it's still not too late to back out of this.'

I shake my head. 'No. I love you, Marc. Thinking about this interview makes me more sure of that than ever.'

'You weren't sure before?' Marc's smile becomes even more dangerous.

'I was sure. But this interview makes me realise I don't care what people think of me. I only care about being with you.'

Marc squeezes my shoulders. 'I hope I won't disappoint you, Sophia. There are things about me ... my life ...'

There's a knock at the door.

'Are you ready for this, Sophia?'

'Ready as I'll ever be.'

'Come in,' Marc barks at the door, not taking his hands from my shoulders or his eyes off mine.

The door opens, and a young woman in a beige coat, with blonde frizzy hair tied back in a ponytail, comes into the room.

'Oh! I'm sorry. Is this a bad time?' Her voice is a little high and wobbly, like she's gargling something.

'Not at all,' says Marc. 'We're ready for you.'

The woman smiles, and pink lipstick stretches right across her face, almost to her ears. She looks kind, and I feel relieved.

'Good to see you again, Marc.' The woman bounds forward and shakes his hand. Then she holds her hand out to me. 'Arabella Price – *Gossip* magazine. You must be Sophia. *So* nice to meet you. This must be very nerve-wracking for you.'

I nod and try my best to smile. I like her energy.

'Well? Shall we take a seat and get started?' Arabella takes off her coat and throws her black handbag by a chair. She's wearing jeans, riding boots and a pink v-neck sweater, and sinks into the armchair like she's in her living room.

I nod and swallow, realising I'm still wearing my coat. I take it off, fold it and place it on the windowsill.

Marc guides me to a sofa, and the two of us sit down opposite Arabella.

Marc feels solid beside me. Calming. And he looks totally relaxed. I'm so proud of him. I let my fingers weave into his, and he squeezes them tight.

I smile inwardly, and I know he's smiling inside too.

'So.' Arabella takes an iPad from her handbag. 'How are you feeling, Sophia?'

'Nervous,' I admit. 'There are lots of girls who want to be with Marc. I have a feeling plenty of people are going to hate me. Especially considering how we met.'

Arabella nods. 'Tell me about that.'

Marc leans forward, but he doesn't let go of my hand. 'I can't pretend I like how things are. I wish Sophia hadn't met me. She doesn't deserve all the rubbish that comes with being part of my world. The gutter press and the garbage they write. They can write what they want about me. No one thinks I'm a decent man, anyway. But I hate the idea of her reputation being dragged through the gutter.'

'*I* think you're a decent man,' says Arabella. 'You give millions to charity. You founded Ivy College to help struggling young actors. I'd say you were a very *decent* man.' Her eyes dart to me for a moment, then return to Marc. 'Of course, people are going to question what sort of man starts a relationship with a student.'

'They should,' says Marc. 'Believe me, I've asked myself all the questions there are to ask. But the bottom line is, I love Sophia. And this is her choice.'

'It's her choice?' Arabella perks her head up. She looks at me, her head tilted expectantly.

I nod. 'He never ... I mean, it was all me. My choices. I wanted to be with him. Marc didn't want any of this.'

'Marc has a reputation,' says Arabella. 'As the strong, controlling type. What do you have to say about that?'

I can't help but smile. I glance at Marc, but I can't read what he's thinking.

'Oh, he's strong and controlling alright,' I say. 'But I think he's softer than people realise.' I try to catch Marc's eye again, but he's looking away.

'What did you think of Marc when you first met?' Arabella asks.

I think back to that first audition. 'He was very charismatic,' I say. 'I could see why he was a big star. But ... maybe he seemed a little arrogant, too.'

'Marc Blackwell? Arrogant.' Arabella is smiling now. 'Never!'

I notice Marc has a quiet smile on his face.

'He's not arrogant, though,' I say. 'Bossy, yes. He thinks he knows what's best for everyone. But he's not full of himself. I'm not sure he thinks very much of himself at all, deep down.'

Marc turns to me, and our eyes meet. There's that lost look again. That confusion. And I know what I just said is true. Beneath that cool, cold exterior, there's much more to Marc Blackwell than meets the eye.

'I'd say you're right on the money.'

Oh? Jealousy rears its ugly head. What does she know of Marc?

'So tell me,' Arabella continues. 'When did you fall for him?'

'I can't pinpoint it exactly,' I say. 'Just little by little, I started seeing more of him. And of course I got a crush, just like every other student. I never thought in a million years he'd be interested in me.' I smile, thinking of the time he rescued me from the lake. 'Maybe he took pity on me.'

'Nothing could be further from the truth,' says Marc. 'Believe me, Arabella. None of this was planned. If it had been anyone other than Sophia, I would have left the college, or just ... ignored my feelings.'

Arabella is watching him closely. 'My, my. Marc Blackwell, you've got it bad, haven't you?' She's teasing him.

'Have it bad doesn't come close to describing it,' Marc says, his voice quiet.

'I've never seen you this way,' says Arabella, cocking her head. 'Your eyes look all mushy.' She leans forward. 'So what is it about our lovely Sophia that has the famously cold Marc Blackwell head over heels?'

'I'm sure I'm not the only person to have fallen head over heels for her,' says Marc. 'Sophia is so natural. So genuine. A beautiful person, inside and out. The whole world will love her, given the chance.'

'I've never heard you talk about anyone this way,' says Arabella. 'And I must say, it's rather lovely. And unexpected.'

'Don't get used to it,' Marc snaps. 'I'm doing this interview for Sophia. So that we can set the record straight, and hopefully at least some of the mongrels will leave her alone.' He jumps up from the sofa. 'Getty was at the college gates this morning.'

Arabella puts a hand to her mouth. She glances at me. 'Oh no.'

12

'What?' I ask.

'He's dangerous,' say Marc. 'Everyone in the industry knows the lengths Giles Getty will go to get a story. He'll stop at nothing. He hires actors to set people up. Alters pictures. The man is a criminal. But as long as he sells papers, no one stops him.' He glances at me. 'And there's more. Where women are concerned. I've known him a long time.'

'We're not all like Giles Getty,' says Arabella, her eyes going watery and nervous. 'Some of us are decent. Some of us just want to tell the truth.'

'That's what I'd like you to do,' I say. 'I want you to tell our story how you see it.'

'The truth?' Arabella smiles. 'Well, there's a word I don't hear very often in this business. I'd be delighted to write the truth about you. Tell me more about how you two met. I'm guessing ... on campus?'

'Actually, it was at Sophia's audition,' says Marc.

'Do tell,' says Arabella, putting her palm under her chin.

'When I saw Sophia perform, there was something about her that just ... shone.'

'She's a beautiful girl,' says Arabella.

'There are lots of beautiful girls,' says Marc. 'Especially on drama courses. It wasn't to do with what she looked like. It was ... something else.'

'Love at first sight?' Arabella raises an eyebrow.

'Perhaps. She was ... quite something.'

'Did you think it would be a problem?' asks Arabella.

'The only thing I allowed myself to think about at

that stage was her talent. What Ivy College could do for her. But, as I'm learning, nothing concerning Sophia is straight forward.'

Arabella turns to me. 'And how about you, Sophia? Were you attracted to Marc at that first meeting? Arrogance aside?' Her eyes crinkle.

I smile and look at my lap. Attracted isn't even the word for it. I felt utterly drawn to him. 'I was ... captivated by him,' I admit. 'Like most women are, I guess. By his intensity.'

'Yes, he is very intense, isn't he?' Arabella laughs.

I look at her, trying to work out if there was ever a relationship between the two of them. I hate myself for feeling this way. For this stupid jealousy.

'Yes,' I admit. 'He's such an amazing actor. I had no idea what he saw in me at first. I still don't.'

'I mentioned before that our Marc has a reputation,' says Arabella. 'As being something of a control freak. Of liking his own way. Does he get his own way with you?'

Wow. She really is going in for the kill. 'He likes being in charge,' I admit with a smile. 'But everything he does comes from the best place. I truly believe that.'

'You seem like a nice, normal girl,' says Arabella. 'Doesn't it bother you? Being with such a powerful man? Someone so domineering?'

'I guess I'm hoping we'll reach a middle ground,' I say.

'And if you don't? I've known Marc a long time. What if everything has to be on his terms?'

I feel like all the air has been sucked out of me. 'I guess we'll cross that bridge when we come to it.'

Arabella's eyes crease up, and I see pity in them. Does she know something I don't? What if she's right? What if, despite Marc losing himself a little in the bedroom, he always has to be in charge?

'And when you met again on campus,' Arabella asks, 'what happened?'

Marc turns. 'Arabella. Remember how young Sophia is. We have to think about her reputation. What people will think of her. It might be best if we don't lead readers into this territory.'

Arabella makes a note on her iPad, and I can't work out if she's annoyed or not. A second later, her head pops up and she's smiling. 'Well then. If you want to keep it light, I guess we're all done with the words. The photography studio will be ready for you this afternoon.'

'We'll be there.' Marc walks towards the door and holds it open. 'Thank you, Arabella. I hope you understand my reasons for not wanting to go into detail.'

Arabella nods. 'I do.' She picks up her coat and heads to the door. 'Nice to meet you, Sophia.'

'You too,' I call after her. I feel bad for her. There was no need for Marc to chastise her like that.

Marc closes the door behind her and reaches me in two long strides.

'I know what you're thinking.'

'What am I thinking?'

'That I was too firm.'

I frown. 'Yes. That's exactly what I was thinking. She was nice, Marc. You didn't need to cut her off like that.'

'Yes. She is. But ... even nice people can have their own agenda.'

'Do you know something about her that I don't?' Ugh. Why did I let myself say that? I can hear the sticky, dark jealousy in the words, and I know Marc hears it too.

Marc stands in front of me, hands on his hips. 'Meaning?' The words are stern, but there's a hint of a smile on his lips.

'Meaning ... I just wondered how you two know each other so well, that's all.'

'I haven't fucked her, if that's what you're asking.'

Oh. I'm so relieved. 'It wasn't.'

'It was.' Marc's smile grows.

I can't help smiling back and feel my lips sliding over my teeth. 'Okay, it was. But can you blame me? She seemed to know plenty about you.'

'She doesn't know a thing. No more than any other journalist.' Marc checks his watch. 'I have to make a phone call in the other room. When I come back, I want you completely naked. I want to finish what I started in the lift.' With that, he strides out of the living area into a neighbouring bedroom and slams the door closed.

My heart is still yammering away after the interview. Trust Marc to be so calm and collected that he can shift his mind so easily.

I'm a little tempted to listen in to his phone conversation. What's so important that he needs to march off like that? But no ... I'd be mortified if he caught me, and we're building a relationship. No sneaking around.

I look down at my clothes, wondering what he would do if he came in and I was still fully dressed. Would he be angry? Annoyed? Or ...

Will he stop loving me if I don't let him stay in charge?

The words jump into my head, unbidden, and I don't like them. I don't like them at all.

13

I hear Marc's low murmuring through the door, and then a shout:
'*When?*'
I strain to listen, but nothing else is clear.
When what?
The bedroom door clicks open, and Marc strides back into the living area. He looks at me, sees I still have my clothes on, then paces back and forth.

God, he's gorgeous. I mean, just mesmerizingly gorgeous. If I wasn't sitting down, I think my knees would give way.

'You're dressed,' he remarks, his voice low.
'Yes.'
There's a chiming sound from the hallway, and Marc hesitates. Then he strides down the hallway and opens the suite door.

I blink in surprise at what's standing behind it.

There, in the doorway, is a bellboy staggering under an enormous vase of white roses. But they're not just any white roses. They're the same white roses I saw in reception – the frilly ones with thick green stems, complete with the same glass vase.

'You're an hour early,' says Marc, ushering the bellboy into the living room. 'But welcome nonetheless. Put them on the mantelpiece. Thank you.'

The bellboy places the roses over the fireplace, arranging them so they fan out towards the room.

'Marc, these are ... they're so beautiful,' I breathe.

Marc slides a ten pound tip into the bellboy's hand, and the bellboy gives a little bow and heads for the door.

I stare at the perfect white flowers, smelling their beautiful fragrance.

'Why did they bring these?' I ask.

'They're for you,' says Marc. 'I thought you'd appreciate a little nature around the place.'

I put a hand to my mouth, feeling a smile spread from ear to ear. 'For me?' I stifle an astonished giggle. 'They're just like the ones in reception.'

'They *are* the ones from reception.'

'You're kidding me. How did you ...?'

'I've been coming to this hotel for a long time. You like them?'

'I love them. Can't you tell?' Sometimes, I get so happy, I feel like my smile is going to rip my face in half, and that's how I'm smiling now.

I throw my arms around him.

'Thank you,' I say, planting kiss after kiss on his cheek. 'I can't believe you did that for me. It's so thoughtful. I feel really special.'

'I love that such simple things make you happy,' says Marc.

'*Simple* things?' I say. 'A giant vase of roses from the Carlo Hotel reception area? Hardly simple.' I stroke the soft petals. 'No one ever got me flowers before.'

'No one ever bought you flowers?' Marc asks.

'My dad used to buy me daffodils sometimes, but I don't think that counts.'

'None of your boyfriends ever bought you flowers?'

'Never.'

'They were idiots.'

'Oh ... no, they weren't. Just young, that's all. You don't buy flowers for people when you're young.'

'Are you calling me old, Miss Rose?'

'Yes, Mr Blackwell. You're very old. Didn't anyone ever tell you?'

'Funnily enough, no.' Marc moves a stray piece of hair from my eye. 'I'm glad you like the flowers.'

'I don't *like* them. I love them.'

'Is that right?'

I nod.

He looks right into my eyes. 'I'm going to ignore the fact that you haven't undressed and take you to the bedroom anyway. But I want you to keep totally still. Is that understood?'

'You're going to ... you want me to keep *still*?' I ask.

He nods, sharply. 'And silent.'

'*What?* Why?'

'To increase your pleasure. And mine.'

He scoops me into his arms so quickly that the bottom falls out of my stomach, then carries me into a bedroom and drops me onto a crisp white duvet. I'm aware of a soft canopy of flowery fabric draped above the headboard. But mostly, all I see is Marc.

He removes his t-shirt and hangs it over an antique arm chair. As he paces around the bed, easily, slowly, he watches me.

He's not performing. This isn't an act. This is real, honest to goodness Marc Blackwell, and oh my god he's hot.

He comes to the foot of the bed and takes my foot in his hand.

I feel his long, strong fingers through the fabric of my shoe and see his toned chest rising and falling. The scars on his knuckles are very white right now as his fingers work my feet.

He pulls the shoelaces free, then slides my foot carefully from my Converse. Dropping the shoe to the floor, he removes the other shoe, every movement careful and gentle, but controlled.

Shoes dispensed with, he takes my ankles and pulls

me slowly down the bed. I slide along the duvet and look up at him, wondering if I'm going to try to keep still or not.

Deftly, with one hand, Marc undoes the metal button on my jeans, then slides the zipper down with his whole palm pressed flat against me. I wiggle a little.

'Keep still,' he says. His tone is gentle, but firm. He's very definitely in charge right now, no matter how soft and slow he's being.

'I can't help it,' I murmur.

'And keep quiet.' He takes the ankles of my jeans and pulls hard so the denim shoots over my thighs, burning a little as he rips the fabric free of my legs. Then he drops the jeans to the ground.

14

Oh.

With two flicks of his wrists, Marc pulls my socks off. He stands back, my socks dangling from his fingers, and looks at my feet.

I flinch a little. I've never been a big fan of my feet – they're very pale and slim, and I have really long toes. They're still nicely pedicured, thank God, after our trip to Marc's island, but I know there'll be bits of black cotton stuck between my toes.

'Marc -'

'No speaking.'

'I didn't agree to that.'

Marc raises an eyebrow. 'Rebelling, Miss Rose?'

'No, I'm just ... trying to have a normal relationship with you.'

'And what's normal, exactly?'

'I guess, being equal.'

Marc picks up my foot and runs his thumb back and forth along the arch.

Oh, that feels good. Why does it feel so good? It's sending salty little shocks up my legs.

'And you don't think we're equal?'

'Do you?'

Marc places my foot gently on the bed. He surveys me for a moment, looking up and down my body. 'Being equal doesn't mean being the same.'

His hand falls to my thigh, and his fingers work their way slowly up, up my leg. The touch is so light that it's making me crazy. I tense in anticipation. 'Meaning?'

'Right now, we're playing different roles.'

His fingers reach my panties, and he runs his thumb

around the elastic, pulling the panties taut as if he's testing the fit.

'Different roles?'

Marc pulls at panties down with his thumb, slowly, so the cotton strokes my hips. I give a little shudder.

'Different roles,' he says again, and it feels like the words are stroking me too. 'I'm in charge and you do what I tell you.'

He puts both hands firmly on my thighs, and in one swift movement, flips me over so I'm lying on my stomach.

'Oh!' A powerful shock hits me right between the legs.

'And your body tells me you like things this way.'

'But you can't always be in control,' I say, wishing I sounded stronger. 'Or we'll never have a real relationship. You have to let go.'

'I thought I already had.' Marc pulls me towards him so my legs come to either side of his hips. I can feel his belt buckle and the stiff material of his trousers at the top of my thighs. 'I've let go more with you than anyone else.'

He unfastens my bra, and I struggle my arms free of the straps.

Oh my god, I know what's coming. And I want him so badly. But I know if we go down this road, I'll be taking a step away from what I *really* want.

'Marc? Please ... can we talk about this?'

'I need to be in charge right now,' Marc whispers, his voice practically a growl. 'And you need it too.'

His hands come to either side of my thighs, and he rubs up and down, up and down, letting his palms slide over my buttocks on the upward stroke. His touch is firm. Hard. He's taking no prisoners, and I'm pushed into the bed with every caress.

My body tells me this feels so good, but my head is screaming, *Stop, stop*!

The strokes slow down, and I listen for the clink of Marc's belt buckle, or the ripping of a condom packet. But I don't hear anything.

Talk to him now, Sophia. Tell him you want him to lose himself in you. To be vulnerable. Tell him before you lose yourself in the moment.

Marc pushes my legs wider apart, and I feel the soft bristles of his cheeks against my inner thighs. He pulls my panties to one side.

Oh no. No, no, no. He can't do this to me, it's not fair. I want to cry out, 'Wait, stop!' but it's too late. He has me exactly where he wants me, and there's no escape.

15

His tongue starts circling where he would have entered me, pushing inside and out, and it feels so good.

I let out a long breath, swept away by the softness and intimacy of what he's doing. His tongue feels gentle. Loving. All the things I'm looking for right now. And then of course, there's the heat that's building up.

Maybe we can talk later.

He works his way down, until he's at where I'm most sensitive. The place where I feel all the electric shocks and soft warmth and waves of pleasure.

Something about the softness of his tongue makes me feel on fire, and I can't stop myself wriggling and moaning and gripping at the bedclothes.

'Oh. *Oh*. That feels *sooo* good.'

Suddenly, his tongue stops moving and the warmth of him is replaced by cool air.

'I told you to keep still. And to keep quiet. Do I have to tie you to the bed?' He snaps my panties back into position.

Ouch! 'Marc -'

'Keep still.'

Now's my chance.

I flip myself over and see him kneeling at the foot of the bed. He's still wearing his cargo trousers, but one glimpse at his groin tells me he's as hot as I am, and about ready to explode too.

'Sophia, I told you to keep still.' His tone is light. Curious. And he's frowning that intense Marc Blackwell frown, one eyebrow a little raised.

I scoot over the bed towards him and drop onto his lap, my legs on either side of him.

'That's a very long way from keeping still,' says Marc, his voice softer now.

I kiss him, my lips swollen from the heat of us. Marc's lips are red too, and as I press mine against them, his eyes close and his forehead twitches in confusion.

He wraps his strong arms around me and pulls me to his bare chest. 'A very, very long way. There'll be consequences.'

I can't work out if he's teasing or not, but I don't stop to think about it. As our tongues feel each other, I'm aching for him to be inside me.

I reach down to his belt buckle, but Marc grabs my hand – gently, but firmly.

He pulls back from my mouth. 'No,' he says. 'I need to be the one to finish this.'

He picks me up and drops me on the bed again.

'Marc, I -'

'Today, I need to stay in control.'

I look up at him, and his eyes tell me all I need to know. He *needs* to be in control right now. Maybe not tomorrow, or forever. But right now, he needs it like a junkie needs a hit.

Why? Is it something to do with Giles Getty?

I watch as his breathing gets longer and slower, and his eyes grow more focused and strong with every breath. He frees himself from his trousers and pulls a condom from his pocket, tearing at the packet, then stretches it over and down, until he bulges against the plastic.

He leans over me, his hands on either side of my shoulders. His arms are long and straight, supporting his weight, and his chest tenses up.

Our eyes meet, and I'm lost.

He moves his hands to my knees and pulls them apart. Not slowly, not gently. He's caught his prey, and he's going in for the kill. He pushes aside my panties and ...

Oh.

As he plunges in, I gasp. His pace is unrelenting, back and forth, back and forth, not giving me any let up, any moment to think.

He's watching me intently, seriously, with those eyes that have lived a thousand different lives and seen things most people will never see.

Harder, harder he moves until I turn softer under him. I'm losing it. The room is fading to white, and I'm in a red hot world of pleasure.

He's such a tight fit that every fast stroke sends sparks through my whole body.

I want to cry out. To tell him to slow down. But I have no chance. He's determined, and there's only one way this story will end.

Going deeper and deeper, he pulls me up to his chest and wraps steely arms around me, holding me so tight that I know there's no escape.

'Marc. Marc. Oh Marc,' I cry out as the hotness turns to burning and I'm swept away by pleasure.

In response, he pushes so deeply inside me that my world goes blurry. Everything feels so tight and good, and I can't hold it together any more. Any minute now, I'm going to come.

Suddenly, Marc pulls back. 'Wait,' he says.

'Wait?' I'm grasping him, desperate, trying to pull him back inside me.

'Stay exactly where you are.'

Marc pulls right out of me, dresses and leaves the room.

'*Marc!*'

16

Moments pass.

Just as I'm getting really impatient, Marc returns with a pair of silver handcuffs dangling from his fingers. They look heavy duty, and I wonder for a fleeting moment if they're real police issue ones.

I swallow. 'Where did you get those from?' I ask.

'The car.' Marc stands at the foot of the bed watching me, still obviously trying to get his breathing under control.

God, he's so handsome. But my heart skips a beat as I eye up the handcuffs. I feel the familiar Marc Blackwell turmoil of emotions: fear, excitement, confusion and lust, all mixed together in one sexy bundle.

'I'm going to handcuff you to the radiator and fuck you until you can't see straight.'

Oh. My body shivers at those words.

I pull myself up on the bed. 'Marc -'

'Off the bed.'

We're back here again – Marc taking charge. Marc dominating me. My mind is in turmoil, but my body knows exactly what it wants. It's betraying me, and my legs swing off the bed.

I want him. So badly. In whatever way he chooses.

Marc scoops me up and carries me towards the window. There's a stout metal radiator underneath it – an old-fashioned one, like the sort we used to have at school.

He lays me on the floor, and I feel the heat from the radiator against my scalp and soft carpet under my back.

Marc presses his palms against my legs, and I shiver. There's no defying him now, and we both know it.

I'm belted into the Marc Blackwell ride, and all I can do is hold on tight.

He's watching me with such force that I'm unable to tear myself away from his eyes. I see the hunger in them, but he's fighting his urges, forcing himself to slow down. That's what the handcuffs are about, I realise. They're helping him stay in control. Which is something I seem to have lost the ability to do.

I struggle up towards him, but Marc's strong fingers take hold of my ribs and lay me back down.

Marc takes the handcuffs, and the heavy metal links clink together. I swallow, hard.

'I'm sure you remember how pleasurable it can be to be restrained.'

I gulp, feeling my hair grow static against the carpet. 'I hadn't forgotten.'

Marc grabs my hand. He hits a handcuff against my wrist, and I feel metal encase it. There's a clicking sound as Marc squeezes the cuff tightly shut.

I watch him admire my wrists for a moment. Then he feeds the other cuff around the pipe connecting the radiator to the floor. Taking my free wrist, he fits the handcuff around it.

I'm now totally in his power.

My arms are above my head, restrained by the cuffs and held tight to the radiator. I move my hands and hear the clang of metal on metal. I really am held fast. If I move too much, I'll burn my hands on the radiator pipe.

Having restrained me, Marc gets to his feet and paces back and forth. He has that powerful look in his eyes, that hunter look, but I can also see by his heaving chest that he's struggling to hold it together.

My breasts move up and down against my ribcage. I lay there, naked and wanting him, but unable to do anything without his say so.

'Wait there.' Marc heads for the door.

'Wait?' *Are you kidding me?* I fidget in the cuffs and am rewarded with a radiator burn along my fingers. 'Ouch!'

Marc raises an eyebrow. 'Do as you're told and you won't get hurt.' He vanishes through the door.

Oh, I'm so frustrated now. This is too much. There's teasing, and there's taking things too far. I try to slow my breathing. To still the rush of hot blood racing around my body. But it's too much. I want him, I want him, I want him.

Minutes pass and my body is going into a frenzy. Knowing he's near, but not being able to have him, is driving me wild. Too wild.

I buck and pull against the handcuffs in a hopeless attempt to free myself, but all I manage to do is burn my hands.

Just when I think I can't bear it any longer, Marc's tall, broad silhouette appears in the doorway.

'Are you trying to torture me?' I shout.

'A little. But in a good way.'

'In a *good way*?'

'Your orgasm will thank me for it.'

'Where did you go?'

'The hotel jewellery shop. I had to buy something for you.'

17

Marc's left hand is closed around a black velvet box, and I eye it suspiciously.

'What do you have?' I ask.

'Something to prolong the torture. Or the pleasure. However you want to look at it.'

'Oh, Marc. Please. No more. I can't bear it.'

'From where I'm standing, you don't have a lot of choice.'

I glare at him. 'You'd let me go if I asked you to, and we both know it.'

'Is that what you want?'

I struggle against the handcuffs. 'Maybe.'

'Well, hurry up and make your decision, Miss Rose. I don't have all day. It's this way or no way. Do you want me to release you or not?'

I break his gaze, my eyes dropping to my heaving breasts. 'No.'

'I thought so.'

'So what's in the box?'

'Something to make things even more unbearable for you.' He gives me his spiky, mischievous smile and opens the box.

I see a long pearl necklace on pink satin.

Marc kneels between my legs and slips the pearls into my panties. Then he puts his palm flat against them and moves the pearls around and around.

'*Oh*,' I moan as the pearls rub against me. 'That feels good. That feels *so* good.'

I look at him, my eyes hungry. He's still fully dressed, kneeling by my thighs, but I see hardness in his trousers.

'No yet,' Marc growls, and I sense this is taking all his self-control too. He puts his palm flat against my panties, pushing the pearls harder against me. I feel their cool, smooth surface rub around and around.

'Oh. Oh God, oh God.'

Suddenly, Marc whips my panties down.

The pearls drop down towards my buttocks.

Marc pulls my panties free, then lifts my thighs towards my chest so I feel a cool breeze around my backside.

He rests my legs over his shoulders, then slides the pearls between my buttocks and right up, up, feeding them one at a time up my backside ... oh!

I almost leap off the floor, and my eyes go crazy and wide. It's such a weird feeling, having them in there, and I'm not sure I like it at first. I feel a few pearls hanging free, rolling around between my buttocks.

'Relax.' Marc lets his palm linger around my backside, then grasps my hips firmly with both hands and manoeuvres his crotch to meet mine. 'You'll enjoy it soon. I promise.'

The pearls are moving around as Marc manoeuvres me, and they're starting to feel really good.

I squirm against the carpet, but that just makes the feeling more intense. My legs are still over his shoulders, and he grips my thighs tight so I can't move too much.

Then he drops a hand to his trousers and frees himself, one long rod of hardness pointing right at me.

For a moment, I honestly don't think I can take him inside me. Not with the pearls moving around. But as he inches himself between my legs, I realise I am so, *so* ready that it's barely a struggle for him to slide inside.

When he's all the way in, I feel so full and good that I can hardly breathe. He's having trouble keeping it together too. I've never seen his jaw locked so tight or his eyes so intense and focused on mine.

Our eyes hold each other as we both try to breathe carefully. Slowly. But it's difficult. I know he's going to move in a moment, and waiting is a delicious agony that's getting harder and harder.

Marc's gaze drops to my breasts, and he trails the back of his hand over them and down to my stomach. Then he slides a hand around my waist and holds me firm.

'Ready?' he breathes, his eyes flicking up to my face.

I nod and swallow.

'Can you still see straight?' He gives me that stomach-melting quirky smile.

'Just about.'

'Enjoy it while it lasts.'

He moves his hips around in a circle, touching parts of me that have never been touched before.

18

'Oh God, oh God,' I moan.

With the pearls moving too, it feels like my whole body is alive with pleasure.

'Oh. *Oh*,' I cry, closing my eyes and letting the sensations overcome me.

Marc stops circling and begins moving back and forth, getting deeper with every thrust. Even with my eyes closed, I feel his stare burning my eyelids. I'm his now, all his, and he has no intention of letting me go.

Shivers of friction and pleasure wash over me until I don't know up from down, and as for seeing straight ... I'm way too dizzy.

I feel Marc's fingers tighten around my waist and hear him cry out – a long, low moan that sends waves of pleasure through my chest.

He's moving harder now, and I feel us both getting lost in each other. There's nothing but our two bodies moving together and my wrists rubbing against metal.

Marc pushes my thighs further against my chest and gets even deeper inside. So deep that I inhale sharply, feeling a sting of pleasure as my backside tightens.

'Oh my god.'

'Wait.' Marc barks. 'Not yet. Don't come yet.' He reaches up to my backside and takes hold of the loose pearls. Then he pulls. Hard. And the whole string slides out, pulling and rubbing me in all the right ways.

It's too much. I can't take it. My body explodes in pleasure, and vibrations roll around my hips and thighs.

'Marc. Oh God, Marc.' I come hard, feeling myself throb against him and holding on tight. The pleasure is so great that, for a moment, I can only see white and orange. But as the world comes back to me in pieces, I turn to see Marc's eyes are tightly shut and he's breathing hard.

Marc moans as I tense and release around him. He grips my thighs tight and pushes himself deeper and deeper.

As warmth laps at my body, my eyes flicker open and I see Marc, his jaw clenched and his eyes squeezed closed. He's frowning, but I can see it's a frown of pleasure.

'I want you to come,' I murmur, wishing I could reach up and stroke his face.

'Not yet.' Marc thrusts deep inside me with such strength that it moves me up the carpet. I feel friction burn my buttocks and hear Marc let out a long moan.

I squeeze and release myself around him, over and over again, pulling him inside me.

'Sophia,' he groans. 'Wait. Sophia. No. I can't stop myself. I can't stop.'

His jaw unclenches, and he lets out a long, low groan as he pushes himself deeper.

He falls onto me, still moaning and moving his hips back and forth. I feel him soften and hear his breathing begin to slow.

His forehead creases up, then relaxes and his body feels loose in my arms.

I wrap my legs around him and pull him tight against me.

We're so close right now, it's like we're the same person. The whole world has disappeared. There are no problems. There's no real life. Only the two of us. And when we're together like this, everything is okay.

After a moment, Marc's eyes flick open, and he reaches up to the handcuffs and presses something that makes them spring open.

My hands free, I wrap my arms around Marc and he rolls onto his back, pulling me on top of him. I lie on him, feeling his hard body and seeing his beautiful face, lips slightly parted, eyes soft but staring, inches from mine.

'That was amazing,' I breathe, watching his dark eyelashes flick up and down.

Marc doesn't reply. Instead, he reaches up to stroke hair from my face, but his eyes tell me that his thoughts are elsewhere.

I rest my head on his shoulder and see the amazing pale skin and tiny scars spread across his chest. I put my hand to the scars, feeling his dark chest hair under my fingers.

'Marc?'

I feel as though I've broken something in him, but I don't know what.

Marc doesn't say anything. Instead, he just clutches me tighter, and I feel him beginning to slip out, centimetre by centimetre.

We lay like that for a long time. Too long. Something's wrong.

19

When Marc finally lifts my body from his, he stares at the ceiling.

His eyes tell me he's scared. He lost control and he didn't want to. It frightens me, that look.

There's a stray eyelash on his cheek, and I reach for it. He doesn't stop me, but he doesn't react either. It's like he's gone numb.

'Make a wish,' I say, holding out the eyelash.

For a moment, Marc doesn't say or do anything. Then he pulls himself up onto his palms.

He blinks, smiles a soft but distant smile, and blows at the eyelash.

I feel like maybe he's come back, just a little bit, but not all the way.

'What did you wish for?' I ask.

'Nothing you'd want to know about.' He sounds almost like Marc. My Marc. The one who climbed up my balcony last night and made love to me. But not quite.

'I would.'

Marc sighs. 'I wished that some things about me will always stay hidden from you.'

'I don't want anything to be hidden,' I say.

He laughs. 'You say that now. But trust me, sometimes ignorance is bliss.'

So I have lost him. For now, anyway. I feel sad.

'When are we having the photographs?' I ask, realising that this, like everything else today, has been arranged by Marc.

'3pm. Not here. A studio near the Thames.'

'Why not here?'

'I didn't think it would be a good idea to publicise that we're in a hotel room together. It just ... doesn't set the right tone. The shoot should be tasteful.'

With that, he bounds to his feet and climbs into his boxers. Even when I'm feeling not quite right about him, as I am now, I still love seeing his body. The mounds where his buttocks peak out the top of his underwear, and the pale curve of his back, and everything so toned and tight and hard and manly. So different from me.

'I'm not so sure me and tasteful go together,' I say.

Marc smiles. 'Oh Sophia, Sophia. Everything about you is tasteful. You're genuine. Natural. And you don't even see it, do you?'

'What should I wear?'

'Whatever you like, but I think you should accessorise with pearls.'

I laugh. 'Marc, I'd really like to talk to you about -'

'Sophia, I can't have a deep and meaningful conversation right now.' Marc opens a wardrobe and takes out suit trousers and a shirt.

'How did your clothes get here?' I ask, seeing more suits hanging in the space.

'They didn't. I had the concierge buy new clothes and hang them while we were being interviewed. There are some in here for you, too. But they don't look like they'll be to your taste.' He checks his watch. 'I'm meeting someone, and I'm already late.'

Someone?

'Who? The woman at your house?' I feel sick again.

Buttoning up his shirt, Marc stoops to give me a quick kiss on the forehead. Too quick, like he's dismissing me. 'Just someone, okay? Trust me, you're better off not knowing who right now.'

He picks up his cargo trousers and reaches into a pocket. Taking out a burgundy leather wallet, he unrolls it and hands me a gold credit card.

'Take this,' he says. 'The pin number is 1966. Old and New Bond Street are just around the corner. Designer clothing shops galore. Go buy yourself whatever you think you need.'

He hesitates as he places the card on the bedside table. 'And Sophia?' I hear his uncertainty.

'Yes?' I sit taller.

He shakes his head. 'We'll talk later, okay?'

I nod dumbly, feeling him draw away from me and into himself.

'*Who* are you meeting?' I hear myself ask again, hating how desperate the words sound.

'Someone from my past,' says Marc. 'Who I'm hoping might help me straighten out my future.'

I wish I could capture the look on his face when he says those words. Capture it, bottle it, hold it close to my heart forever. Because when he says *my future*, I see in his eyes what I mean to him. Just for a second. And then the light goes out, and I lose Marc to coldness once again.

'I'll have someone drive you to the studio, okay?' he says. 'Be in the room at two thirty. Until then, have fun. Buy whatever you like.'

He throws the room key on the bedside table. And then he's gone.

20

Who is he meeting? *Who?* Oh, I'm driving myself crazy, especially as my brain gnaws at the thought of the woman in his house. I pace the suite, walking around the hallway, through the living area and master bedroom in a circle until I make myself dizzy.

After too many circuits, I slump onto the couch in the living area and decide to call Jen.

When I pull out my iPhone, I notice I have thirty-seven missed calls. I've never had more than three missed calls in my whole life. I scroll through the numbers. Most of them are London numbers I don't recognise, but plenty are from Jen, Tom, Tanya and my dad.

Jen picks up on the first ring.

'Soph? Oh my god, I've been calling and calling. Where are you?'

'The Carlo,' I say.

'The *Carlo*? As in, the Carlo Hotel London? As in, by royal appointment to the Queen, the Carlo?'

'Um ... yeah.'

'Holy Jesus fuck! What are you doing there? Oh wait. Stupid question. You're with Marc Blackwell. So I'm guessing you're messing up the sheets.'

'*Was* with Marc Blackwell,' I say. 'He's gone. To meet someone. I don't know who. We just had an interview with *Gossip* magazine.'

'*Gossip* magazine?' Jen practically screeches the words. 'Oh my god. You've just become media royalty. Did you do a photo shoot?'

'Not yet,' I say. 'We're supposed to do one this afternoon.'

'What are you going to wear?'

'I haven't decided yet. Marc gave me his credit card to go shopping. He sort of suggested Old and New Bond Street, so I guess he wants me in designer things.'

'OH MY GOD!' Jen screeches. 'What are you doing on the phone to me? You're wasting time! Go spend, spend, spend.'

'Do you think it's going to last? Him and me?'

There's a pause. 'You *are* from two different worlds.'

'Yes,' I say. 'Two very different worlds. Jen, I don't fit in here. This isn't me. Shopping for designer clothes isn't me.'

'Did he say you *had* to get something designer?'

'No. He just mentioned that the shops are near here.'

'Did he say it like he *wanted* you to go to those shops?'

I think for a moment. 'No. But maybe he meant ... I felt like that's what he wanted.'

'Do you love him?' Jen asks, serious now.

'Yes,' I say. 'Or at least ...' I think about what he said earlier. About being careful what I wish for and getting to know him better, and the woman at his house. 'What I know of him. But perhaps there are things I don' know.'

'That's a good start,' says Jen. 'Hey – do you want me to come help you find something to wear? It's no trouble; I'm in London today anyway.'

'No, no, you're working. I'll be fine.'

21

I know it sounds pathetic, but I have to really work up courage to leave the hotel room. Marc speaks the language here, but I'm a foreigner and I feel out of place.

Staff nod at me as I head through the lobby, and I slap on a smile and murmur, 'Hello' as I pass them. I notice all the other guests ignore the staff, but that just feels rude to me. I may not have been brought up with much money, but I was always taught manners cost nothing.

As I hop down the steps outside, I realise I don't have a clue where I'm going. There's a grey-haired doorman by the revolving door, so I ask him where Old Bond Street is.

'Just over the road,' he says, dimples appearing in his weathered cheeks. 'Can't miss it.' His accent reminds me of my Grandpa Jack, and I smile.

'Do you come from East London?' I ask.

His face breaks open into a grin. 'Highbury. Why ... do you know the area?'

'Know it?' I smile back. 'I used to visit Walthamstow every Christmas. My grandparents live there. We'd watch the football at Highbury.'

'Oh right? Football lass, are you?'

'Not really, but I used to love watching live games.'

'We've got something in common there, then. I can't stand the game usually, but seeing it live is different. A world away from this place, eh? The old football matches. Pie and Bovril and all the singing.'

'You can say that again,' I say.

He reaches out a white-gloved hand. 'Bill.'

'Sophia.' I shake his warm glove and feel at home for the first time today. 'Really good to meet you.'

'I saw you come in earlier,' says Bill. 'With our Mr Blackwell. He's been good to us over the years – don't you go believing what the papers say.' He glances up the street. 'Mind you, if you need any help while you're here, you just come to me. I'll look after you. And if that fella of yours steps out of line ...' He raises his arm and backhands the air. 'You just come and find me.'

We both laugh.

'Thanks Bill.' Maybe I should practise that backhand. It looks effective.

I cross the road and find myself at the foot of Old Bond Street – and a different world.

22

Okay. So I know about Gucci and Dolce and Gabbana from *Sex and the City* episodes, and I know celebrities wear designer labels for important events. But I'm from a small village, near a small town, and have never seen *real* shops selling designer clothes. Unless you count Nike as designer.

As I walk down Old Bond Street, I'm getting an education. For a start, I've never seen shops with security guards outside. This is a first. And second, I've never seen such amazing window displays.

I see a giant Christmas tree in one window, all sprayed white and hung with fake diamonds. Another window has hundreds of snowflakes suspended on wire around a display of party dresses. Beautiful.

I pass a shoe shop where a lady hands out pink cocktails to shoppers. Wow. And I see diamonds and watches and handbags on sale that cost more than my dad's cottage.

I think of Marc's credit card, still resting on the bedside table. I couldn't bring myself to take it. I'm just not the sort of girl who goes charging up money on someone else's account. I've got my own credit card, and I'll pay back the balance by working, like I've always done. Okay, so my credit limit is only a few hundred pounds, but that'll be enough to get something, I'm sure.

I walk past shop after shop. As I pass different window displays, I find reasons not to go inside.

Too smart. Not quite me. Too fancy. Too young. Too old. But the truth is, I'm not comfortable going in these designer places. I feel like the second I step over the threshold, everyone will know I don't belong.

Sophia, you're being ridiculous. Just walk into a shop. This one. This one here.

I see a window of gold shoes, white suits and sunglasses on skinny mannequins in the window. Swallowing hard, I walk inside the store.

Where to start?

A shop assistant walks over. She's wearing the exact same outfit that's displayed in the window, right down to the sunglasses. She glances down at my jeans and shoes.

'Just looking?'

'Oh ... um. Yes. For the moment.' I scan the store for sale rails. Old habits die hard. There are none. Of course there aren't. It's the run up to Christmas.

I see a rail of dresses and walk over to it. The assistant follows me.

'This is nice,' I say, my hand touching a fitted grey dress with silver embroidery.

The assistant whips off her sunglasses. Her eyes look mean. 'Just so you know, the fitting room is only for people *seriously* considering buying something.'

My hand falls away from the dress.

'She *is* seriously considering buying something,' says a deep voice.

Oh my god.

I turn to see Marc, white shirt, black suit, impossibly handsome. If he stood very still, he could easily be part of the window display.

23

My eyes widen. 'What are you doing here?'

The shop assistant's mean little eyes practically bulge out of her head. 'You ... You're ... Marc Blackwell. *Marc* Blackwell. I ... I'm so sorry. I hope I didn't sound rude. It's just ...'

Marc glares at her. 'We won't be needing any of your assistance, thank you. You can go exercise your bad manners elsewhere.'

The assistant blinks a few times, stumbles a little on her gold high heels, mumbles, 'Sorry', and scuttles away.

'You forgot this,' says Marc, reaching into his pocket and pulling out his credit card.

I'm so happy to see him. I want to fling my arms around his shoulders, but I guess it's a little too public.

'I didn't forget it,' I say. 'I just ... didn't feel right about taking it.'

Marc frowns. 'Why not?'

'Because ...' How can I explain what I don't understand myself? 'It just felt wrong. That's all.'

'It felt wrong letting me look after you?'

'No ... I ... I suppose it didn't feel like you looking after me. It felt like me not being an adult.'

'It wasn't intended that way.'

'I know.' I shake my head. 'I know you're coming from a good place.'

'Will you just take the damn card?'

'Are you asking me, Mr Blackwell, or telling me?'

'Asking.' One side of Marc's lips quirks up. 'But don't get used to it. It won't become a habit.'

'Oh? You're sure about that?'

'Quietly confident.'

The rest of the world disappears for a moment, and it's just Marc and me, standing together.

'How did you find me?' I ask.

'Housekeeping rang to say my credit card had been left in the bedroom. So I thought I'd better come looking.'

'Didn't you have to meet someone?'

'They understood I had an urgent engagement. But I have to go back to them now.'

'Right.' *Who is it, who is it, who is it?*

'Would you like me to send someone from the hotel to help you?' He gives that quirky smile again, leaving me weak at the knees. 'Act as your bodyguard?'

'I already have one.'

'Yes, you do.'

'Not you,' I say.

Marc's eyebrows shoot up. 'Do I have competition?'

'You certainly do. She's very good.'

'She?'

'Yes, *she*. My best friend, Jen. And you'll have to meet her approval if the two of us are going anywhere. So I guess you should meet soon.'

'Oh, I'm guessing she'll approve of me,' says Marc. 'Women almost always do.'

I laugh. I guess he's allowed to be a little arrogant about the effect he has on women.

He rests his forearms on my shoulders, and I smell that gorgeous, soft, musky woody smell that comes from his body. Like sweet pine after the rain. It almost makes me swoon.

'I have to go now,' says Marc, his voice as deep as a well. 'But I'll be back before the studio session. And when I am, I'd love to meet this bodyguard of yours.'

I inhale again, breathing him into me. 'I'll call her right now.'

24

Jen and I meet outside Vivienne Westwood on Conduit Street. She's carrying two Starbucks in paper cups as she hurries towards me, and she's dressed in a sharp grey trouser suit and fawn coloured coat.

'I knew I should have come earlier,' she calls, making fast clicks with her high heels. She hands me a Starbucks and pulls me into a one-armed hug. 'Shopping fuel,' she says, nodding at the cups. I can smell mine is hot chocolate and see cream melting through the sipping hole.

'Come on. Let's get you some shoes.' Jen drags me into Vivienne Westwood by the elbow, and I smile at being on the familiar Jen shopping train, charging along at one hundred miles an hour.

I'm guessing takeaway drinks aren't technically allowed in the store, but no one would argue with Jen in bulldog mode. She steams into the shop like she owns the place and starts talking to the assistants in designer clothing speak.

'What cut would you say this is? Isn't this a lot like the summer season you did back in 1998? I'd call this nude, wouldn't you?'

It's a different language, and I watch in awe as she talks about seasons, colours, 80's comeback collections and 'occasion' wear.

She packs me off to the fitting room with three stunning, amazing outfits that look like works of art, and has an assistant hold my coffee while I change.

The third outfit I try on is the winner. It's a bright-blue fitted dress in thick fabric with little black leather 'Z' shapes sewn all over it. It's dressy but daytime dressy, and fits me like a glove. It sucks my waist in an extra

Where the Ivy Grows

inch too, and the detail around the bust makes me look bigger. All good.

We team it with black ankle boots covered in buckles, and we're done.

I slip my cashmere coat over the whole outfit, and I feel good. Really good. Like I fit in on Bond Street. Or, at least, I can hold my head up high.

'Marc wants to meet you,' I tell Jen as we leave the store, arm in arm. My jeans and shoes are stuffed into a Vivienne Westwood bag, and they look marked and dirty now I've got my new clothes on.

'I want to meet him too,' says Jen, her voice steely. 'After what was printed this morning, I need to have some serious words about his PR team.'

'The *newspapers*,' I say, stopping. 'I haven't even seen them yet. What did they say?'

'They're ... not *too* bad,' says Jen, but I've known her long enough to tell when she's doing a PR spin. 'I have them with me. Take me back to your hotel, and you can read them yourself.'

25

The papers aren't good. Actually, that's an understatement. They're nasty. Most of them seem to have gone for the 'slutty student seduces her teacher' angle, and talk about me like I'm some crazed nymphomaniac who won't leave Marc alone.

Jen and I are in my suite at the Carlo, sitting on the living area carpet with newspaper pages everywhere.

When we arrived, a butler brought us up afternoon tea, 'Courtesy of Mr Blackwell', but we're not paying much attention to the tiered silver tray of scones, sandwiches and pastries. The newspapers are our focus.

As I read the *Daily News* story, I find myself blinking in shock.

'Oh my god. Jen, have you read this? They've interviewed someone from my college.'

'Where?' Jen leans over my shoulder and reads the headline and the first paragraph. '*Marc's Sexy Student*. Sultry student, Sophia Rose, has bedded one of Hollywood's hottest bachelors.' She gives a little laugh, but then she frowns as she reads on. 'Who's Cecile?'

'She's on the same course as me,' I say.' I can't believe she's saying all this rubbish.'

Under the headline, there's a picture of me from my audition cards looking all doe eyed. I cringe. I guess they must have got that photo from my old university website. The shot of Marc and me, to my relief, is very grainy and fuzzy.

We both look startled, but there's no body language between us – nothing that would suggest we're an item. For all anyone knows, Marc could be paying an innocent visit to a student's home.

That's if Cecile hadn't given an interview.

I read the article again, my teeth gritted.

'Sophia was after Marc from the moment she arrived at college,' says fellow student, Cecile Jefferson. 'She didn't care about the course. Only meeting the famous Marc Blackwell. She did everything she could to get his attention, hanging around after classes when everyone had left.'

Thanks a lot, Cecile. You've given the gossip mill plenty to be getting on with.

'I can't believe she did that,' I say. 'It's all so untrue.'

Then I see the journalist who covered the story. Giles Getty. No wonder he was at the college gates this morning.

'She'd better pray I never get a hold of her,' says Jen, reading the paper over my shoulder. 'Slandering my friend like that. Does she even know you? Have you ever met?'

'A few times,' I admit. 'She fancies Marc. That's all it is. She's just jealous.'

'Soph, you've got to toughen up. This isn't campus gossip, it's a national newspaper. She's spreading bullshit about you to the whole of the UK.'

I sigh. 'But what can I do about it, Jen?'

'Well, for a start, you can get a decent PR firm behind you.'

'Really?' I raise an eyebrow. 'Know any decent PRs?'

We both laugh.

'But seriously, Soph.' Jen crosses her arms. 'They shouldn't have let the papers print this stuff. Marc needs to find someone better. I'm not saying use me. But someone better.'

I think about that. 'I'll talk to Marc.'

'When do I get to meet Prince Charming, anyway?'

'Any minute now.' I glance at the carriage clock on the mantel piece. It's dwarfed by the giant vase of roses. 'He said he'd be here at two.'

As if on cue, the clock chimes 2pm, and the front door opens. I know it's Marc without looking. Trust him to arrive *exactly* on time.

26

'Sophia?' he calls, and I sense an urgency in his voice.

'In here,' I reply.

Marc strides into the living area and looks visibly relieved to see me. 'I'm glad you got back safe.'

He kisses me on the forehead.

'I wasn't in the wilds of Africa,' I say, smiling. 'I only went across the street.'

He notices Jen and strides forward, his hand out. 'You must be the best friend I've heard so much about. Pleased to meet you. Sorry it has to be under these circumstances.'

'Yes,' says Jen, shaking his hand. 'I read the papers this morning. Not the best of starts for you two.'

'It's being dealt with.'

Jen and I look at each other, and I can see her trying to work out whether to bash his PR team now or later.

'Did your team have a damage limitation plan in place?' Jen asks.

'Yes,' Marc replies. 'But they didn't go in strong enough. I had words with them this morning. They'll go in stronger next time.' He pours himself black coffee from a silver flask that came with the afternoon tea.

Jen clears her throat. 'Don't you think it's a little late to go in strong? Post publication? If it had been me, I'd have pinned the papers down right away. I wouldn't have let them get away with what happened this morning.'

Marc turns to her and raises an eyebrow. I can't tell if he's annoyed or not, but if he is, there'll be fireworks. Jen isn't one to back down.

'Oh? And what would you have done to stop those stories?'

'Threatened legal action. Pulled in some favours. Bargained to make the story more favourable. It looks to me like the papers ran exactly what they liked. There was no pressure on them. Nothing to stop them.'

'Jen's in PR,' I explain.

Marc takes a seat on an armchair opposite us and sips his coffee. He's relaxed. In control. The suave businessman.

'You're saying my team should have blackmailed the press into running a better story?'

Jen gives a tight smile. 'Not blackmailed. Bargained. Offered something in return for a favourable report.'

'Something?'

'More photographs, but ones that show you favourably. Or an exclusive interview.'

Marc's lips push out into a thoughtful pout. God, he's sexy. Even when he's frowning, my body responds to him.

'Well, now. That would have been a good idea. Who did you say you work for?'

Jen's tight smile turns into her full-beam, blind you with her white teeth, megawatt smile.

'Prometheus PR. But I'm starting my own firm soon. It's just a matter of time.'

'Interesting.' Marc's gaze flicks to me.

'Don't think I'm trying to sell my own services though,' says Jen. 'All I care about is Sophia.'

'Then we have something in common. I'm listening to what you're saying. It sounds like you know your line of work extremely well.'

'Speaking of work, I'd better go,' says Jen, leaping to her feet. 'I told them I'd be back an hour ago.'

She kisses me on the cheek and makes a phone sign

with her hand. 'Call you later, okay babe? Nice to meet you, Marc.' She snatches up her coat and heads out the door.

Marc sets down his coffee. 'We should get moving too. Ready for the photo shoot?'

I nod. 'Ready as I'll ever be.'

He takes my hands and pulls me to my feet. 'New dress?'

'You only just noticed?'

'I rarely notice what you're wearing. It's *you* I notice, not your clothes.'

'You noticed I wasn't wearing a coat on campus. Remember?'

'That was different. I didn't notice your clothes. I noticed you were cold. Clothing aside, you look extremely desirable, Miss Rose. A little too desirable for my liking. I'm not sure I'll be able to keep my hands off you during the photo shoot.'

'I thought that was the point of the pictures,' I say, feeling a shiver go through me at the thought of his hands. 'For you to have your hands on me. So we look like a couple.'

Marc drops his head to my ear. 'If that's the case, I'm going to have a hard time restraining myself.'

Yes! I feel like singing. Little by little, I'm getting closer. I'm chipping away at that famous self-control of his.

'Won't the photographer tell you what to do at the shoot?' I say with a raise of my eyebrow. 'Do you think you can handle that?'

'I don't take orders well,' says Marc, letting his hand slide onto my lower back. 'But I think I can manage. For you. And who knows? Maybe I'll be able to work in a few orders of my own.'

27

The photography studio isn't what I'm expecting at all. I'd sort of pictured this huge bungalow type building with a rubber floor and tons of camera equipment and lights everywhere. But actually, the studio is just a room inside GMQ headquarters – the company that publishes Arabella's magazine and a bunch of other gossip magazines and newspapers.

It's completely white, with no windows, and it's teeny tiny. Pokey, really. The floor is covered with long sheets of white paper, and there's just one light mounted on a silver tripod.

A giant screen stands in one corner, and I see cardboard boxes of props behind it.

There are no cameras on tripods, or men skulking around setting up lights. Just one photographer – a really happy looking guy with a brown beard and Led Zeppelin T-shirt.

Marc strides towards the photographer, shakes his hand and slaps him on the shoulder. 'Danny. How have you been?'

'Marc, good to see you.' The photographer clasps Marc's hand. 'Keeping busy. How about you?'

'Ask me again at the end of the week.'

The photographer turns to me. 'You must be Sophia. I'm Danny. Good to meet you.'

I smile. 'Nice to meet you too.'

'Well.' Danny drops Marc's hand. 'You two want a tea? Coffee? Doughnut?'

He gestures to a counter of polystyrene cups, instant coffee, plastic water bottles and spilt sugar. There's a box of doughnuts covered in pink frosting. 'Marc, I've got twenty Marlboros if you fancy one later.'

Marc shakes his head.

'Have you given up?'

'I've barely smoked since I met Sophia.'

I smile. 'Is that true?'

Marc raises an eyebrow. 'I've replaced one drug with a much better one.'

'So I'm a *drug*?' I grin.

'Yes. A very addictive, beautiful one.'

Danny clears his throat. 'So. Sophia. Drink?'

'Just water for me, thanks,' I say.

'No worries.' Danny grabs a plastic cup and sloshes water into it. 'How about you, Marc? You remember the coffee from last time, right? Tastes like gravy browning, but stick in enough sugar and it goes down okay.'

Marc slides his hands into his trouser pockets. 'I hadn't forgotten. I've already texted the deli downstairs to bring us up some fresh ones. Latte with hazelnut syrup for you, hot chocolate for Sophia.'

Danny glances at me and gives a little wink. 'I haven't worked with him in months, and still he remembers how I take my coffee. Behind closed doors, he's not half as bad as they say.'

28

'Oh, I still have my moments behind closed doors.' Marc's eyes flick in my direction, and I give him a frown and a 'not here' glance. Oh Marc, Marc. How can you melt my insides with a few well chosen words and one look?

'Don't we all,' says Danny amiably, seemingly oblivious to the simmering Marc just created inside me. 'Are you two all costumed up?'

'Costumed up?' I ask.

'Is that what you want to wear?' He points his camera at my dress.

I look down. 'That's what I planned.'

'Great. You look great. Right, I had a few props in mind.'

'Props?' Marc raises an eyebrow.

'See what you think.' Danny disappears behind the giant screen, and we hear clunks and bangs as he rummages through the prop boxes.

There's a knock at the door, and a delivery boy leans his head into the studio. 'Drinks for studio two?' He has a tray of paper cups in his hand and wears a Daryl's Deli baseball cap.

When he sees Marc, his mouth drops open, but he recovers himself, straightens his cap and holds out the cardboard tray.

'Great timing. Thanks.' Marc takes the tray.

'Can I have your autograph?' the delivery boy stammers. He must be all of seventeen and has bright red spots on his cheeks.

'Of course.' Marc sets down the tray on the white paper floor and pulls a parker pen from his pocket.

The boy holds out a napkin. 'Will this do?'

'Oh, I think we can do better than that,' says Marc. He kneels on the floor and signs the white paper covering, then carefully tears off a corner and hands it to the boy.

The boy looks so overjoyed, I think he might faint. 'Thank you, Mr Blackwell, thank you, thank you.'

'You're welcome,' says Marc. 'Here. Have this, too.' He hands him the pen.

'Really?' The boy's voice grows high pitched. He does a funny sort of bow and backs out of the room. 'Thank you. Thank you.'

'Don't mention it,' says Marc, his eyes softening.

The boy grins and closes the door, and I picture him leaping into the air outside.

I smile at Marc.

'What?' he asks.

'I just never thought of you as the 'talk to fans' type.'

'Just because I like my privacy, doesn't mean I don't appreciate the people who put me where I am today.'

'Yes, but ... I didn't realise you could be so sweet.'

'*Sweet?*'

There's that electricity again. How can he have this effect on me, from the other side of the room?

'Yes, sweet,' I say. 'You were very sweet just then.'

Marc smiles one of his dangerous, curvy smiles. 'Not a word many people use to describe me, Miss Rose. But still, I'm curious. You thought I wouldn't speak with my fans?'

I shrug. 'I wouldn't have pictured you signing autographs like that. It was nice of you.' A grin is sneaking onto my face. I know things are getting dangerous. Hot dangerous. But I can't help it. I'm loving teasing him about his softer side.

In two strides, Marc is beside me.

'Any more of that talk, Miss Rose,' he whispers, 'and

I'll put you over my knee.'

My face flushes, and the grin leaves my face.

Danny appears from behind the screen, and Marc and I turn to him.

'What do you think?' Danny asks, holding up a huge black umbrella. 'I thought the two of you could stand under it together. I can add a rain effect afterwards. Just the two of you together, in the storm. Very London, don't you think?'

'I love that idea,' I say quietly, glancing at Marc. 'It's ... sweet.'

Marc frowns at me, but his eyes are smiling.

29

'So, I'd like the two of you standing close together,' says Danny, handing Marc the umbrella. 'But I don't think it should be a soppy 'arm around the shoulder' sort of shot. I'd just like the two of you side by side.'

I stand by Marc's shoulder, feeling awkward, and not knowing what to do with my arms. I wish he *would* put his arm around my shoulder. But I think I understand what Danny is trying to do. He's going for subtle. Elegant. Not a cheesy family portrait.

Snap, snap, snap. Danny takes shot after shot, from every different angle.

Every so often, he comes up to us and adjusts things – my hair, Marc's jacket, the way we're standing. But mostly he just snaps away, saying, 'Great, you look great. Beautiful.'

It's hard work standing in one position, and my body is soon aching from the effort. Just when I'm thinking about asking for a glass of water, the door creaks.

I see Arabella in the doorway. She's wearing black-rimmed glasses, and her hair is tied more tightly in its ponytail, with no strands escaping around her face.

She smiles when she sees us. 'Wow,' she says. 'There's certainly chemistry between you two. I can feel it from over here.'

I look at Marc and see he's half smiling, half frowning. 'What brings you down here, Arabella?'

'Not you, Marc Blackwell, if that's what you're asking.' She gives him a teasing smile, which I don't like at all. 'Actually, I wanted to talk to Sophia. There have been some developments.'

'Developments?' Marc snaps.

Unease stirs in my stomach.

'What sort of developments?' Marc's body moves protectively against mine.

'We've heard on the grapevine that Sophia's going to be offered a part,' says Arabella. 'In the new *Beauty and the Beast* musical. In the West End.'

I stare at her.

'Beauty and the Beast?' says Marc, slowly. 'At Tottenham Theatre?'

'That's the one,' says Arabella.

'Who gave you this information?' says Marc.

'It was leaked by the director's assistant,' Arabella replies. 'No one is supposed to know yet. The leading lady had a breakdown. Personal problems. And they want an understudy who can get them a bit of press attention, and I guess Sophia will do just that.'

I think I'm about to have heart palpitations.

'No, that can't be right,' I say. 'How can that be right? I've never even auditioned ... no one has seen me perform ... I can't sing.'

'Welcome to show business,' says Arabella. 'They don't care if you're any good. Notoriety is much more valuable than talent.'

'She *is* talented,' Marc barks.

'But I really can't sing,' I say. 'A musical? I mean, that's way out of my league.'

'You *can* sing,' says Marc. 'But that's irrelevant.' He turns to Arabella. 'When will they make her the offer?'

'They're making calls right now, trying to find out who her agent is. So I'd say, as soon as they can get a hold of her. It changes the interview slightly. We don't want to look out of date, so I need to know whether Sophia will take the part.'

'With Getty sniffing around, this is a bad time,' says Marc. 'It wouldn't be clever to accept.'

I smile. 'Marc, I can make my own decisions.'

'I'm aware you can make your own decisions. But this is a new world you know very little about. Anyway, this part hasn't been offered for the right reasons. And the male lead – he's not what I would call a high calibre actor.'

'Do I detect a hint of jealousy, Marc Blackwell?' says Arabella.

'Jealous? Of Leo Falkirk?' Marc frowns and slips his hands into his pockets. 'Hardly.'

'*Leo Falkirk* is the male lead?' I squeak.

Marc raises an eyebrow. 'Please don't tell me he was on your bedroom wall.'

'No,' I say. *But he was on Jen's.* 'But he's just ... well, really famous. I'm flattered anyone would consider casting me beside him. I'm nobody.'

'It's all far too dangerous,' says Marc. 'That particular production of *Beauty and the Beast* only has two actors. Belle and Beast. All eyes would be on you. Lots of press attention. Including Getty. You're not ready.'

Arabella looks from me to Marc to me again. 'You're sure?' she says. 'I mean, lots of young actresses would kill for that role. And to play beside Leo. Whatever you might think of him, it's quite the opportunity.'

'They'll be others,' says Marc.

'Maybe you've forgotten, but being a young, unknown actor is no picnic,' says Arabella. 'Are you sure you're not giving Sophia the wrong advice for your own purposes?'

Marc frowns. 'My own purposes? I'm trying to keep her safe.'

'Oh come on, Marc. She's going to have to experience the real world soon. With all its ugliness. She's not a bird in a cage.'

I swallow and try to stand up straighter. Arabella's

right. Most actresses would be over the moon to be offered this part. I shouldn't turn it down just because Marc says so.

'Well?' Arabella asks me. 'Will you take the part or not?'

I chew at my thumbnail. 'I'd like to, but I need time to think.'

Beside me, I feel Marc stiffen.

'You're sure you don't want to make a decision now?' Arabella seems almost annoyed, and I can understand why. I'm holding up her article.

'I wish I could, but I can't make a decision like that straight away.'

'The director will approach you soon,' says Arabella. 'One way or another. When she does, give me a call, okay? Tell me what you decide.'

'Okay.' I nod.

'Oh, and one last thing,' says Arabella. 'The press know you're at the Carlo. There's a gang of paparazzi outside.'

'How could they know?' says Marc.

Arabella shrugs. 'Someone must have told them.'

30

Marc and I leave the studio hand in hand, both thinking our own thoughts. As we weave through the corridors and downstairs towards reception, I feel Marc's grip loosen.

'Marc?' I say as we walk around a half-circle staircase. 'Are you angry at me for considering the part?'

He's frowning and barely glances at me. 'I couldn't be angry at you if I tried. You should know that by now. But ... I'm concerned about you.'

'Concerned?'

He nods. 'Concerned that if you don't take my advice, I won't be able to keep you safe.'

'I have to live my own life, Marc. I have to make my own decisions, even if I make the wrong ones.'

Marc's hand slips from mine.

We reach the first floor, and I see a ladies room.

'I have to use the bathroom,' I say. It's not true, but I need a few moments alone. And I want to phone Jen.

Marc gives a curt nod. 'The limo is waiting out front. I'll meet you in the back. It's probably better we leave here separately anyway.'

So cold again.

In the bathroom, I pat my eyes and smooth my hair down. My nose and lips are red, and I know I'm on the verge of tears.

It's okay, I tell myself. *You and Marc are just starting out. There'll be obstacles. When you overcome them together, you'll be stronger.* That's what my mother always used to say. But I guess she never met anyone like Marc Blackwell.

My phone has no signal to call Jen, so I just stare at

myself for a moment in the mirror, thinking, thinking. Then I see someone come out of the cubicle.

I freeze.

Oh my god.

It's Cecile.

Cecile from Ivy College.

She's wearing very tight white jeans, high-heeled riding boots and a blue blouse tucked into her waistband. Even in jeans, she looks fancy.

I hold my head up as high as I can, and turn to her. 'What are *you* doing here?'

Her eyes widen when she recognises me, but only for a second. Without saying a word, she waltzes up to the sink and turns on the taps.

'Well?' I ask as she washes her hands under running water.

'The same thing as you,' she says. 'Doing a newspaper story.'

'You're here to tell more lies about me?'

Cecile flicks her fingers into the sink and reaches for a paper towel. 'The truth is different, depending on where you're sitting.'

Anger races around my chest. 'You know what you said wasn't true. Why would you want to bad mouth me like that? I've never done anything to you.'

'I beg to differ,' says Cecile, drying her hands. 'You always knew I wanted Marc. It's me he should be with. Who are you anyway? Some small girl from a small town. I mix with all the right people. I wouldn't be an embarrassment to him. Some girl he has to dress up.' She looks icily at my dress. 'I'm guessing that outfit is Marc's choice?'

I look down at my dress, momentarily wrong footed. It wasn't Marc's choice, but it wasn't exactly mine either. I mean, yes, I picked it. But I would never have even visited that store if it wasn't for Marc.

'You're just jealous,' I mutter.

'You didn't play fair,' says Cecile. 'You pretended you didn't want him, then snuck in when my back was turned. So now it's my turn. I'll do whatever it takes to win Marc. And if that means telling the world what you're really like, then so be it. He'll work out what you are eventually, anyway.'

'I'm not like you,' I say. 'Things just happened. It wasn't planned -'

'That's not how it looked to me,' says Cecile. 'Or anyone else. You're just some little nobody sleeping with Marc to get famous. That's what *everyone* thinks. The newspapers. Everyone. It's not as if they had to force the story out of me. They'd pretty much written it before they even spoke to me.'

Ouch. Is that what everyone thinks? I haven't spoken to Tom and Tanya yet – are they believing what they've read in the papers?

'You've made your bed,' says Cecile, gliding towards the door. 'And now you'll have to lie in it.'

I search my brain for some witty retort – something that will put her in her place. But I can't think of one. It'll come to me later, and I'll replay this little scene, wishing I'd said something clever and cutting.

The bathroom door slams, and I'm left staring at it, feeling helpless, furious and alone.

31

Fuming, I head down to the GMQ lobby. I don't get angry often, but when I do, I find it hard to think straight.

Ahead, I see Marc's limo through the automatic glass doors. Two wheels are mounted on the pavement.

I'm so wrapped up in anger that I don't notice the other person in the lobby until I feel a pressure on my elbow.

'Sophia.' It's a man's voice.

I turn. Oh my god.

It's Giles Getty.

He's taller than he looked at the college gates this morning. Not as tall as Marc, but tall, nonetheless, and my eyes are level with his soft shirt collar. He's dressed in that fashionable media way – black jeans, loose, creased blue shirt and a navy suit jacket.

He looks normal enough. Almost handsome. But his eyes are bulging and wild, and I can see he's having a hard time keeping still. He's agitated. Not at peace.

I look down at my elbow and see hairy fingers gripping my cashmere coat.

'Please take your hands off me.' I try to make my voice as firm as possible, even though I'm not feeling very firm at all. The truth is, there's something very frightening about this man.

'Just wanted to talk, that's all. You don't mind talking, do you?' He's speaking quickly. Too quickly.

His grey eyes dart back and forth.

'I need to go,' I say, pulling my arm free. 'Marc's outside.'

'Hey. Wait. Wait.' He blocks my path, bouncing from

one foot to the other. He reminds me of a boxer in the ring before the fight starts. All energy and fury. I can't see the limo anymore. 'Look, I've known Marc for a long time. Years. I'm just interested in the new lady in his life, that's all. Is that so bad?'

He sticks out his bottom lip a little, I guess to look cute, but he doesn't look cute at all. His eyes are bulging more than ever. 'How about a glass of champagne?'

'No, I really have to go.'

'Your friend Cecile's here. Did you know?'

'She's not my friend.' I try to walk around him, but he moves to stand in my way.

'Wouldn't you like to make some money, Sophia?' When he says my name, it feels like a snake has slithered around my shoulder. 'I've heard about your background. Seen your family home. Not exactly a wealthy upbringing. I can set you up with the right people, show you how to tell a good story.'

'Haven't you told enough lies?'

Getty laughs, a long, throaty laugh. 'We have a caped crusader in our midst. Truth, honesty and justice? I wouldn't have expected Marc to settle for anything less. Tell me Sophia, what's he like in bed?'

My hands start to shake, and I try to move around him again, but he sidesteps in my way.

'Does he tie you up and spank you like he does the other women?'

I look around the lobby, but there's no one. The reception desk is empty. Did Getty plan this? Me in the empty lobby?

'You must know, Sophia, that you're just a novelty to him. A toy. You won't last. Nobody does. Sell your story and make some cash while you still can. Like I say, I've known Marc a long time.'

'Too long.' The words boom around the lobby, and

Marc appears behind Getty's shoulder. 'Move out of her way.'

Getty turns around. His eyes look ready to pop out of his head. 'Well, well. The hero of the hour. But you're not really a hero. Are you?' He's talking more quickly than ever, and his face has gone white.

'I hardly think you're in a position to judge heroism. Move out of her way. Right now.'

Getty steps aside. 'Pardon me. Just doing my job.'

'Go do it somewhere else.'

'It's a free country.'

Getty whips his camera out and takes a snap before either of us can react.

I'm momentarily stunned by the flash of white, but Marc launches forward, pushing Getty aside and pulling me to him. He bundles me towards the automatic doors.

'God damn him,' he shouts as we charge down the steps to the waiting limo. Marc opens the limo door and helps me inside. I fall onto leather, hearing the door slam behind us. 'I won't let him do this. Not this time.'

32

The car pulls out, and I'm thrown onto the leather couch.

Marc sits opposite me and leans across to take my hands.

'Are you okay?'

I swallow. 'A bit shaken up.'

'Christ, I'm such an idiot. I should have seen this coming. I've known Getty for long enough.'

'How?' I ask. 'He said he knew you too. How do you know him?'

Marc shakes his head and drops my hands. 'It doesn't matter.' He stares out of the window and mutters, '*How* did he know you were there?'

'Maybe just coincidence?' I say. 'I think he brought Cecile to GMQ.'

'There's no such thing as coincidence. Not where Getty is concerned. No, he knew. Why didn't I stay with you? I thought ... I thought GMQ was safe. Getty doesn't have any connections there. I was certain. Christ, what a fool I am. And now he's got his picture.'

'Is that such a bad thing?' I say. 'I mean, maybe he'll leave us alone now.'

Marc laughs. 'Leave us alone? As long as he can get money for our pictures, he'll keep taking them. And if and when the papers lose interest in the real story, he'll just set up what he can and make the stories up himself. Anything to get at me.'

'But why? Why does he want to get at you?'

'Let's just say we have a past, and leave it at that.'

'Where are we going?' I ask as the car charges out of Central London.

'The only place I can keep you safe,' says Marc. 'My town house.'

'But I thought you said ... don't you have a visitor?'

'Well, we'll just have to deal with that when we get there.'

Marc looks out the window and doesn't say anything more.

33

On the pavement by Marc's townhouse, a pack of photographers jostle and fight for position. I slide down the seat when I see them. The windows are tinted, but it still feels like they can see in.

When the photographers see our limo, they charge towards it, shoving cameras against the glass and banging on the windows.

'Marc! Marc, is Sophia in there with you?'
'Is it true she's only with you to get famous, Marc?'

I remember Arabella's words, 'A bird in a cage', and that's exactly how I feel. A very frightened bird.

Concern creases Marc's forehead, and he leaps across the car to sit beside me. He puts an arm around my shaking shoulders, and I bury my head in his chest, trying to drown out the banging and shouting.

We drive through the gates, and the photographers don't follow. I guess they know better than to trespass. I see them through the back window, milling around, cameras dangling from their hands.

As we drive down into the underground garage, the sunshine disappears and all I can see is dark and concrete.

'How long will we have to stay here?' I ask. 'Hidden away.'

'A few weeks. A few months. It really depends.'

'A few *months*?'

'Sophia, I just want you to be safe,' Marc whispers into my hair. 'I can look after you here. I've spent years getting the security right.'

I nod, climbing out of the car into the dark, underground space. His words should make me feel comforted, but …

I don't want to be stuck in a house, no matter how safe it is, for weeks or months on end. I need sunshine.

Marc's cars are spread around the garage, shiny and expensive looking. I can almost hear them purring.

His Ford Mustang is parked in the corner, shiny and raring to go. I notice the wasp yellow car again. The one that doesn't suit Marc at all. Marc's leather shoes click on the concrete behind me.

'You still haven't told me why you keep your father's car,' I say, turning.

'Keep your enemies close, isn't that what I said?'

'You did, but that's not much of an explanation.'

'I don't like talking about my past.'

'Marc, I want to know about you. If we're going to do this for real, you're going to have to get used to opening up.'

'You're not going to leave this alone, are you?' He heads to the stairs.

'Probably not.' I catch up with him and take his hand. 'Tell me about your father. How did he die?'

'Cancer,' says Marc, curtly. 'Long and drawn out.'

'And ... do you ever regret not being there? At the funeral?'

'No, I don't,' says Marc. 'The only regret I have, where my father is concerned, is that I didn't protect my sister better.'

'But you were so young. Just a child.'

'It doesn't change the way I feel.' Marc's lips clamp shut.

'So tell me about the car.'

'I keep that car because my father bought it with my childhood earnings. Does that go some way to explaining things?'

'A little, but ... not really.'

Marc lets out a long breath. 'What do you remember

about your childhood?'

'All kinds of things. Playing with Jen. Going to football matches with my grandpa. School plays. Christmas. Camping in the woods. And bad things too. My mum dying, and my dad falling apart. But I try not to focus on that.'

'All I remember of being a child is working. And this car was paid for with that money. So I suppose you could say this car is my childhood.'

'That's ... sort of sad, but also sort of beautiful,' I say, squeezing his hand. 'So that's why you keep it? Because you don't want to let your childhood go?'

'No. I keep it because I never want to forget what my father did to me. I want a constant reminder.'

'Marc, is that completely healthy?'

Marc shrugs. 'Probably not. But that's who I am.'

'And I love who you are.'

We reach the top of the stairs, and suddenly Marc turns to me and slips his hands around my back. He kisses me, a long, slow kiss that makes me cling to him. His lips move gently over mine, and his tongue slips forward, stroking and caressing. I'm lost in a world of senses – his hands running around my lower back, his chest pressed against mine and his beautiful smell.

It's such a tender kiss. So unlike Marc's usual kisses, but I still feel his hunger.

Suddenly, Marc breaks away, leaving me a little disorientated and wobbly legged. I feel like a giddy schoolgirl. He scoops an arm around my back, opens the door to the house and leads me into the large hallway.

'Why the kiss?' I ask, smiling.

'Are you complaining?' Marc raises an eyebrow.

'Not at all.'

'Let's just say I was struck by how much I can love a girl in such a short space of time.'

My smile grows. 'I love you too.'

I see the familiar pictures of buildings along the hall, and the red carpet running along and up the sweeping staircase.

There's a clinking sound from the kitchen.

'Marc?' calls a voice. A woman's voice, musical and light.

34

'Your visitor?' I say, hoping my tone doesn't betray my jealousy.

Marc nods.

'Who is she?'

He doesn't answer. Instead, he grips my waist, and we head into the kitchen. 'You're up. I thought you'd still be in bed.'

In *bed*?

At the kitchen counter, I see a tall, skinny woman with very long, straight brown hair that comes to her waist. The bones of her knees and shoulders show through a floaty, flowery dress.

Her eyes are watery blue and pale, and there are worry wrinkles around her eyes.

She starts to cry when she sees Marc – deep, wracking sobs that shake her skinny chest.

'Marc. Oh Marc. I'm so sorry. I'm so, so sorry.'

He goes to her, and she flings her arms around his waist. 'I told them where you were, Marc. I didn't mean to. They phoned. They pretended to be from the college. I told them where you were. Where you were going.'

She looks up and notices me.

'Oh! You must be Sophia.' She tries for a smile. 'I'm so sorry. What a mess.'

Marc turns to me.

'Sophia,' he says gently. 'This is my sister. Annabel.'

I think of the family photo in Marc's box upstairs, and the young brown-haired girl in the picture. This woman looks more than a little like that young girl. But the names on the back of that photo were Joan, Mike, Marc and Emily. No Annabel.

Does Marc have another sister?

Annabel pulls herself free and pushes hair back from her face. I see a long red and purple bruise down her left cheek, by her ear.

Marc notices it too and crouches down, taking her chin in his hand.

'If that doesn't heal up soon, I'm calling the doctor.'

She turns away.

'You have to leave him for good this time,' Marc says. 'Do you understand me? You can't go back. I don't care if he says he'll marry you. You have to think of your son.'

'I know. I know, Marc.'

She pulls herself from the stool.

'Sophia, I'm so sorry.' Her legs look barely able to hold her weight. 'I so wanted to be well and healthy when I met you, but ... I'm a wreck again.'

'It's fine, really.' She's so frail that I want to take care of her. Wrap her in warm clothes and feed her up.

As she walks towards me, hand out to shake mine, she stumbles a little.

I leap forward, and Marc does too. We both grab her, me around her rib cage, Marc by the shoulders.

'You need to rest,' says Marc.

'You need to *eat*,' I say, helping her back onto the stool. 'Let me make you some soup.'

'No, please.' Annabel shakes her head. 'Honestly, what must you think of me? I so wanted to make a good impression on you.' She glances at Marc and manages a weak smile. 'The girl who has my brother head over heels.'

'Let me fix you something,' I say, making sure she has a firm seat on the stool. 'Tea at least. Or hot Bovril.'

I go to the fridge and see its chock full of gourmet stuff – potted crab, sides of ham, smoked salmon and a basket of exotic fruit tied with ribbons.

'Do you have any chicken soup?' I ask Marc.

He comes to my shoulder and looks into the fridge. 'Rodney stocked up in case Annabel felt like eating. I don't know if chicken soup was on his radar.'

'Do you think you could manage some soup?' I ask Annabel.

'I can try.' Annabel gives Marc the tiniest of smiles. 'She's beautiful, Marc. Just like you said. Inside and out. I can see why you like her.'

I feel a smile in my stomach and glance at Marc, but he's giving nothing away, so I open and close cupboards, looking for hearty, warming foods – the sort you want when you're ill and shaky. I don't know what's wrong with Annabel, but chicken soup helps most things.

There's nothing in the cupboards but gourmet spreads, exotic spices, speciality flours and warm champagne.

I go back to the fridge and find a packet of Harrods roasted chicken legs and some fresh tarragon. There are odd bits of vegetable in the fridge door – a bunch of carrots with big leafy stems, a Savoy cabbage and a packet of Jersey Royal potatoes.

I rummage in the cupboard for flour, noticing Marc watching me, a half smile on his face.

'Chicken soup,' I say, taking down a knife and chopping vegetables on a marble board. 'And I'll bake some soda bread too.'

35

Thanks to Rodney's organisation, the kitchen is easy to use, and I soon have a pan of soup boiling on the stove and soda bread baking in the oven.

When I serve Annabel her bowl of soup, she takes a spoonful and smiles.

'Mmm,' she says. 'I haven't had anything like this in a long time.' She looks at Marc. 'I'll bet you haven't either. A home-cooked meal.'

'On the contrary,' says Marc. 'Sophia cooked me a meal just the other day. At her father's house.'

'If it was as delicious as this, you were lucky,' says Annabel.

'It was sublime.'

I blush when Marc says that. He's probably eaten at some of the world's best restaurants, but still he enjoyed my cooking.

'Do you think you could manage some bread?' I ask Annabel, stooping to check my little loaf in the oven.

'It smells so good,' says Annabel. 'I'd love some.'

I take the loaf from the oven and cut a little slice for Annabel. I don't butter it –that might be a step too far – but she seems happy to dip it into her soup.

There's colour in her cheeks now, and she's sitting up much straighter.

'What must you think of me, Sophia?' she says, scraping her spoon on the bottom of the bowl. 'A grown woman, a wreck like this.'

I think about what Jen told me, before I started Ivy College. About Marc's sister being a heroin addict. I don't care if she is. I don't judge people. But I wonder how Giles Getty is involved in all this.

'Don't call yourself that,' I say. 'Think of your son – he wouldn't want his mother talking about herself that way.'

Tear's slide down Annabel's face. 'I'm no mother. My son is with foster parents.'

'God, you poor thing,' I say. 'That must be awful for you.'

Annabel nods and sniffs. 'It was my choice. I asked them to take him. Until I can get myself free of this stuff and his father, he's better off in care. I need to get well this time. I have to. Or they'll take him away permanently.'

'You should sleep now,' says Marc, frowning. 'You need to rest.'

'Yes,' says Annabel, clambering up from the stool. 'Thank you so much, Sophia. Not just for the food.' She looks at me, and her eyes are big and earnest. 'For caring.'

'Here, I'll help you,' says Marc.

'No, no.' She waves him away. 'Please. I feel bad enough about meeting Sophia like this. You stay here. I'll be fine.' She gives him a weak smile. 'You know I will be – you've seen me like this plenty of times before.'

'And I'm concerned each and every time.'

'I know,' says Annabel, limping out of the room. 'And I love you for it.'

'Why didn't you tell me?' I ask gently, picking up Annabel's bowl and taking it to the sink.

'Tell you?' Marc takes a seat on a stool, one leg dangling towards the floor.

'That your sister was your house guest. And that she was sick.'

'Sick? That's one word for it.'

'I was thinking all sorts of things.'

'Oh?' Marc raises an eyebrow. 'You were jealous?'

I look at the floor. 'Maybe. A little. My mind was playing tricks.'

Marc lets out a long, low laugh and my stomach grows soft.

'I always thought dark feelings were for people like me.'

'Perhaps I'm not the angel you think I am.'

'You are. But perhaps you won't be by the time I've finished with you.'

'Meaning?'

'I think you know exactly what I mean.'

I feel my stomach flip over, and the familiar melting, crazy-making feeling that has me falling into Marc's arms whenever he snaps his fingers. But I resist it. There are serious things to discuss.

'I don't know why it had to be such a big mystery,' I say. 'Was she who you were talking to on the phone? When we were in the hotel?'

Marc nods slowly, watching me.

'And the person you so badly had to meet up with? The person who could help you with your future?'

'I need Annabel to be better. To break free of her boyfriend and move forward. Until she does, there'll always be a part of me who's angry. And as long as I'm angry ... there'll be a barrier between us.'

'So why didn't you tell me?'

Marc opens out his hands. 'I didn't want you to have to deal with ... something like this ... so early on. I wanted you to meet her when she'd recovered.'

'Recovered?'

'From her heroin addiction.' He rests his chin on his elbow, still watching me.

'I heard about that,' I say.

'I didn't know if it was true.'

'It's true. She's going through withdrawal right now. Day four. There's light at the end of the tunnel.'

'How can we help her get better?'

Marc smiles and shakes his head. 'And you wonder why I love you? She's nothing to you, and yet you want to help her. Most people would think 'junkie scum' and run a mile.'

'Of course I don't think that. She's a human being. We all have our problems. And I want to help, if I can. She's your sister. Why wouldn't I want to help?'

'It's going to take a bit more than a few bowls of soup, Sophia.' He puts his head in his hands. 'Sorry. That came out wrong. I didn't mean ...' He looks up. 'I love that you did that for her. But we've been battling this for years. Years. She wants to stop, but something always drags her back. Not something, some*one*. Her boyfriend.'

'The one you punched out?' The words are out of my mouth before I can stop them.

36

Marc's eyes widen. 'How did you -'

'Jen,' I say. 'She works in PR, remember?'

'Ah, yes. The PR bulldog. Of course. She certainly knows her stuff. She was my chief suspect when the press knew our location.'

'*Jen*?' I'm outraged. 'She would *never* do *anything* like that. We're like sisters. How could you even think that?'

Marc's top lip curls into a sexy smile. 'Jealous and a hot temper? I'm seeing new sides to you today, Miss Rose.'

I blow out air. 'It's been a difficult day.'

'I accept that.' He holds his hands up, still smiling. 'Maybe I don't trust as easily as you. But don't worry, I've learned my lesson. It's clear Jen means a lot to you. I take back my comment.'

'Thank you.' I hesitate. 'Marc?'

'Yes?'

'Who's Emily?'

Marc stares at me for a moment. 'How do you ...'

'I saw the name Emily on your family picture. In the box in your bedroom. Do you have another sister?'

'No.' Marc shakes his head. 'Emily was the name our mother gave my sister. But when our mother died and we moved to the States, my father renamed her. Emily was too plain for him.'

'That's ... awful,' I say. 'He sounds ... a little crazy.'

'Not crazy, just spectacularly self-centred. The worse example of a human being.'

There's a vibrating sound, and Marc slips his phone from his trouser pocket. He frowns when he sees the number, but still takes the call.

'Minty. Yes. Yes, I heard.' He frowns, thick eyebrows pulling together. 'So they thought they'd go through me? Well, as it happens, Sophia's right here. No, that won't be necessary. There's no decision to make. Tell them she won't take the part.'

He hangs up.

'Marc?' I feel uneasy. 'What just happened?'

'That was the *Beauty and the Beast* musical. They couldn't get hold of you, so they phoned my publicity person instead.'

'And you told them ... *what*, exactly?'

'You heard what I told her.'

'You told them *I wouldn't take the part*? Without asking me? Am I hearing you right?'

'Exactly right. It's not safe.'

I step back from him, not quite knowing where to turn or what to do. 'How could you ... you had no right.'

'I have your best interests at heart.'

He moves towards me, but I take another step back, shaking my head. 'I can't believe you did that. Marc, you have to phone them back. Tell them that it's my choice.'

'I see no reason for doing that.'

'You see no reason?' I can barely get the words out, I'm so angry. 'No *reason*?' I feel like I'm falling, and the kitchen goes blurry. 'I can't be around you right now,' I hear myself say. 'I need to be alone.'

I storm out of the kitchen into the hallway, before I realise there's nowhere to go. The paparazzi are outside.

I turn a circle in the hallway.

'Sophia.' Marc appears beside me.

'Stay away from me, right now,' I say. 'I mean it. I'm not a child. What gave you the right ... do you have any respect for me *at all*?' Today's events are whirling round and round my head, and Giles Getty's words keep coming back to me.

You're just a toy to him.

'Sophia, you need to understand -'

I put a hand up. 'Please, don't try to explain.'

Marc looks at me for a long time, his hands slipping into his pockets. He doesn't look angry, just ... disappointed. Thoughtful. Like he wants to reprimand me but doesn't know how. Little lines have appeared above his nose.

'So you want to be by yourself?' he says eventually.

'I need to think ...' But the truth is, I can't think. Not when I'm so angry.

'As you wish.' Marc marches past me to the door leading to the garage. His hand falls to the door handle. 'Rodney is upstairs. He'll get you anything you want. You can use my bedroom if you want to be alone. You know the way.'

'Where are you going?'

'To give you some space. I'll call you later.'

The door bangs, and I hear the roar of a car – something sporty and fast.

I'm left alone in the hallway, startled and very, very confused. I know I said I wanted to be by myself, but for Marc to leave like that ... it makes me angrier than ever.

37

I sit on Marc's bed like a sulky teenager, staring at my phone. In spite of myself, I'm waiting for his call. But I might have known Marc would be true to his word. He really is giving me space, at least for a while.

I text Jen:

'Marc just decided I shouldn't take a part in a big musical. Beauty and the Beast. He didn't even ask me.'

Jen replies:

'No way! That's a big part. What a cave man. He can't do that. Please tell me you told him where to go.'

I text back:

'We got in a fight, and now he's left. He didn't seem to get why I'm angry.'

Jen replies:

'Men. They're all crazy. And they say women are the mad ones.'

As I read Jen's last message, there's a soft knock on the door.

'Sophia? It's Annabel. Can I come in?'

I pull myself off the bed and open the door a fraction. 'I don't mean to shut myself away,' I say. 'But I've got a lot to think about.'

'Did my brother do something?' Her eyes are big and concerned. She looks better than before. Sturdier on her feet, but still frail.

'He made a decision for me without asking. I know he had my best interests at heart, but it was wrong.'

Annabel nods, her head all loose like a puppet. 'Can I come in?'

I hold the door back. 'Please.'

She takes a seat on the bed.

'I don't want you and Marc to fight.'

'We're not fighting exactly,' I say, taking a seat beside her. 'He left.'

'That sounds like my brother. Checking out whenever things get too difficult. That's just his way of coping. But think of it this way – if he wasn't like that, he might have ended up like me.'

She glances down at her skinny hands, and I notice bruises around her fingers.

'Don't be so hard on yourself,' I say. 'It doesn't sound like you've had things easy.'

'I've never heard him talk about anyone like he talks about you,' says Annabel. 'He's *different* since I last saw him. I hear it in his voice. His face is different. He looks lighter. Softer. You must be the difference.'

I shake my head. 'I *wish* I could have that effect on him. But ... he found it pretty easy to leave just then.'

'He has his issues. But the way he talks about you ... you're an angel to him. You're saving him.'

'If I were an angel, I wouldn't get jealous or angry or scared. Or confused.'

'He's not as complicated as he seems, you know,' says Annabel. 'He's frightened too. The way he takes charge of everything – that's just his way of coping.'

I think about that. It makes sense. I guess he's scared of me taking this part. Scared that he'll lose control and I'll get hurt. But I can't live my life that way.

'Look, I'll leave you to think,' says Annabel, pulling herself up from the bed and letting out a long yawn. 'I'm going for another sleep. Whatever happens, I'm glad Marc met you.'

She leaves the room.

I check my phone again, in case by some miracle Marc called and I didn't hear. He hasn't, but Annabel's words have softened me.

I tap out a message.

'Sorry for the fight. Can we talk?'

Immediately, a text from Marc appears.

'On my way home.'

There are no kisses, but Marc doesn't send kisses. I let out a long sigh. When he gets back, we'll get everything sorted out. I'll make him understand. I know I have to. Because if I can't ... oh, that doesn't bear thinking about.

38

I'm going stir crazy in Marc's bedroom, so I head downstairs, clutching my phone.

I guess Annabel must still be sleeping, because there's no one in the kitchen or living area.

Marc's house is warm in temperature, but it feels a little cold. I can't put my finger on it. The pictures of buildings don't help, nor the lack of colour. The curtains and light shades are expensive, but plain. Unremarkable. Like the house was decorated for a business conference.

I head into the kitchen. Through the patio doors, I notice the garden is still overgrown and in sore need of love and attention. Ivy climbs up trees and creeps up walls. It's beautiful, but it needs to be cut back a little and clipped into a better shape.

The trees are yews and holly, so they're still green and bushy, but they've been left to grow completely wild, and their green leaves are blocking out the sunlight.

In my palm, my phone vibrates, and I answer straight away, thinking it will be Jen or Marc.

'Hello.' The voice is very posh. Plumy. And female. 'Is this Sophia Blackwell?'

'Yes,' I reply. 'I'm Sophia.'

'This is Davina Merryweather.'

There's a pause, and I'm guessing she's waiting for me to recognise her. But I have no idea who she is.

She coughs politely. 'I'm directing *Beauty and the Beast* at Tottenham Theatre.'

'Oh.' My hand shakes a little, and I clamp my other hand over it. 'Right. Yes. I was told ... It's nice to speak to you. How did you get my number?'

'I have my ways.' I can hear her smiling down the

phone. 'Look, I wanted to talk to you in person. I was ever so disappointed that you didn't want the part. And I thought ...' She gives a little laugh. 'Maybe I could persuade you. We're getting a little desperate, and the marketing team thinks you fit the bill.'

I clear my throat. 'Actually, I never said I wouldn't take the part. My ... I mean, Marc answered for me.'

'Did he, indeed?'

'He thought he was acting in my best interests.'

'How very 1950's.'

'Yes. So. What I mean to say is, I haven't decided one way or another about the part.'

'So you're interested?'

'Interested, yes. But I'm still thinking things over. Can you give me a little time?'

'Not much time. We'll need to know by close of business today. 6pm.'

'I understand.'

'Well. My number should have come up on your phone. Call me back with your decision.'

The line goes dead.

I let the phone slide from my ear, realising that I *have* heard of Davina Merryweather. I saw her on a BBC documentary about musical theatre, years ago. I guess she must be pretty famous. I wonder if Denise Crompton knows her.

I wish I had more time to think. But 6pm today ... I don't have long.It's late afternoon, and a pinkish light is shining over London, but in Marc's garden, the light is lost in the overgrown trees.

I see a pair of green wellies near the patio doors and slide my feet into them. They're four sizes too big, but they'll do. I'm guessing they're Rodney's.

He probably uses them to wade through wet grass and empty the bins.

Out in the garden, the air is chilly, but the sky is bright white and clear. I take a look around, breathing in the beautiful fresh smell of plants and soil.

The grass is knee height and full of dead dandelions, and the small patio near the door is green with mould. I wonder if Marc has ever even set foot out here. Probably not. Buildings are his thing. Not nature.

There's a rickety shed in the corner with a loose door, and I see shears, a spade and trowel hanging inside.

By the time I've clumped over the grass to the shed, I've already formed a plan for tidying this space.

The ivy is staying, of course. It's beautiful. I love that ivy can stay pretty and green and silver all year round, in the harshest of weather. But the trees need cutting back so the sunlight can get through, and the grass needs trimming so sunlight can get to the soil. I'll also dig a little vegetable bed, if there's time, and ask Rodney to buy seeds and bulbs.

I take out the shears and start cutting the thin tree branches and feathery leaves. Once I've cut enough to let some daylight through, I set to work on the grass. There's no mower, so I use the shears again, crawling on my hands and knees.

I leave a few clumps wild, so there are some dandelions to decorate the garden. Then I use the spade to dig a neat little rectangular vegetable bed and turn over the soil so the sun can get to it. There are a good few worms crawling up, which tells me the soil is healthy.

When I stand back, cheeks flushed with the exercise, mud under my fingernails, I feel proud of what I've done. The garden looks so much better. Fresher. Lighter. More beautiful. Not perfect, but at least a little bit loved.

I sense someone watching and turn to see Marc through the glass. He has his hands in his pockets.

39

I smooth my hair down, suddenly self-conscious, and plod towards him in the welly boots, my feet slipping and sliding out of them as I walk.

'Maybe I should hire you full time,' says Marc as I close the patio door and stamp the boots on the mat.

'You *should* hire someone,' I say. 'It's criminal to have a space like that and not use it.'

'You want me to have someone dry clean your dress?'

'Oh, shoot.' I look down and see grass stains and mud on the Vivienne Westwood dress. Sometimes, I get so carried away with gardening that I forget basic things like eating, drinking and changing my clothes. The dress isn't ruined, but it does need a clean. 'We need to talk.'

'Okay.'

We look at each other.

'Have you had time to think?' Marc says.

'About?'

'About taking the part. How foolish it would be.'

I'm shaking my head. 'I don't believe this. Marc, do you even understand why I was so angry before?'

'You didn't like me making a decision for you.'

'Exactly right.' I go to the sink and wash mud from my hands. 'Can't you just apologise and we'll move on?'

'I don't see why I need to apologise for keeping you safe,' says Marc, taking a stool.

'I know you only want what's best for me,' I say, 'but you're not my teacher right now. This is real life. You have to let me make my own choices.'

'As long as they're the right ones.'

'*No*, Marc. You have to trust *me* to decide what's right and wrong. I won't always get things right. But you have to let me make my own mistakes.'

'That's ridiculous,' says Marc. 'You're clearly not in the mood to have a rational conversation. And until you are, we may as well put this discussion on hold.'

Oh, I'm fuming now. How *dare* he?

'I *am* having a rational conversation. It's you who's not making any sense.'

'Sophia, there's no point talking about this. We clearly don't agree.'

'Davina Merryweather phoned me while you were out,' I say.

'She phoned you?' He jumps from his stool, and it tips back and forth behind him.

'Yes, she did.'

'And what did you tell her?'

'It shouldn't matter to *you* what I told her. It's my decision to make.'

Marc slaps his hands on the counter. 'Are you saying you took the part to spite me? Sophia -'

'Is that what you think of me? Thanks for your trust. No, I didn't take the part. To spite you or for any other reason. I told her I'd think about it.'

'It's not safe for you to take that part. Not with Getty lurking around.'

'Marc, he's only a photographer -'

'All I want is to protect you.' Marc rocks back and forth on his shoes. 'If you take this part, you'll be in alien surroundings. Vulnerable. Alone.'

'So you're saying I can't take care of myself? That unless I have you looking after me, I can't do *anything*?'

'Christ.' Marc tips his head back and looks at the

ceiling. 'Sophia, don't you understand? Now we're out in the open, it's dangerous out there. I brought you here so I can protect you.'

'So I can never leave?'

'For the time being, it makes sense that you stay here.'

I remember Giles Getty's words again.

'I'm a human being Marc, not a pet. You can't keep me here because *you're* scared.'

'Sophia, you're being a child.'

'No. You've got that wrong. I'm trying to be an adult. And live a normal adult life.' I charge past him. 'I need to be by myself. Can you please ask Keith to give me a ride?'

'Where are you planning on going, exactly?'

'I don't know. My dad's house, maybe. I need space. I need to be somewhere where someone doesn't try to control my life.'

'Control your life?' Marc frowns. 'All I'm doing is trying to keep you safe.' His blue eyes flicker with pain.

'Really? Because all I see is someone who's afraid. So afraid that he's making decisions on my behalf.' I put a hand to my forehead. 'I need some space.'

'At least let me arrange somewhere for you to go. It's not safe at your father's house. Getty can find you there.'

I hesitate. I don't want my family dragged into all this. 'Okay. Well. I'll find somewhere else then.'

Marc takes a step towards me.

I look away from him. 'Marc, please. I can't -'

'Ivy College is safe. Go back to your old room. Carry on with your studies. I won't come anywhere near you if space is what you want. It'll be like I don't exist.'

I feel that pain in my chest again. I don't want him not

to exist. It hurts to even think about not seeing him. But I do need space right now. I can't think straight while I'm here. And I know he's right about Ivy College. I'll be safe there.

'Okay.'

40

I watch the grey road ahead as Keith drives me to Ivy College. We're not chatting, like we usually would. Instead, I stare out of the window, watching London slide past.

It starts to rain – tiny patters at first, but then the sky turns blue-brown, and great torrents of water slosh over the car windscreen.

'Lovely weather,' Keith remarks.

'Lovely,' I murmur. Funny how life can change. This morning, I was full of hope. Marc and I had a future. Now, I'm not sure about anything. My lips feel like they have magnets in them, pulling them down, and there's a burning in my stomach.

I want Marc, but how can things ever work if he wants to keep me trapped, never making my own choices?

I hear tinkling classical music and distractedly notice my mobile phone is flashing. It's Davina's number.

I take the call. 'Hello?'

'Sophia? Just checking in.'

'Oh, hi.' I glance at Keith.

'Have you made your decision?'

I think about Marc and how he wants to keep me safe. And then I think about a life where I never make any decisions for myself. I don't know what Marc will do if I take the part. Maybe he'll break up with me. Or maybe it'll make us stronger. Either way, I need to show him that I can make decisions on my own. Good ones. Decisions that help my future. I try not to think about Getty.

'I'll take it,' I say. 'Yes. I'll take the part.'

'Wonderful!' A pause. 'You don't sound very happy.'

'No, it's just ... I have things on my mind.'

'We don't have much time. Can you come see us first thing tomorrow?'

'Yes, great. See you tomorrow.'

I'm about to hang up, when I hear, 'Sophia!'

I bring the phone back to my ear. 'Sorry. Yes?'

'Aren't you going to ask where to meet? And what time?'

'Oh. Right. Yes, of course.'

'7am at the Tottenham Theatre. We'll have a driver collect you. Just give me your address.'

'Ivy College,' I say.

'Ivy College? You're not staying with Marc?'

'Not right now.'

'Oh.' There's a pause, and I can almost hear the cogs in her brain working.

'Is something wrong?' I ask.

'No, no. Actually, Ivy College is perfect. What's your email? I'll send you the script and some MP3s.'

I tell her.

'Great,' she says. 'See you tomorrow.'

It's still raining when Keith drops me off in the college car park. I thank him, pull my coat over my head and run across the gravel.

There are no students in the grounds, but the meal hall is all lit up. I guess everyone must be inside having dinner.

I should eat too, but I'm so not hungry, it's ridiculous. My stomach is like a screwed up piece of paper, and sadness has crept right into my bones.

I hurry across the grounds, seeing gravel fly up around my feet, and feeling rain on my legs and face.

When I reach the accommodation block, I feel tears coming. What a difference a day makes ... isn't that what the song says? This morning, I left this building hand in hand with Marc. Things weren't perfect, but we had a future.

Now, I just don't know.

My room is cold and dark, but it suits how I'm feeling, so I leave it that way. Changing into pyjamas, I climb under my duvet and let lazy tears slide down my face.

I don't even have the energy to cry properly. Water is just sort of leaking out, and the tears feel cold and grey, like everything right now.

When I realise sleep is impossible, I water my plants and check my phone.

Marc has called five times. And sent a text message.

'Sophia, let me know you're safe.'

41

My thumb is poised, ready to text back, but I hesitate. What should I reply? As I'm thinking it over, there's a knock at the door.

The phone slides from my hand, falling with a clatter to the floor. I pull the duvet around me, jump to my feet and skid in my socks towards the door.

I *told* him to give me space. Doesn't he get it?

'What do you want?' I snap, pulling open the door.

I see Tanya, the smile sliding from her pretty, pale face. There's rain all over her cheeks and glasses. She's wearing waterproof trousers, a V-necked beige sweatshirt and an anorak.

'Sorry, Soph, I just –'

I shake my head. 'No, no. Sorry, Tanya. I thought you were ... someone else.'

'I saw you on the balcony,' says Tanya. 'Have you been hiding in here all day?'

'No. I was with Marc before.'

'I saw the newspapers. Pretty heavy, huh?'

I nod. 'You can say that again.'

'I haven't seen Cecile yet, but when I do ...' Tanya pounds a dainty little fist into her palm.

'I saw her today,' I say. 'At the GMQ newspaper offices. Selling another story.'

Tanya rolls her eyes. 'The poor little rich girl didn't get Marc. And you did. So now she's bitter. Are you going to let me in, or leave me standing on the doorstep like a Jehovah's Witness?'

The tiniest of smiles tugs at my mouth. 'Come in.'

'Great.' Tanya barges forward and flicks on the light. 'It's dark in here. And freezing.'

I shield my eyes.

'Let me get a fire going.' Tanya stoops by the grate and makes a little fire with a magazine and a few logs. 'What are you doing here, freezing cold and in the dark? Are you okay? You look awful.'

'Thanks a lot,' I say, trying for a smile.

The firelight glows on Tanya's pale cheeks, casting a shadow from her glasses over her forehead. There's something so lovely about the way her cheeks bunch up under her eyes. So friendly. It's good to see her.

'You know me, I say it how I see it. What's happened? Has that bastard done something to you?' She shakes her glasses and wipes them on my duvet.

I bite my lip. 'No.'

'Are you upset about the newspapers?' She moves a strand of red hair from her wet face. 'Because none of us believed that crap. You do know that, don't you? There's no need for you to be hiding up here.'

'It's not that,' I say, slumping onto the bed. 'Sorry I didn't return your calls. There was a lot going on today.'

'We guessed as much. Don't worry. It would take more than that to offend us. So? You're *not* upset about the newspapers?'

'I didn't like what they wrote, but ... it's fine.'

'So what's wrong?' She pushes her glasses up her nose 'You look like your whole family just died.'

I put my head in my hands. 'Marc and I had a fight.' I feel tears against my fingers.

'What happened?'

'I got offered a part in a musical. *Beauty and the Beast*.'

'*Beauty and the Beast*?' Tanya sits on my duvet and crosses her legs. 'You're kidding me. How come? Oh wait ... I get it. Because of lover boy.' Her eyes drift towards the window.

'Yes,' I admit. 'But Marc thinks it's not safe for me to take the part. Because of all the journalists. He turned it down.'

'*He* turned it down? *Your* part?'

'I know. That's what the fight was about.'

'So what did you do?'

'I took the part. The director phoned me herself.'

'Did you take it to show Marc who's boss?'

'No.' I shake my head. 'That's not why. I ... guess I want to test him. Us. To test us. And to show Marc I can make decisions without him.'

'You think this is a good decision?'

'I ... hope so. It's done now. I'll just have to *make* it a good decision.'

'So you'll be starring in *Beauty and the Beast*.' Tanya sounds distant, and her eyes are back on the window again.

I hear my phone and feel my pillow vibrating.

'That has to be your phone,' says Tanya. '*Vivaldi's Spring*. That ringtone suits you down to the ground.'

'Is that what this music is called?' I say, watching the pillow. 'I just picked it because I liked it.'

Tanya pulls my phone from under the pillow. 'It's him. Marc.'

I feel sick.

'Do you want me to answer it?' Tanya asks. 'Tell him to get lost?'

'No. But I'm too upset to talk to him right now. Just make it go to answer phone.'

She does.

'Will you still go to his classes?'

'He's not teaching me,' I say. 'We agreed to that way before.'

'That sounds smart. So. When do you start rehearsing

Beauty and the Beast?'

'Tomorrow,' I say, catching my reflection in the French doors. 'And I look awful.'

'Well, if anyone can carry off the red-eyed, crumpled look, it's you.'

'Thanks.' Tiredness overcomes me, and I let out a long yawn.

'Shall I leave you to sleep?' Tanya asks.

'I guess I should try.'

'You look so sad. Is all this just over one argument?'

'Yes. Pathetic isn't it? But that one argument was a big one.'

'It'll all come out in the wash.' She pats my back decisively. 'You'll be fine. Will I see you tomorrow?'

'I might make Denise's class in the afternoon. But I'm not sure yet.'

'Okay.' Tanya shuffles off the bed. 'Look, I'm right downstairs. If you need anything, anything at all, just give me a call. Or Tom.' There's a pause, and I sense she wants to tell me something. But instead, she takes a roll of toffees from her pocket and offers me one.

'Toffee?'

'Thanks,' I say, 'but I'm feeling a bit sick.'

She takes one herself and begins to chew. 'We're here for you, Soph. Don't forget that.'

'I won't.'

When Tanya leaves, I check my emails. There's nothing from Marc, but Davina has sent over the script and some music files. She wants me to learn half the play by tomorrow. Whoa. That's a lot of lines.

I'd better get started.

42

When I wake the next morning, I'm shivering. It takes me a moment to realise I've flung off the duvet in my sleep and am lying on the bed in just an old t-shirt and panties.

My chest feels heavy, and there's a sickly feeling in my stomach. I have no peace from thoughts of Marc. They're waiting for me before I even open my eyes.

I hug my knees to my chest and look out at the orangey brown leaves. In autumn, I love going early morning leaf kicking, but today it's a struggle to sit upright.

I dress in old clothes lying on the floor and drink a glass of water, but I feel too sick for hot chocolate or food.

Sliding my phone from under my pillow, I check to see if Marc has called or sent a message. He hasn't since yesterday, but as I scroll down the call list, I see missed calls from a London number.

Shit.

Davina. Tottenham Theatre. What time is it?

9am.

I hardly *ever* sleep in. Why did today have to be the day? What time did Davina say? Seven. Shit, shit, shit. I call the number, but there's no reply.

I'm about to try again, when my phone rings.

'Hello?'

'Hey babes, how are you?' It's Jen.

'Not great. I should be at the theatre right now. I slept in.' I rub my eyes.

'You took the part?'

'Uh huh. Told them I'd come for rehearsals at 7am today.'

'So what are you doing talking to me? Get yourself to that theatre right now. Do you want me to call you a cab?'

'No, it's fine. I'll walk. It's only a few streets away. A cab would take longer.'

'I'm glad you said yes,' says Jen. 'You show them. Show them all.'

'I need to show Marc, most of all.'

Inside, a little voice says, *Marc says it's dangerous. And you know you can't sing.*

'You go, girl,' says Jen.

'I wish I had your courage,' I say.

'You're braver than you think,' says Jen. 'Trust me. I've known you a long time.'

The Tottenham Theatre is a truly beautiful building. I don't know when it was built, or anything like that, but it looks like a giant wedding cake – all pink and white, with little stone flowers stuck all over it.

I feel a pang of sadness as I realise Marc would probably love this building.

Even though it's early, the main doors to the theatre are open, and I walk into the lobby, wondering where I might find Davina.

I needn't have worried – she's right there, pacing the red carpet, barking into a mobile phone. I recognise her voice immediately.

'No, *now*,' she shouts. 'This is an emergency.'

She's a very tall woman, with jet black hair cut into a sharp bob. She has a really straight fringe, a pointy little nose and bright red lips, and is dressed in a sort of woolly shawl and a long pencil skirt with tan leather boots. The shawl is probably really expensive, but it looks like something you'd see in a charity shop.

When Davina sees me, she drops her mobile to her

chest.

'*Sophia*!' The way she says my name, I know she's happy to see me, but also a little mad. '*Where* have you been?'

'I called,' I say. 'I really am sorry. I slept in. I don't usually -'

'Do you realise how little time we have?'

She shoos me towards some wooden double doors. 'We've been rehearsing without you for hours. Leo's ... well, it would take a freight train to make him stressed, but it hasn't been the easiest of mornings. You should have told us you were on your way. We had photographers ready.'

'I did call. I should have kept trying. Sorry. Photographers?'

'Well, of course. We planned to take some shots when we picked you up, but we've blown that now.'

'What sort of photographers?'

Davina raises a thin black eyebrow. 'Sophia, my dear, do you live in a cave? *Press* photographers. So we can get some good headlines for the play.'

'Oh. Right.' Headlines. Of course. Silly me.

'We missed some good shots,' says Davina, sounding annoyed, pushing me through the double doors into the theatre itself.

I can't help catching my breath when I see the auditorium. It's huge and beautiful, with tiered seats running up so high that it's a wonder the people at the top can see the stage. Yellow tassel fringes run along the tiers, and an enormous crystal chandelier hangs from the ceiling.

I see a huge, curved stage, decorated with a menacing forest backdrop – all twisted trees, evil-looking birds and grey branches.There's a very broad, very handsome man on stage with chin-length, sun-bleached blond hair. Leo Falkirk.

43

'Leo!' Davina calls out. 'She's here! Your leading lady.'

Silence. Then a long shout that makes me jump.

'Oooo – eee! At long last.'

The man takes a great leap from the stage and lands squarely in the aisle. He bounds towards me.

Wow. Leo Falkirk. The real one. From the movies.

Even with images of Marc churning around my mind, it's impossible not to notice how good looking Leo is. He's big and broad, with muscled brown arms under a white 'surf shack' t-shirt, and long legs in ripped jeans. His sun-bleached hair is tucked behind his ears.

I've seen a few of his movies. He usually plays the lovable rogue in romantic comedies, and although he's no Marc Blackwell, he's certainly very likeable.

Leo heads towards me, hand outstretched, and I let him shake mine.

'Hey, good to meet you.' His accent is pure Texas, and as warm as syrup on toast. 'I can't wait for you to be my girl.' He smiles and his brown eyes twinkle. 'On stage, of course. Off stage, you're someone else's girl, right? That's what's going to get us all this great publicity.'

'So I'm told.'

'Tell me,' says Leo, 'how is Mr Blackwell?'

He hasn't let go of my hand, so I slide it from his warm grip.

'He was in one of my first movies, did you know that?' Leo strokes blond stubble on his chin. '*Gideon's Wish*. Did you see that movie?'

'Once. Years ago. Marc was amazing.'

'He sure was amazing,' says Leo. 'Acting with him

was ... quite something.'

'You were in that movie?'

Leo laughs. 'Kind of. I played the skateboarder in the waiting room. Remember him?'

'No.' I smile.

'It wasn't a speaking part. But I was happy to get it. Hell, happy isn't the word. Over the moon. I told all my friends back home, and my parents held a party. They couldn't believe their little boy was in a Hollywood movie. They still can't.' He grins. 'I can't believe it either. One day this will all go pop, but I plan to enjoy it while it lasts. So anyway. I remember Marc. He was a good guy. Kept himself to himself. Didn't talk a lot. But when he did, everyone listened.'

'That sounds like Marc.'

'When the movie wrapped up, he treated everyone to dim sum and champagne at this amazing Chinese place. And I do mean everyone. All the stunt guys. Costume people. Even bit parts like me. I'd never had anything like dim sum before – I couldn't believe this big star was treating me. I never forgot that. Things like that, the press never write about. But I guess, I don't need to tell you.'

'Shall we start rehearsing now?'

'Sure.'

Last night, I got a good feel for the script. I didn't manage to memorise everything Davina wanted, but I think I learned enough.

Today, we're scheduled to rehearse scene twelve where Beast shows Beauty around his castle.

Leo and I throw out a few lines, and I soon discover we work well together. He's so easy to be around, and he puts his heart and soul into his performance, just like I do.

But when Leo mentions trying out a song, my mouth goes dry.

'I'm not sure I'm ready for that yet,' I say.

'Come on, try it,' says Leo. 'Davina's out there making calls.' He jabs a thumb at the lobby. 'No time like the present. And if I can sing, I'm sure you can.'

'Where did you do your musical training?' I ask.

'Promise you won't tell?'

'I won't tell.'

'The school choir.'

I laugh.

'How about you?'

'I've hardly done any,' I say. 'I was really surprised when they offered me the part.'

'I'm sure you'll be great,' says Leo. 'With practise.' He bounds off stage, and I hear magical, other-worldly music float through the sound system.

It's beautiful, and I recognise it.

'Davina sent me that track yesterday,' I call out. 'But ... this version sounds a little different.'

Leo bounces back on stage. 'It's been arranged by Geraldine Jones. I love it too. How come you aren't singing?'

'I sort of missed my cue,' I say. 'I got a bit lost in the music.'

'Shall I start it again?'

'Yes, please.' I take a deep breath and shake my arms. 'Okay. Ready.'

Leo starts the music again, and I clear my throat.

I sing the first few lines, '*Lost in this castle, my heart feels afraid ...*' and then I stumble. The next line. It's *like a bird in a cage.*

My throat grows tight, and I put a hand to it. Tears come, and I shake them away, furious with myself.

'Like a ...' I try, but I can't get the line out. More tears prickle, and I run down the stage steps to my bag, rummaging inside, looking for tissues. My bag is such a hopeless mess that all I can find is chewing gum, loose coins, a beaten up notepad and a whole load of chocolate wrappers.

'Hey, are you okay?' Leo asks, appearing behind me. 'You were doing great. What happened?'

44

I shake my head. 'Nothing. I just ... that line. I found it hard to say.'

'Some of these songs are pretty emotional, huh?'

I nod.

'Hey, let's take a break.'

'Good idea.'

We take seats in the fifth row, Leo resting his long legs on the seat in front. We're a few feet back from the stage, and the set looks completely beautiful from where we're sitting. All dark, twisty trees, like a gothic fairytale. It's a bit spooky, but I like that.

'You did good,' says Leo. 'You have a pretty voice.'

'Thank you. I know it's not the strongest, but maybe with practise ... I need to speak to Denise Crompton. She'll help me.'

'Denise Crompton? As in *the* Denise Crompton?'

'She's a teacher at Ivy College.'

Leo slaps his forehead. 'Of course! She and Marc are great friends, right?'

Damn it! I'd just stopped crying. Now I'm off again, tears leaking down my cheeks.

'Did I say something wrong? Is something up? Was it ... because I mentioned Marc?' Confusion pulls at Leo's blond eyebrows.

I know my silence speaks volumes, but I can't manage to get any words out.

'Did you two have a fight or something?' The little dimples disappear from Leo's cheeks.

I bite my lip. 'We're ... it's complicated right now.'

I hear a cough behind me, and turn to see Davina. 'Complicated?'

'Oh! Davina.'

'What do you mean, *complicated*?'

'We ... there are things we need to talk about.'

'But you're still together?' Davina barks.

'I think so, but ... I don't know right now.'

'You don't *know*?' Davina's eyes narrow. 'Sophia, without Marc, you're nobody. You do understand that, don't you? You're no good to us without Marc.'

'I don't know what to tell you,' I say, humiliation rising. 'I can't promise Marc and I are still together. I'll understand if I'm not right for you anymore. I didn't mean to mislead anyone.'

'Hey.' Leo puts a hand on my shoulder. 'It's fine. We need a leading lady, and we've got one. What's the problem?'

Worry wrinkles appear around Davina's eyes. 'She's ... look, I don't mean to be rude, Leo, but we hired her for the publicity. If she can't bring us that, what good is she?'

'Don't you read the papers?' says Leo. 'She beat thousands of actors to get into Marc Blackwell's college. Which should tell you she's a pretty decent actress. We were lucky to get anyone at such short notice. You've been on the phone all morning, and no cigar. Am I right?'

Davina puts red fingernails to her forehead. 'You don't get it, Leo. Publicity is our lifeblood. Without it, we die. We'll have to find someone else. Short notice or not.'

She stalks towards the stage, taking a front-row seat and tapping at her mobile phone.

'Thanks for sticking up for me,' I tell Leo. I sigh. 'So much for me making good decisions.'

'Good decisions?'

I shake my head. 'Oh ... nothing.'

Leo leans in closer, his green eyes soft and kind.

'You can talk to me. I'm not Davina. I won't sell a story on you. Have you made some bad decisions, or something?'

'Maybe. Marc thought I shouldn't take this part. So I wanted to show him ...'

'Show him that he was wrong?'

'Does that sound very childish?'

'No. It sounds like you're laying down some ground rules.'

'I guess it doesn't matter now. I'm just sorry I let Davina down.'

Leo puts his whole arm around my shoulder. 'Don't worry. Her bark's worse than her bite. She hated me at first. Now she wants me to come to her daughter's sweet sixteen party. Anyway. I have an idea.'

'An idea?'

'Yep. To get Davina all the publicity she wants.'

Leo's arm feels nice. Comforting. I wonder what Marc would think if he could see me now. My stomach begins to churn.

I lean forward. 'Publicity?'

Leo's green eyes twinkle. He really is cute, in a tanned, boy band sort of way. I'll have to make sure Jen gets to meet him.

'Sure,' Leo grins. 'You really do have the most amazing eyes. Did anyone ever tell you that?'

'Oh.' I look down, embarrassed. 'Thank you.'

'Don't go all shy on me, it's the truth. Wait there.' Leo leaps up and heads down the aisle. 'Hey Davina. Hey!'

45

'Yes, Leo?' Davina looks up with a sugary smile.

'I've been thinking.' Leo winks at me over Davina's shoulder. 'You want publicity, right?'

'Yes.'

'So how about this? Sophia and I head out for a coffee. The press see us. Snap, snap, snap. The gossip mill starts turning. *Leo gets close to his leading lady.* And hey presto. We've got ourselves a cover story.'

Davina drums her fingers on a wooden armrest. 'I suppose it could work. It's a possibility. And lord knows, I've had the worst luck trying to find another lead. It seems this is the time of year everyone checks into rehab. Okay, fine. Go try it. I've already told the press Sophia's here.'

Leo swaggers back towards me, flashing the lovable rogue smile that makes him perfect for all those romantic comedies. 'See? No worries.'

I chew a thumbnail. 'Are you serious? You actually want to go out and purposely get papped?'

'Yep. Welcome to the world of show business.'

'But ...' I think about Giles Getty. 'Mightn't it be a little dangerous?'

'Live by the sword, die by the sword. Look at it this way, what choice do we have right now? I need a leading lady, Davina needs publicity and you need to show Marc what you can do. Right?'

As Leo and I head into the box office, my feet feel heavy.

'Are you sure about this?' I ask.

'Too late now.' Leo points up ahead.

'They've already seen us.'

I follow his finger and see a dark mob of photographers outside the box office.

'I guess Davina must have called them when you arrived,' says Leo. 'You should be proud. I'm not interesting enough to get *that* many photographers in one place.'

'Oh my god.' I grip his arm. 'What should we do? We can't walk through them.'

'Why not? All they want is a picture.'

'I just ... maybe I'm not ready for this sort of attention. Not yet.'

'Come on. You'll get used to it. They're not that bad.'

'To you, maybe. Did you see the stories they wrote about me?'

I look at the mass of photographers, jostling each other, thrusting their cameras between shoulders and over heads, jeering and shouting.

Their words seep through the box office doors.

'Sophia. Sophia. Is it true Marc ties you up, Sophia? Does he like to be in charge? Do you have to do as he says? Sophia, where's Marc right now? Does Marc know you're with Leo?'

'Rough questions,' Leo breathes. 'Don't worry. They'll back off when we go out there.'

'Are you sure?'

'Pretty sure. Only one way to find out.'

He pulls open a door, and we drop down onto the single step outside.

The shouting is magnified, and I put my hands to my ears. It's too much. Too intense. Everyone is surging forward, and I want to run back inside.

I'm aware of the door closing behind us, and being jostled back and forth. I grip Leo's arm tighter.

'Hey, it's okay,' he whispers. 'Just play along, and then we'll go back inside.' He slings his arm around my shoulder, and my hand drops from his arm.

I know it's for publicity. I know that. And I know I should just play along, but it just feels wrong. The only person I want putting his arm around me is Marc.

I take a step forward, ducking out from under Leo's arm, but I forget we're on a step. Tumbling forward, I feel a leather jacket under my fingertips, then I'm thrown back and forth in the crowd.

Hands grab me and cameras are thrust in my face. I try to shield my eyes from the bright lights, but flash after flash leaves my vision swimming.

Before I know it, I'm lost in the crowd of photographers, and hear Leo calling my name.

'Leo,' I call back, but I can only see photographers. One is taller than the rest, with tapered sideburns and black hair.

Oh my god.

Giles Getty.

He's far back in the crowd, but he's pushing the other photographers aside, getting closer.

There's a look of fury and triumph on his face, and he's moving his jaw round and round in a restless, twitchy way.

A hand grips the back of my sweatshirt, and my hair catches on something – a zipper, I'm not sure, and I twist and turn, watching Getty push his way forward.

Getty holds up his camera and takes snap after snap of my terrified face. He looks amused. Excited. I hate for my face to be exposed to him like this.

I try to cover my face, but doing that throws me off balance.

My hair rips free and I lurch backwards, my feet stumbling over pavement.

I fall and shut my eyes, steeling myself to hit the ground. But it doesn't happen. Instead, I'm lifted into the air.

I open my eyes and find myself staring up into the blue eyes of Marc Blackwell.

46

The cameras go wild, snapping and flashing, but the photographers are backing off. Keeping their distance. Something about Marc makes people obey, and the look on his face right now says get the hell away.

His blue eyes are dark and cloudy, his cheekbones taut, and his brows almost one straight line. I feel he could turn people to stone just by looking at them.

I see white sky above me, and London's buildings as Marc carries me through the crowd. His arms feel so strong. I'm lowered down and see the shiny black of Marc's limo.

There's a click, then I'm carried inside the limo and placed on a leather couch. The limo door slams shut, daylight disappears and the car starts moving.

I pull myself upright, my trainers skidding over the leather seat. I see Marc sitting opposite, watching me.

'Thank you for getting me out of there,' I say. 'I was ... it was scary.'

'Would you like to tell me what the hell you were playing at?' Marc's clasping his hands together, his fingers and knuckles a bloodless white, the scars on his knuckles standing proud.

I sit up, dusting hair from my face, my hands shaking.

'We ... Leo thought ... the play needed publicity.'

'Leo thought?' Marc's blue eyes darken.

'It was just a stunt. That's all.'

'He had his arm around you.' I see the tendons stand out on Marc's neck.

'Yes, but ... I mean, no. I tried to slip away from him. That's how we got separated.'

'What the hell were you doing there? At the theatre?'

'I ... I was rehearsing.'

'Rehearsing?'

'Yes. I took the part.'

Marc's neck grows tight. 'Now do you see why it's a bad idea? Taking this part?'

We're back on this again. 'I know what I just did was stupid. A mistake. But taking the part -'

'Don't argue with me, Sophia.'

I take in a deep breath and let it out. The motion of the car is calming me a little, but my hands are still shaking.

'I'm not arguing.'

'Can't you see you've behaved foolishly?'

'Yes. Just then, but ... you've never made a mistake?'

'I've made plenty of mistakes. When I had no one to guide me.' Marc's face softens. 'Let me take you back to the townhouse. Or at least Ivy College.'

'So you can keep me like a bird in a cage?'

Marc laughs. 'A very *safe* bird in a cage.'

I stare out of the window. London is beautiful today. We're driving by townhouses, and there are red and orange leaves scattered all over the pavement.

I sigh. 'What would happen, Marc, if I forgot all about this part and headed off into the sunset with you?'

'You'd be safe.'

'But would I be happy?'

Marc's eyes register pain, and I know I've hurt him.

'I'm not saying you don't make me happy,' I say. 'But Marc, if I walk away from that part, it'll always be 'Marc knows best'. You'll never respect my decisions. I'll always be following your lead.'

'Is that such a bad thing?'

'Yes,' I say. 'I want to be with you. But I want to show you that I can make my own decisions too, and they can work out just fine. Okay, I just did a stupid thing. But I'm learning. And if you won't let me learn on my own terms, there's no future for us.'

'I can't sit back and watch you put yourself in danger. I want you to give up this part.' He frowns at the passing townhouses.

'Marc, I can't live like that. Doing what you tell me. I'm a person, not a toy.'

'When have I ever given any indication that you're a toy?'

'It was ... something Giles Getty said.'

'Oh, *really*. And you'd rather take advice from him than from me?' He's mad now, his chest swelling up.

'I don't want to take advice from anyone, necessarily. I want to live my own life. I want to try out this part – it's a great opportunity.'

'You're in danger now that we're out in the open. I need to protect you. I can't sit back and watch you get hurt.'

'Who says I'll get hurt?'

'I do. You'll be right in the spotlight. Exactly where Getty can get to you.'

'No. I'll be inside a theatre. Marc, this is a relationship. Not a classroom. It's not like you set the rules and I follow them.'

'Oh no? You seem to enjoy my rules in the bedroom.'

'That's different.' My cheeks redden. 'If you need to be in charge of me *all* the time, it won't work.'

'Sophia, I need to keep you safe. You either have to accept that or ...'

'Or?'

'We end.'

47

Oh, those two little words. They hurt me more than any words I've ever heard in my life.

'We end?' I stammer. 'Are you saying that if I don't give up this part, you'll break up with me?'

Marc turns to stare out of the car window. I can't see his eyes, and I think he wants it that way. 'If we're not together, the press will leave you alone. So I can keep you safe that way, at least.'

'You'd really do that? You'd really end our relationship if I don't give up this part?'

'It's the only way I can protect you.'

'I can't give up the part,' I say. 'I've already said yes. I'd be letting too many people down.'

'Then we can't be together.' Marc doesn't look at me.

'What? You're ... you don't mean that.'

'Yes. I do. I have to keep you safe.'

'Stop the car,' I say.

Marc gives a little shake of his head. 'Not here.'

'STOP THE CAR,' I shout, clambering forward and knocking on the tinted driver's glass.

A section is pushed aside, and I see the back of Keith's head and his fingers on the glass.

'Everything okay back there?'

'Please. Keith. Would you stop the car?'

'Okay dokey. Let me pull over.'

I don't look at Marc as the car slows to a stop.

'Sophia. Wait.'

I pull at the door handle and stumble out onto the cold London pavement. Townhouses tower over me, and I feel very small and alone.

'Sophia.'

I turn to see Marc.

'Will you *please* get back into the car?'

'Why? What's the point?'

'I at least want to make sure you get back to college safely.'

'I'm not going back to college. I'm going back to the theatre. To rehearse. Please, Marc. Don't make this harder than it already is.'

That seems to hit the right mark. He takes a step forward, then back, his feet uncertain, a hand pushing through his hair. 'I ... believe me, Sophia, I have no desire to hurt you. I never wanted this for you. I never wanted to put you in danger.'

I swallow. 'I know. But I guess we just don't work in the real world.' I don't mean those words. I only say them because I want Marc to contradict me. To tell me it's not true. But he doesn't.

'I'll let my people know our relationship is ... at an end.' Marc looks at the pavement, then turns and heads back towards the car.

Ouch.

I put one hand to my stomach, the other to my mouth. I can't believe he just said that. I want to tell him to wait. To say I'm sorry. I'll do whatever he wants if only we can be together. But I know I can't do that. I feel tears sting my eyes.

When Marc reaches the car, he turns to me. 'Let me drive you there in the car. Give me that at least.'

I shake my head, tears streaming down my cheeks. 'If we're really over, I can't be with you.'

'Then take a taxi.'

'I want to walk.' I gulp at the air.

Marc's fists are clenched, and his cheeks have gone hollow. 'Don't you understand? I just want the press to leave you alone. They won't do that if we're together.'

'It seems a pretty easy choice for you.' I wipe away tears with the back of my hand.

'Come back to the car. Please.'

'*No!*' I turn and run, darting down an alleyway.

Narrow buildings give way to daylight, and I emerge on a busy shopping street and fall in with the crowd. I'm shaking and crying, and everyone is looking at me, but right now I don't care.

48

The pain in my chest grows. This is the end. We just broke up. Before we even really started. Marc was right all along.

I run fast and far enough so I know Marc can't follow me. Then my pace slows and the tears stop. I realise how cold I am – Leo and I went outside without coats. Rubbing blue fingers, I weave in and out of shoppers. They're just going about their normal lives, unaware that part of mine has just ended.

I wander the streets for a long time. Hours. I see restaurants and fast food places fill up as people start taking their lunch breaks. Soon, I feel totally numb. I think it's the cold at first, but then I realise it's coming from inside. From my heart.

Suddenly, Tottenham Theatre is right ahead of me, but I have no idea how I got here. Did I purposely walk this way? I don't remember.

There are no paps outside, and the theatre looks weirdly dark and empty.

I try the doors. They're locked.

What?

Turning a full circle, I see tourists and shoppers milling around.

My phone bleeps, and I slip it from my pocket. I have five missed calls from Marc, and a text from Davina:

'THEY GOT THE PICTURE!! Front page of tomorrow's Daily Sport. Rehearsing at the theatre is proving too difficult, re paparazzi. Marc Blackwell has arranged for us to relocate at Queen's Theatre, Ivy College, where he can provide security. See you there, Davina.'

My mouth falls open. I don't believe this.

I dial Marc's number, pacing up and down the pavement.

Marc answers on the first ring.

'Sophia.'

'You moved the play to Ivy College?'

'I thought it a good idea for the time being. My team will break the news of our separation to the press tomorrow, but they'll still be a few weeks of fall out. They'll still want pictures of you for a while. You'll be safer in the college and nearer your studies.'

'Thank you,' I say stiffly. 'I ... appreciate that.' I ache for him to say something more. That we can be together after all.

But instead he says, 'I won't bother you on campus. You go your way, I'll go mine. It'll be like we were never together.'

Never together. I feel a lump in my throat and want to throw up.

The line goes dead.

49

Queen's Theatre, Ivy College. Where Marc and I shared our first kiss. My legs are shaky as I walk through the doors.

It's the weirdest thing seeing Davina and Leo on the Queen's Theatre stage. They look at home, but not at home. Of course, they both belong in a theatre, but *this* theatre is different.

'Sophia!' Davina calls in her high-pitched voice. 'Up, up, up on stage, right now. We don't have time to mess around.'

Images of Marc's beautiful face and strong body creep into my mind as I head towards the stage steps. Marc and I, on stage together, swept away by a kiss that should never have been.

'Come on, come on!' Davina shouts.

The kiss tingles through me as I walk up the stage steps. Marc, so dark and intimidating, raw and sexy. Me, held tight in his arms, lost and found.

'Hey.' Leo takes my arm. 'Sorry about earlier. One minute you were next to me, and the next ... poof!'

'I sort of slipped, and then we got separated.'

'Stick with me next time,' says Leo. 'But for the record, they got the picture we wanted. It'll be all over the papers tomorrow.'

'I think they got more than they bargained for,' I say, thinking of Marc carrying me through the crowd.

'Right,' Davina yells. 'Let's start. Right now. Scene twelve. Beast shows Beauty around the castle. Let's go.'

I scrabble through my memory for lines, my head a mess.

'No, no, no.' Davina grabs my arm. 'She wouldn't stand there. Over here. Beast has to call her over.'

'Oh. Okay,' I stumble as she drags me across the stage.

There's a pause.

'Line!' Davina shrieks.

'Oh ... sorry. I didn't realise you wanted me to start already.'

Davina rolls her eyes. 'I'm dealing with an amateur. Leo – you're the professional. You start. Little Miss Rose is having trouble speaking.'

'I'm not -'

'Line!' Davina interrupts.

Leo throws me an apologetic smile, then launches into the script. 'Of this house, you are now mistress,' he says, bowing down almost to the ground.

'I have no desire to be so,' I reply. 'Only to be set free.'

'Stop, stop,' Davina says. 'Sophia. I need character. Show me character.'

In two lines?

I try again, but Davina cuts me dead.

'Christ, have you never been on stage before? I need bigger. Bolder. For God's sake, Sophia, you're useless.'

The rehearsals go on that way, with Davina picking at everything I do.

Leo is the golden boy, and she heaps praise on him, but I can't do anything right.

By the end of the day, I'm tired and unhappy. I've had enough of being criticised, and I miss Marc so much, it's unbearable.

Usually, I love being on stage. I can forget all my worries while I'm acting. But today was hell. This has to get better.

'Okay,' Davina shouts. 'We're nearly done for today.' She clicks her fingers. 'Let's finish on a song. Sophia. Song. *Forever and You*. Let's hear it.'

Oh no. The bird in a cage song.

Just get on with it, Sophia.

Davina snaps on some music, and I pat my chest, lift my chin up and draw in my breath.

I start singing, and I'm okay. Not great, but okay. I stumble a little on the 'bird in a cage' line, but I recover.

'Terrible,' Davina shouts. 'Just terrible. Like amateur karaoke night. And that bird in a cage line. You completely stuffed it up.'

I stiffen. 'Davina. I'm learning, okay? I'm not a big Hollywood star like Leo. I haven't starred in hundreds of movies. I'm young. I'm inexperienced. But I'm a hard worker, and I'll do everything I can to get things right.'

'I just hope you get better quickly,' says Davina. 'Or this show is going to bomb.'

I think about the newspapers. They'll have a field day if the audience hates me. I want to be good at this. As good as I can be. But in Davina's eyes, nothing is good enough.

Our eyes meet, and I sense how annoyed she is with me.

I twist my hair in my fingers. 'Maybe it's time to take a break.'

Davina raises a skinny eyebrow. 'Agreed. Go away. Practise. And I just pray to God you're better tomorrow.'

50

I leave the theatre almost in tears. I'm angry at myself for getting emotional, but I feel so trapped. It's awful having Davina snip and snipe at me, but ... maybe she's right. I am an amateur. I've never acted professionally. Leo is so much more confident than I am.

I'm lost in my own thoughts, when ... I don't believe it.

Tanya is up ahead.

She sits on a wooden bench, wrapped in a long puffa coat, a white scarf wound around her neck. Tom is beside her, his wheelchair perched on a grass verge. He's flamboyant as always in a top hat and pin-striped jacket, with pink shirt.

'Tanya! Tom!' I don't think I've ever been so happy to see my friends.

I break into a run. 'What are you doing out here in the cold?'

'Waiting for you,' says Tanya, returning my smile.

I throw my arms around them both. 'I'm so glad to see you guys. Soo glad. How'd you know I'd be here?'

'Tom's an eavesdropper,' says Tanya. 'He overheard reception organising the big move from Tottenham Theatre, and we guessed the rest. So? How's it going?'

I let out a long sigh. 'Not great. The director hates me.' I sit next to Tanya, putting my head in my hands. 'Right now, it's really hard work.'

'I'm glad to hear it,' says Tom. 'We'd be very jealous if everything was wonderful.'

'I *was* a little jealous,' Tanya admits. 'It seemed a bit unfair, you getting this great part just because of Marc. But don't worry, I'm over it now.'

'I don't blame you,' I say. 'It's not fair. Marc didn't want me to take the part. He thought it was too dangerous. Maybe he was right.'

'Mr Blackwell was a right grump in our lecture this afternoon,' says Tanya. 'No pleasantries. All business. He nearly bit my head off for doodling. I can't help it if I don't pay attention for long. I'm a creative! We're supposed to be scatty.'

'Speak for yourself,' says Tom. 'I'm incredibly organised and always pay attention.'

We all laugh.

'You ... saw Marc today then?' I venture.

Tanya snaps her serious face back on. 'Yes. And he had a face like thunder, if you want to know the truth. I'm guessing you two are still on the rocks?'

'More than rocks,' I say. 'Mountains. We broke up.'

Tanya flings a hand to her mouth. 'Oh! I'm so sorry.'

Tom wheels himself around so he can pat my arm. 'So soon?'

I nod, feeling tears appear.

'How can that be?' says Tom. 'The two of you, both so beautiful. I would have thought the sexual chemistry alone would keep you going for months.'

'It was Marc's decision,' I say. 'He says it's the only way he can keep me safe.'

Tanya slings an arm around my shoulder. 'Plenty of fish in the sea, and all of that.'

'Tanya.' Tom shakes his head. 'You do know that is absolutely the worst thing to say when people break up.'

'Don't worry,' I say. 'There's no good thing to say right now.'

We hear a crunch of gravel, and I see Leo heading along the shadowy path.

'Sophia?' He reaches the bench. 'Is that you?'

'Yes, it's me.'

'I was hoping to catch you.' He nods at Tom and Tanya. 'These must be your friends. Hello, hello.'

'Tom and Tanya,' I say. 'Meet Leo Falkirk.'

'We know *exactly* who you are,' says Tom, pulling himself up in his wheelchair. 'And it's a pleasure to meet you.' He gives a theatrical bow.

Leo laughs. 'Don't bow on my account. I'm not worth it.'

'You absolutely are,' says Tom. 'I don't waste my bows on just anyone. You ask these two.'

'Uh, Sophia?' Leo fixes his twinkly green eyes on me. 'I wondered. It's been a long day, and I thought ... if you hadn't eaten yet, you want to grab a bite?'

'With you?'

'Sure, with me.' He grins, showing his dimples. 'I know some great places in London. Places the press aren't allowed.'

51

I look at Tom and Tanya. Tanya is giving nothing away, but Tom is grinning and nodding like an idiot.

'Thanks,' I say. 'But I'm really tired. I might just grab a sandwich and get an early night.'

'Oh. Well. Hey, I'll be on campus for another hour or so. They gave me a guest suite here, so I'm going to go grab a shower. Call me if you change your mind, okay? Here's my number.' He hands me a business card with a black and white shot of him on one side, all muscles and brooding eyes. 'Ignore the photo. That was my agent's idea. Maybe see you later, okay?'

'Okay.'

He jogs away over the gravel.

When he's gone, Tanya gives me a little punch on the arm. 'Why didn't you say yes? Are you blind? He looks like one of those Greek statues.'

'I just ... it didn't feel right.'

'Tanya, my love,' says Tom 'Can't you see she's still pining for Marc? She can't just switch her feelings off like a tap.'

'But he's so *hot*,' says Tanya.

'Is he indeed?' Tom raises an eyebrow.

Tanya smiles. 'Not as hot as you. But hot.' Her hand rests on his shoulder, and suddenly something clicks.

'What's going on with you two?' I ask.

Tanya and Tom look at each other, then quickly in opposite directions.

'Nothing,' says Tanya, her hand sliding from Tom's shoulder.

Tom looks at his lap.

Tanya's pale skin has turned a bright red. I don't think

I've ever seen her look so uncomfortable.

A smile spreads across my face. 'Are you two ... has something happened? What's going on?'

Tanya scratches her neck, and looks pointedly at Tom.

'Oh, you know us,' says Tom. 'Boring as usual. Food. Pub. Lectures. Food. Pub. It's a hard life. Missing our friend, Sophia.'

'Shall we go to the pub?' says Tanya.

'Are you sure there's nothing you want to tell me?' I ask.

They shake their heads far too quickly.

'Okay.' I'm prepared to let it go for now. 'The pub sounds good. But I have to learn my lines too. Promise you won't let me get too drunk, okay? I'm so stressed, I can see myself downing two bottles of wine.'

'Promise.'

52

The campus pub is as cosy as always, with its beer barrel stools and rope decoration. There's a roaring fire and mulled wine on sale.

Tom and I take a round wooden table in the corner, while Tanya brings over three steaming cups of wine with cinnamon sticks floating in them.

The wine is comforting, and it feels nice to be here with Tom and Tanya – like when we first came to college and I had no troubles.

As I take a sip of hot wine, Tanya nudges me. 'Look what the cat dragged in.'

I turn to the door. 'Oh no.' It's Cecile, arm in arm with Ryan.

Cecile doesn't even look in my direction. She's wearing the same outfit from earlier – tan riding boots, jeans and a blouse. Her icy blonde hair is tied in an elegant chignon that makes her cheekbones look especially pointy. 'Christ, why is there no champagne in this dump?' I hear Cecile say. 'It's like being in some northern town.'

Beside me, I see Tanya gripping the table, her white cheeks flushed red again. She leaps to her feet.

'Cecile. I want a word with you.'

Cecile blinks, her spiky little face perfectly composed. 'Oh, our resident northern monkey. Don't blame me if they don't serve *proper* drinks up north, Tanya. I'm just telling it like it is.'

'I couldn't care less what you think about life up north,' says Tanya, climbing around the table. 'I care about Soph. You should be ashamed of yourself, spreading all that rubbish.'

Cecile gives a tiny, smug smile. 'It wasn't rubbish.'

'It bloody was, and you know it.'

'If you'll *excuse* me,' says Cecile, draping her arm around Ryan. 'We're celebrating. The *Daily Sport* has just written me another great big cheque for telling the *truth* about Sophia.'

The look on Tanya's face tells me she's about to storm across the bar and punch Cecile on the nose. I grab her arm.

'No, Tanya. It's not worth it. You'll just give her another story to tell the papers.'

'It bloody well *will* be worth it,' Tanya shouts, her eyes fixed on Cecile's. Tanya struggles, and I'm losing my grip on her arm.

Cecile has the sense to look frightened, and she clutches at Ryan. 'Stop her, Ryan. She's crazy! You know what they're like up north.'

That was the wrong thing to say.

Tanya launches herself across the pub, grabs Cecile's shoulders and wrestles her to the floor.

'You lying, two-faced stuck up cow,' she shouts, raising her fist. 'See how much acting work you get with a broken nose.'

'No!' Cecile covers her face, and I charge over and grab Tanya's wrist.

'No, Tanya, don't. She's not worth it.' I manage to haul her off and back towards our table. 'I don't want to see you in the papers tomorrow.'

I push her onto a seat and hold her arms down. 'Please, Tanya. For me. Don't get in trouble over her.'

Cecile pulls herself up and looks warily at Tanya and me. She takes a bar stool, dusts her jeans and checks her fingernails.

The pub door creaks open.

'Sophia, *look*.' Tanya's mouth drops open.

53

Leo Falkirk stands in the doorway.

Poor Leo. The whole pub is staring at him. But I guess he must be used to staring.

He's wearing a thick green duffle coat that looks pretty strange against his tanned face and sun-bleached hair.

I notice Cecile slap a sickening smile on her face and pat her hair. She slides from her bar stool, all long legs and white teeth, and holds out a perfectly manicured hand.

'Leo,' she says, shaking his fingers. 'I heard you were on campus.' She puts a hand to her chest. 'I'm Cecile. I know Duncan Granger.' She gives a smug smile. 'The *Perfect Weddings* director? He comes to all my family parties. My mother plays tennis with him sometimes. It's a dump in here. Full of morons. How about I take you somewhere more interesting?'

'You know Duncan?' says Leo, catching my eye. 'Well, you say hi next time you see him. Good to meet you, Kelly.' He walks past her.

Cecile's lips pull tight, and she glares as Leo comes to my table.

I can almost read Cecile's mind: *What does that girl have that I don't?* And truly, I don't know. I mean, Cecile's beautiful, blonde, rich and well connected. I'm just ... ordinary.

'Hey, Sophia.' Leo slides onto a chair beside me. He grins at Tanya and Tom. 'Hey guys. Good to see you again.'

'Do you ... would you ... like a drink, Mr Falkirk?' Tom asks. 'The mulled wine here is *very* good.'

'Please.' Leo holds up his hands. 'Call me Leo. I'm

good for drinks. I just wandered in here thinking I might find Sophia. I thought I could convince her to come to dinner after all.'

Behind Leo, Cecile's lips practically disappear, and she whispers something furiously into Ryan's ear.

Across the table, Tom mouths, *Go on.*

'We can talk more about the play,' Leo says. 'I know it wasn't the best day. Maybe I can help you get in Davina's good books. You're looking way too sad right now. Let me cheer you up.'

I notice Leo's large, tanned hand on the table and suddenly think of Marc's hands – large and strong too, but with slender, pale fingers. I think of them sliding around my back, winding my hair around them ...

'Yes,' I say, jumping up, my hands on the table. 'Yes, why not? Let's get out of here.'

54

Cecile's face is a picture as Leo and I leave together. We head across campus side by side, but he doesn't try to take my hand or link arms with me, which is good. I'd probably have cancelled dinner if he did. I want a distraction, not a date.

There are paps hanging around the college gates, so Leo orders a special VIP cab with tinted windows, and we drive from the college car park out into London.

I can't help looking at my iPhone every few minutes, but Marc hasn't called or left messages.

'It's not me, is it?' Leo asks as the cab shunts to a stop at traffic lights. He's sprawled in the seat beside me, tapping his fingers on his knee in time to some imaginary tune.

'What's not you?' I let my phone drop to my lap.

'That's making you look so sad.'

'Do I really look that sad?'

'Yes.'

'Sorry.' I sigh. 'No. It's not you.'

'Am I to guess it's Marc Blackwell who's making you sad?'

Stupid tears. Back at the first mention of his name. I put my fingers under my eyes and pat.

'Hey. Hey.' Leo unbuckles his seatbelt and slides over, throwing an arm around me. 'Did I cause that? I'm sorry.'

'No.' I hide my face in my hands and take a few steadying breaths. 'No, it's fine.' I pull my hands away and force a smile.

'Better,' Leo nods. 'Hey, I won't mention the 'B' word again. Okay?'

'Thank you. I'm sorry. I feel so stupid.'

'Don't feel stupid.' His hand squeezes my shoulder. 'Let's change the subject. You know, this is only my second trip to London, but I love this city.' He waves his hand at the passing buildings. 'Bad food, sure. But *great* nightlife.'

'Bad food?' I'm smiling now, wiping tears away.

'Oh, come on. It's terrible. All carbs and oil. I miss Californian food. Have you ever been to California?'

I shake my head.

'You should come. I have a place right on the beach. You'd love California. Best food in the world. Fresh fish, fruit. Smoothies. And the frozen yoghurt – I miss it.'

'You do realise we're going out to dinner in London, don't you?' I say with a smile. 'Are you going to tell the restaurant how bad British food is?'

Leo laughs. 'I won't mention it. I promise. Anyway, we're going to one of the few places in London that *does* do good food.'

'Oh really?'

'Yeah. Soba. Japanese place. You ever been?'

I shake my head.

'You'll love it.'

55

Soba is on the second floor of a big brown building overlooking Park Lane. It's really quiet – a little too quiet for me. I'm used to bustling chain restaurants full of screaming kids.

All the seats are leather, and there are more waiting staff than customers.

'Nice, huh?' Leo says.

I smile, but inside I feel nervous. I'm scruffy in jeans as always, but then so is Leo.

'May I take your coat, sir?' asks a waiter.

'Sure.' Leo hands it over.

If the waiter is at all bothered by Leo's scuffed duffle jacket, he doesn't show it.

'Madam?'

'Yes?'

'Your coat?'

'Oh, of course. Sorry. Thank you.'

We're shown to a table overlooking Park Lane, and we sit for a moment, watching cars zoom past. Leo is really easy company, and I feel fine to sit with him in silence.

'I love cities, don't you?' says Leo. 'So much going on. Such a buzz. I grew up in a small town in Texas where *nothing* happened. First time I went to Houston, I was like, whoa. This is where I want to be. And then the acting thing happened, and LA was like Houston only ten times better.'

'How did you get into acting?' I ask as the waiter presents us with steaming hot towels.

'I did school plays,' he says. 'The usual stuff. And then I did modelling for a sports company and ended up in California for a shoot. Took up surfing, loved it, never went home.'

'You were a model?' I say, surprised. Leo seems too ... I don't know, genuine to do all that preening and posing.

'Sure,' says Leo. 'It was mainly sports stuff, you know. Athletic stuff. Why, did you model too?'

I laugh and shake my head. 'I couldn't think of a worse model than me.'

'Why?'

'Well, for a start, look at my fingernails. I'm not especially good at self-maintenance.' I hold out my hands, showing my bitten nails. 'If I grew them any longer, I wouldn't be able to garden.'

'You like the outdoors, huh?'

'I love it.' I look out of the window. 'There aren't enough trees in London.'

'Not enough ocean, either.' Leo follows my gaze. 'But it's so alive, don't you think? The city.'

I shrug. 'I can take it or leave it.'

Leo smiles. 'You're not like other actresses, you know that? I've never met an actress like you.'

'Is that a good thing?'

'It's refreshing. You're easy to be around. Of course, it helps that you're super pretty.'

A waiter hovers over us with two menus. 'Champagne to start?' he asks. 'Or we have an excellent apple mojito. Perfect with our appetisers.'

'Sophia?' Leo asks. 'You want champagne? A cocktail?'

I glance at the waiter, then back at Leo and whisper, 'I think I'd rather have a beer.'

'You'd rather a beer?' Leo stage whispers back. 'Okay!'

The waiter puts on a polite smile. 'We have excellent

Japanese beer. Two Kirin?'

'Sounds good.'

I open my menu. 'Is all this raw fish?' I ask.

Leo laughs. 'Not all of it. Why? You don't like raw fish?'

'I've never had it before.' I chew a thumbnail.

'You haven't? It's nice.'

I frown at the menu. There are all sorts of words I don't know.

'I'll have the lang-ous-tine as my main,' I say, carefully. 'That's like prawn, isn't it?'

Leo laughs again. 'Sophia, this is like tapas, okay? You order more than one.'

'Oh.' I'm flustered, and the menu slips around in my hands. 'Okay. Well the ceviche ... what kind of fish is that?'

'It's not a fish, honey. It's a dish.'

'Can you just order for me,' I say, shoving the menu across the table, my cheeks burning. 'That'll be much easier.'

'Sure.' Leo takes the menu, just as the waiter comes with our beers. He orders, but I have no idea what. The only word that's familiar is 'caviar', and I take a deep breath, remembering my first dinner with Marc.

'So, how was your day?' Leo asks.

'Awful,' I admit, taking a sip of beer. 'Usually, I love performing. But not when someone picks holes in me the whole time.'

'Try to see things from Davina's point of view,' says Leo. 'She's used to working with professionals.'

'Thank you.'

'Sorry. That sounded harsh. But I can see what she's getting at, even though she doesn't get at it in the best way. There's a big difference between a drama student and an actor. You could use a little polishing.'

'Polishing?'

'Mmm.' Leo nods as he swigs beer. 'Fine tuning. So you're not so self-conscious.'

'But the more she criticises me, the more self-conscious I get.' I pick at the label on my beer.

'You know, doing that means you're sexually frustrated.'

My head snaps up. 'Excuse me?'

Leo points his beer bottle at mine. 'Peeling off beer labels. Sexually frustrated.'

I redden. 'Oh, look. Here comes our food.'

56

The meal is truly delicious. I thought raw fish would taste really fishy, but it doesn't at all. It tastes fresh and delicate, and it's presented so beautifully that I'm half tempted to get my iPhone out and start taking pictures.

We eat delicate slices of raw salmon, spread on a bed of ice chips, and tacos filled with raw beef, covered in lemon juice, washed down with lobster and champagne soup.

'You want to come out with me after dinner?' Leo asks, finishing his second beer. 'Come see a few London clubs?'

I shake my head. 'I need to learn my lines.'

'Very good. You're a star pupil. No wonder ... oh, wait. No. I promised not to go there.'

'What you said about me being unpolished.' I use my fork to push around a piece of prawn shell. 'What did you mean, exactly?'

'Oh, just ... you can tell you haven't acted professionally before. That's all I mean. You're too aware of who's watching.'

'And how do I stop that?'

Leo shrugs. 'Hard to say. I guess it just comes with practise.'

'So maybe, by the time we're ready for the show, I'll be better?'

'You'll be better, but I don't know if you'll be at the level that Davina wants. It takes years to really, truly forget the audience.'

'Years.' I stare out of the window.

'Are you drinking that beer?' Leo asks.

I stare at the half-full bottle by my plate.

'No.'

He reaches across and downs my beer in three large gulps. 'You sure you don't want to head out with me after dinner?'

I smile and shake my head. 'I think the press have enough pictures of me for today.' And there's something else too – something I don't say. *All I'll be able to think about is Marc, anyway.*

'Are you okay there?' Leo asks. 'Looks like you're thinking about something serious.'

'It's nothing.' My fingers reach for my phone.

'He didn't call.' Leo spins a fork on the table.

My fingertips freeze over my iPhone screen.

'Look, you've checked that thing every five minutes all night,' says Leo. 'He didn't call. You would have heard it ring.'

I let my hand drop away. 'And I thought I was being subtle.'

'About as subtle as a rock. But I promised I wouldn't mention the 'B' word, so ...' Leo holds his hands up.

I sigh. 'You're right. He didn't call. Or text.'

'Hey. It could be worse. You could have a glitch with your phone and get 500 text messages a day, like me.'

'You get 500 messages a day?'

Leo nods. 'Sometimes more. My phone's bust. It sends me duplicates. Sometimes triplicates.'

'Can I take a look at it?' I say.

'Sure.' Leo hands over a slim silver touch screen phone.

I take a look through the settings, then discover a software update and press it.

'It's a glitch with the phone,' I say, handing it back to him. 'But there's an update that should fix it. It should work now.'

Leo's eyes widen. 'Wow. Software girl. Who knew

you had such hidden talents?'

I shrug. 'I just like gadgets, that's all.'

'Shame you won't come out dancing with me. You want me to call you a cab?'

I nod, my thoughts drifting to Marc again. Marc would try to drop me off personally. Make sure I was safe. But he also just broke up with me.

'Thanks,' I say. 'That would be great.'

Leo calls the waiter over. 'One taxi cab for the little lady, here. And do you know any good clubs near here?'

The waiter gives a stiff smile. 'Night clubs, sir?'

'Yep.' Leo slaps his back. 'For dancing and romancing.'

'Chinawhite is nearby.' He glances at Leo's jeans. 'I think that might be the sort of thing you're looking for.'

Leo stands. 'You sure you don't want to come with me? Last chance?'

'No, I'd better head back. I should get an early night.'

The next morning, I'm woken by a knock at the door.

'Soph. *Soph*.'

'Tanya?' I rub bleary eyes, glad that I'm not too hung over. My mouth is a little sticky, though, and I grab the glass of water by my bed and take a long gulp.

Setting the glass down, I throw the duvet around me and waddle to the door.

'What time is it?' I ask, pulling the door open.

Tanya's in the hallway with a rolled up paper in her hand, practically hopping up and down. 'Did you READ the paper?' Her glasses are wonky, and her hair is all messed up. She's wearing a navy dressing gown with yellow rope cord around the lapels.

'I only just woke up.' I stand aside so she can come into my bedroom.

Tanya hurries past me and throws herself on my bed. 'That absolute cow Cecile. She's done another number on you.'

I rub my eyes. 'I kind of thought that might happen. She was at the GMQ offices yesterday, so I guessed there might be something today.'

I sit beside her on the bed. My chest feels heavy.

'Let's see.'

Tanya lays the newspaper on the bed. There's a big picture of Leo and me on the front cover, outside Tottenham Theatre. Leo is flashing his big, handsome Hollywood grin, and my eyes are half shut as I try to slip out from under his arm. My hair is blowing everywhere, there's a sheen of oil on my forehead and my unmade-up eyes look pale and tired.

It certainly doesn't look like a romantic picture.

I'm glad.

I blink at the headline.

Is Sophia Cheating?

Oh great. I read the article.

Slummy student, Sophia Rose, set tongues wagging yesterday when she dined with Beauty and the Beast star and Hollywood golden boy, Leo Falkirk.

The news of Sophia's intimate dinner date may come as a shock to Marc, who only yesterday broke the news of his love for Sophia.

Falkirk looks besotted with the pretty brunette, but is he next in line for heartbreak?

'Marc looked totally heartbroken when he taught our class,' says fellow student, Cecile Jefferson. 'You could tell Sophia has really got to him. She's playing games and he's hurting.

'Sophia will sleep with anyone to get to the top. She's completely callous and heartless. She doesn't care who she hurts in her quest for fame. No one here gets why Marc likes her.

She's scruffy and common, and so not good enough for him or Leo. I don't know what either of them sees in her.'

My first reaction is to laugh. It's a slightly hysterical laugh, but a laugh nonetheless.

'God, she just has no morals.'

'Aren't you furious?' says Tanya. 'I am.'

'Don't be,' I say. 'It's pathetic. I just wonder how long it'll take to repair the damage.'

'You've got to stop her doing this,' says Tanya.

'I know,' I say. 'I just don't know how. Yet.'

'You said she was in the newspaper offices yesterday morning?' says Tanya. 'She hadn't even had a lesson with Marc then. And how did they know you went out to dinner?'

'Maybe she rang them up and gave them extra details.'

'What a cow.'

'She'll get bored,' I say.

'But what if she doesn't? Are you going to let her keep dragging your name through the mud?'

'It's partly my own fault,' I say. 'I agreed to do that publicity stunt with Leo yesterday. I guess Cecile must have overheard about the dinner, but ... like Leo said, live by the sword, die by the sword.'

58

When Tanya leaves, I dress in leggings and a sweatshirt and brush my teeth. I catch sight of myself in the bathroom mirror, my brown eyes tired.

Slummy Student.

I spit in the sink, swill my mouth out and hunt around the bathroom shelves for makeup. Eventually I find the pencil case that holds my kohl pencil, mascara and other battered cosmetics.

I apply kohl all around my eyes, then mascara, then foundation, powder and cream blusher, before drawing on my eyebrows. Is that better? Am I less slummy now?

I catch a glimpse of my outfit in the full-length mirror, and turn to the side.

Scruffy and common.

I peel off my clothes, and dress in a long, green jumper dress and flat leather boots.

Will they leave me alone now?

'Hey, what's with all the make-up?' Leo asks as I climb the stage at Queen's Theatre.

My hand goes to my cheek. 'Nothing, I just ... thought I should make more of an effort.'

'For anyone in particular?'

'No. Just me. Does it look bad or something?'

'No, just ... not quite you.'

I spy Davina in the front row, tapping at her mobile phone, a steaming paper cup of coffee by her high heels.

She glances at me, then looks back at her phone.

'Nice to see you on time for a change, Sophia.'

'I'm sorry about yesterday,' I say. 'I'm never usually late.'

'You have a fifty fifty record so far,' says Davina.

I glance at Leo, but he's busy scanning his script.

'Right.' Davina drops her phone into her handbag. 'Let's hope your voice is a little better today. I can dream, at least.'

'I think Sophia's got a great voice,' says Leo. 'Perfect for these songs. Really subtle. Pretty.'

'Well, you and I are going to have to differ on that.'

'I know I'm not a strong singer,' I mutter. 'I need to practise more. I will.'

'Any news about you and Marc?' Davina arches an eyebrow. 'Is it any less *complicated* yet?'

'I ... no. I haven't seen him.' And he hasn't called. Or left a message.

Davina sighs. 'Still. Not a bad article this morning. Right!' She claps her hands. 'Let's get started.'

59

The rehearsal ends up being worse than yesterday. Davina is even more critical, if that's possible. And to top it all off, Marc still hasn't rung. It's been two days now. I don't know what I'm expecting. After all, we broke up. But a part of me still hopes that maybe, maybe something can be worked out.

I go to my room, learn my lines, fall asleep and before I know it, it's rehearsal time again.

The days and weeks begin rolling together. Every morning, I get up at seven, eat breakfast with Tom and Tanya, then head off to Queen's Theatre for an all-day rehearsal.

We're never finished before seven at night, and I'm usually too tired to do much more than learn lines and fall asleep. Sometimes, Tom and Tanya come to my room to watch a movie, but I usually fall asleep halfway through.

I hardly have any time to see my family or Jen, which makes me sad, but I do manage to call Dad and Jen a few times. I really miss cuddling Sam and playing with him. Dad gets him to gurgle a few words at me down the phone, but it's not the same.

During one late night call after a really tiring rehearsal, Dad asks me about Marc.

'I read in the papers that you two broke up,' he says. 'You're not too heartbroken, are you?'

'No,' I lie. 'It's all fine.' The last thing I want to do is make him worry.

Marc has kept his promise. I haven't seen him or heard from him, but the thought of him makes me ache more than ever. Has he forgotten me? Did he ever really care?

It becomes harder and harder to imagine that we ever really had a relationship.

Christmas trimming start to go up around the college, and it makes me feel sad and lonely. I usually love Christmas, but not this year. This year, my aim is just to get through it, and not think about Marc.

Leo and I work our way through the play, but it's slow going. Davina criticises me at every turn and far from improving, I often feel I'm getting worse, making more mistakes. I feel scared to say my lines half the time, for fear of Davina correcting and chastising.

At every opportunity, she pick, pick, picks.

Stand up straighter, Sophia. Give us more character. Give us more charisma. Christ, can't you even do that? You'd have to pay me to watch you right now, you're so amateur.

The worst thing is, I know she's right – at least in part. Okay, so she's delivering her thoughts in the meanest possible way, but that doesn't mean there's no truth at the heart of them.

Leo is no Marc Blackwell, but he's a good actor. Confident. Experienced. Knowledgeable. Beside him, I know very little, and it shows. And the more Davina criticises me, the smaller I feel and the more mistakes I make.

60

After one particularly awful morning a month into rehearsals, Davina calls me a 'total waste of space' and I've had enough. I'm exhausted and broken down.

When we stop for lunch, I head down the stage steps to the front row.

'Davina, can we talk?'

She's resting a biro on her red lips, frowning at a script on her lap.

'What about?' She's wearing bright red glasses today, and they've slipped down to the end of her nose.

'I know I wasn't your first choice of actress.'

'You can say that again.'

'But I'm really trying.'

Davina drops the pen onto the script and fixes me with a long, hard glare.

'Trying. Well. How very high school.' She mock claps her hands. 'As long as you're trying your very *best*, I guess it doesn't matter that you're ruining this play.'

'I don't want to ruin anything,' I say. 'Tell me. Please. Tell me what I can do.'

'Be better.' She says the words slowly and carefully, like I'm a five-year-old, then flicks her eyes to the script. 'Gain five years of experience by tomorrow. Now if you wouldn't mind, *I* have better things to do than babysit *you*.'

I swallow. 'Thanks for your time.' I hurry out of the theatre. I'm halfway across the college grounds before I know where I am, tears streaming down my face.

I look back at the theatre and think, *I can't go back there. I just can't. Not for a while. Something needs to change, or I'm going to completely fall apart.*

My feet carry me away from the theatre, across the car park and towards the woods. Concrete turns to gravel then to soil, and I feel crispy leaves under my feet. The air is fruity and fresh, but for once the stillness of the trees doesn't calm me. Taking deep breaths, I feel only the hopelessness of my situation.

I'm damned if I do, damned if I don't. It's far too late to quit – another actress could never rehearse the play in time for opening night. But if I carry on being torn apart by Davina, I'm going to have some sort of breakdown. My self-esteem has a seriously loose thread right now. One tug and it will all unravel.

I lean into a tree trunk and let sobs overtake me. I'm nearly all cried out, when I hear a twig snapping.

I spin around, red eyed, face all damp, and put a hand to my mouth.

It's Marc. He's standing a few feet away, looking like someone just stuck a knife in his chest. A cigarette smokes at his fingers.

There's nowhere to run, and I have no strength to run anyway.

'Sophia? Are you okay?' He's dressed in a tight black t-shirt and black trousers, and as usual doesn't seem to notice the biting cold. He stoops to stub the cigarette out in the soil, then kicks dirt over the butt.

'You're smoking again?'

'I replaced a healthy drug with an unhealthy one.'

'I thought you were staying away from me,' I say.

'I'm trying, believe me. But I saw you run into the woods and I could tell something was wrong. I'm not superman. I can't see you upset and walk the other way.'

'You were right. I should never have taken this part.'

Marc takes a step forward, and I smell his fresh, clean natural smell.

'Sophia,' he says softly. 'Talk to me. What's happening?'

I'm caught in his eyes, my heart racing, my palms sticky, my body awkward and off balance. It's been over a month, but he still has the same effect on me.

I let out a long breath, trying to calm myself.

'This is my problem,' I say.

'Christ.' He runs a hand through his hair. 'Sophia, tell me what's wrong. Let me help you.'

I shake my head. 'It's too late. Nothing can make this better. I'm just not good enough to play this part.'

'Never say that.' His voice is hard. Serious.

'But it's true. I'm just not good enough. Not experienced enough.'

Marc's eyes flick shut for a moment. When he opens them, they're clearer than before. 'I can help you,' he says. 'Teach you how to be better. To appear more experienced.'

'Teach me?' I gulp. 'Is that possible?'

'If acting is your problem, then yes.' He smiles. 'Funny. When you told me you'd taken the part, I never thought acting would be the issue. It's a far better problem than the Getty one.'

'I don't know if I can risk being around you. Not if we're not together.'

'You've resisted me so far, haven't you?'

I laugh. 'Barely.' My heart is beating so fast now, I think the birds must be able to hear it.

'Davina has a reputation,' says Marc. 'Hard-nosed. You need to feel more confident, that's all. Take charge more. I can help you with that.'

'Rehearsals are hell,' I admit. 'She hates me. I can't give her what she wants, and the more she criticises, the more I fall apart.'

'Well, you have a choice,' says Marc. 'You can bury

you head in the sand and carry on as you are.' He takes a step towards me. 'Or let me help you.'

'Marc.' I fix my eyes on the soil and leaves. 'You must know how difficult that would be.'

'You were strong enough to take the part.' I hear leaves crunch under his feet. He's close now. Too close. 'So it's really up to you. Exercise some self-control and accept my tuition. Or carry on as you are.'

'Marc, I just think ... it probably wouldn't be healthy to be taught by you right now.'

There's a pause. 'Whatever you want.'

I'm still not looking at him. My gaze is on the soil. 'It's so hard being near you,' I whisper.

'Then I should go.'

I shiver, feeling a sudden cold sweep over the woodlands. My chest becomes duller and my body goes cool.

I look up and see that Marc has gone.

61

Alone in the woodlands, I think about Queen's Theatre and what waits for me there. Suddenly, the cold becomes unbearable and shivering turns to shaking. I don't want to go back there and be slowly torn apart. I want to get better. To *be* better.

Suddenly, I'm running through the trees, leaves crunching under my feet, soil flying.

I see Marc ahead by the car park, his long legs eating up the distance between us. His Ford Mustang is parked up under a tree, and he's heading towards it.

'*Marc!*'

He stops, and I see his broad shoulders rising and falling sharply. This is as hard for him as it is for me.

'Wait.'

I reach him, out of breath, a hand to my chest. 'I ... you're right. I do need help. I need to be better. Will you help me?'

He turns and I'm nearly knocked over by his handsomeness in the milky winter light. 'Do you really need to ask?'

I so badly want to touch him. To feel his arms around me. But no. That's not what this is about, and if he's going to help me, I have to be strong.

'Is that a yes?'

'Of course it's a yes. Meet me in the theatre tonight. 9pm.'

62

As I head towards Queen's Theatre that evening, my Ugg boots crunch over silvery trails of ice. It's freezing, but I'm enjoying the cold. Since I saw Marc earlier, my mind has been all over the place, and icy weather always helps dull my thoughts.

I'm dressed in black leggings and a long crimson-coloured jumper, trying to play it cool and casual. Like this meeting is no big deal.

I walk with purpose, no time to think, no time to get emotional. This is just another lesson. I've had lessons with Marc before ... I give my head a little shake.

Don't go there.

The theatre doors loom ahead, and they look darker and taller than ever.

I feel my pace slow, and then ... I stop.

I'm not sure I can do this. My heart beats hard in my chest, and I swallow sickly mouthfuls of nothing.

I turn from the theatre, hearing gravel thrown around under my boot.

Behind me, the theatre door creaks open.

'Sophia.'

I stop dead, feeling Marc's voice in the pit of my stomach.

'Where are you going?' His voice is so deep, it sends electricity skidding around my body.

'I'm having second thoughts,' I say, without turning. Above me, the moon is a silver sliver and I focus on it, my eyes beginning to sting.

I hear gravel crunch, and sense him behind me.

'Come inside the theatre.' I feel his heat on my neck. And oh, that voice. He must know the effect it has on me. How it makes my heart flutter and my knees turn to treacle.

'I'm not sure I can,' I admit.

Now I hear his breathing – low and tight. The hairs on my neck stand up and I close my eyes and take in a deep breath. I smell him. That fresh, clean smell that makes my senses go crazy.

'You're stronger than this,' says Marc, his voice firm. He's in teacher mode now.

'I don't think so.' I shake my head, tears coming.

'Yes, you are. Turn around.'

'Marc -'

'I said turn around.'

I swallow and turn, my eyes are damp and red. I'm level with his smooth, square chin.

'There's something you want,' says Marc.

I keep my eyes fixed on his chin and shoulders. He's wearing a black buttoned up shirt with no tie.

'Something I want?' I stammer.

'You want to be stronger. A better actress.'

'Yes, but -'

'So tonight, that's what you're going to learn. Look at me.' He clicks his fingers – a powerful snap right in front of my eyes – and I look up before I can stop myself.

He's frowning. Serious. 'You can do this, Sophia.'

'I ...'

'Yes.' The word broaches no argument. 'You can. Come inside. Before you catch your death out here. Come on. No more of this nonsense.'

I close my eyes for a moment. He's right. It would be pathetic to walk away now. 'Fine. Okay.'

63

'After you.' Marc holds the theatre door open.

'Thank you.' I pass through the door, not looking at him, and head inside. The lights are low. Intimate and shadowy. I walk towards the stage and climb the steps.

Behind me, the door creaks closed. The creaking echoes around the empty theatre, and I hear Marc's footsteps click along the dusty floor.

Once on stage, I turn to see Marc in the aisle, hands on his hips.

'Eager to get on stage, Miss Rose?'

Even in the shadowy light, there's no mistaking how attractive he is. He moves so easily, head held high, cheekbones catching the low light. I want to run my fingers through his thick hair. I want to feel him, all of him, everywhere.

No.

I need to get a hold of myself.

'Not really,' I admit. 'I just ... I guess I wanted to get up on stage before I talked myself out of this.'

'It's hard for me too,' says Marc. He's closer now, his face washed in white light from the stage. Sharp cheekbones, beautifully straight nose and the tiny shades of hollows in his cheeks. 'But I promised myself I'd be strong. And you can be strong too. I know you can.'

'I'll try.'

'No.' Marc is right by the stage now, fierce eyes locked on mine. 'You won't *try*. You'll *do*. You will *succeed*. Is that clear? There's no room for failure in my classes. If a student fails, I fail. And I have no intention of failing.'

I'd forgotten how strict he could be. How stern. And what a good teacher. His words inspire something in me – a strength in my chest. Yes. I will succeed. I can do this. We both can.

'I read the *Beauty and the Beast* script,' says Marc, taking a seat in the front row, crossed legs straight out in front. 'Memorised it. I liked it. There's more to it than I realised. And I know exactly the scene I'd like you to rehearse. Scene fifty, where Beauty tells Beast she's fallen in love with him.'

'You're kidding me.' I shake my head. 'Are you trying to make this harder than it already is?'

'Believe me, Sophia, this is the best scene for you right now. Let's hear the line.'

I let my arms drop down and turn a circle on stage, pulling the lines into my head. 'Okay. Yes, okay, I'm ready.'

'Go.'

I let the frown fade from my face and clear my throat. 'You're beautiful,' I say, waving my hands at an invisible Beast. 'So kind and thoughtful. I didn't see it at first, but now it's clear. I see the person inside, and he's a prince.'

I read the rest of the scene, surprised that it flows more easily than it ever has with Davina. When I'm finished, I feel a little glow in my chest. I'd almost forgotten how good it feels to perform.

'Okay.' Marc leaps to his feet. 'Good. Sophia. Plenty of emotion. Sincere. If I were your director, I'd be happy.'

'But ... Davina isn't happy with me at all. Do I need to be more ... sensual, or something? Like you said when you were teaching me?'

Marc shakes his head. 'This isn't a sensual part. It's more subtle. You're perfect for it, in many ways.'

'I was better just now. Better than I've been with Davina. I don't know why.'

'Because you felt more confident.'

'So what's going wrong? Why can't I be confident with Davina?'

'Because you're inexperienced.'

'That's what Leo said.'

'What Leo said?' Marc's blue eyes narrow.

'Marc ... just so you know, there's nothing between Leo and I -'

'Your personal life doesn't interest me right now,' Marc interrupts. 'On with the next scene. Let's try fifteen.'

I deliver my next lines more confidently, Marc's words of approval ringing in my ears.

'Good,' says Marc when the scene is finished. He watches me for a moment, and I get that 'rabbit caught in headlights' feeling.

'What?' I ask.

'Just thinking. About how my experiences might help you.' Marc runs his fingers back and forth along the velvet arm of the chair, and I find myself watching them.

No! Keep it together, Sophia.

'Your experiences?' I ask, hoping my thoughts haven't shown on my face.

'Yes,' says Marc, still trailing his fingers back and forth. 'The first big movie I did, I was self-conscious. Like you are with Davina, I'm guessing. It was a tough part, and I knew I was punching above my weight. My father lied about my experience, and as usual it was down to me not to show him up.'

My chest feels soft. It's so strange to think of Marc as a boy. Especially a boy who was vulnerable. It breaks my heart.

'You must have hated your father,' I whisper.

'I wasn't sad when he died. Put it that way. But ...

let's get back to you.' Marc stands suddenly, and heads towards the stage. 'I was telling you about one of my experiences. The more nervous I felt, the poorer my performance. Is that how you feel with Davina? Self-conscious? Nervous?' He climbs the stage steps.

I nod, feeling anxiety churn around my chest as he gets closer.

64

No. Please. No closer. I can't bear it.

'You're inexperienced, Sophia.' He circles me, forcing me to turn and watch him. 'So you're not taking charge. You need to take charge. Do you see what I'm doing now?'

'Apart from making me dizzy?'

Marc's lips flick into a spiky smile, and my stomach turns to mush.

'Am I?' he says.

'Yes,' I say, still turning.

'And yet you're still watching me.'

My eyes drift to my feet. 'It's ... sort of automatic.'

'Exactly right. You didn't mean to. You didn't even think about what you were doing. I took charge. And you followed my lead. I made you look where I wanted you to look. But that kind of power only comes when you stop worrying about what people think, and start *telling* them what to think.'

'But how did you learn that?' I ask, risking looking up. Marc has stopped circling me now, and stands with his hands slipped in pockets.

'I got lucky,' says Marc. 'I had a good mentor.'

He pulls a sleek, black leather wallet from his pocket and unfolds it, sliding out a scuffed business card with blue biro scrawled on it. 'I still keep the card he gave me.' He reads from it. '*Show 'em who's boss and knock 'em dead kid, Baz.*'

'Who's Baz?'

Marc smiles. 'Baz Smith.'

'Baz *Smith*? As in the gangster actor?'

Marc nods.

'He was your mentor? He helped you?'

'More than anyone will ever know.' Marc slides the card back into his wallet. 'He saw a struggling young boy and made him into a man.'

'How?'

'Oh – plenty of ways. The most memorable being throwing me in a street fight with some punk kind from Manchester who beat the daylights out of me.'

'He did *what*?'

'Baz is into no holds barred stuff. Proper bare knuckle fighting. One day, he took me along to a fight and threw me in the ring. I was beaten black and blue before I started fighting back. That day changed me. After that fight, everything was different.'

'Different, how?'

'I realised I had it in me to take charge of a situation. And that I could either let life, and my father, beat me down. Or I could fight back.'

I so badly want to throw my arms around him, but I stand firm. 'You never told me this before.'

'There's plenty you don't know about me.'

'Like about your sister?'

'Yes.'

'How is she?'

'She's doing okay. She's checked into a place that will help her psychological rehabilitation. Here in London. It's a good sign. The counselling is going well.'

'Good. I'm glad. I'd like to see her again. I'd like to help her if I can. I wish you'd told me about her before.'

Marc smiles. 'Trust you to be thinking of my sister at a time like this. Let's get back to you.'

'Marc -'

'*Right* now.'

There's no arguing with him, and we both know it.

'Are you going to throw me in a boxing ring?' I joke, but the look on Marc's face makes me nervous. 'Marc?'

He checks his watch. 'Time's up for today. We'll start again early tomorrow. I'll have Keith collect you. 6.30am. We'll be done in time for your rehearsal.'

'Collect me? We're not rehearsing here?'

'No. See you tomorrow.'

And with that, Marc stalks out of the theatre.

65

'Please tell me where we're going,' I ask Keith as the car whizzes through central London. It's 6.40am and pitch black. I'm nervous.

'I'm under strict instructions not to say,' says Keith. 'But I think you're going to have fun.'

'I wouldn't be so sure about that,' I say, thinking about Marc's boxing ring story. I'm gripping my knees so hard that my knuckles have turned white.

I watch the shadowy city of London fade to countryside and see wooden fences and bare fields.

The car slows by a collection of red brick buildings, and I press my face to the window. There's a large country house with Georgian windows and what looks like a barn and stables.

Pinkish yellow light flows along the horizon, throwing the most beautiful coloured shadows over the buildings.

'Is this a farm?' I ask.

'Indeed it is,' says Keith. 'Marc's farm. One of his many land investments.'

The car turns on to a path of bumpy, hard mud and bounces along, past the house, until we reach the stables.

We turn a corner, and I see Marc by the stable doors. My heart catches in my mouth, but I swallow it down again.

Remember, Sophia, he's your teacher today.

Still, I can't help noticing how handsome he is in the morning light. He's wearing black cargo trousers and a grey V-necked sweatshirt.

There's a large brown paper bag by his feet with a

Where the Ivy Grows 197

boutique clothing store logo on it.

'Here we are,' says Keith, pulling the car to a stop.

'Thanks,' I say, wrapping my coat around me and climbing out of the car. I march towards Marc, my thin trainers feeling hard rocks on the ground.

'Good morning, Miss Rose.'

'Good morning, Mr Blackwell. So.'

'So?'

'What are we doing out here in the countryside?'

'I'm about to show you. Come with me.' He picks up the brown bag by its rope handles.

'What's in the bag?'

'Patience, Miss Rose.'

The stable has a huge metal door, and Marc unbolts it. There's a deathly creaking sound as metal grates along brick.

I hear a noise. *Bang, bang*. Like someone punching metal. And smell straw and horse manure.

BANG, BANG! Louder this time.

'What's that noise?' I ask, taking a step back.

'See for yourself.' Marc strides into the stable, his trainers crunching stones on concrete. It's cold inside, and I see puffs of mist up ahead.

66

Cautiously, I creep after him, seeing straw bales and empty enclosures where I'm guessing horses are usually kept.

Marc stops by an enclosure, and the huge black nose of a horse appears over the half-door. Marc lifts his hand to the horse's mouth and strokes its jaw.

The horse jerks left and right, but after a minute or two, Marc's stroking calms him down.

'He's beautiful,' I whisper, coming closer – but not too close. Big horses scare me. 'My mother used to take me horse riding.'

Marc runs a firm hand down the horse's nose, and it whinnies in approval. 'Yes, I know.'

'How?'

'I saw a photo of you riding. At your father's house.' Marc unbolts the enclosure, holding up a steadying hand to keep the horse from charging forward.

I can tell this horse is fiery by the way he smacks his hooves and shakes his mane.

Marc picks up the brown paper bag and holds it out to me. 'For you,' he says. 'Riding gear.'

'Oh no. You're kidding me. You want me to ride this horse? *This* horse? He's huge. And he looks like he has a temper.'

'Whoever said this horse was a he?'

'It's a girl horse?'

Marc smiles. 'No. A male. He's called Taranu. It's a Welsh word. It means thunder. And he's extremely strong and wilful, like his namesake.'

'Marc – I can't ride him.'

'You can and you will. And he'll teach you a lot.' Marc

slaps his shiny, black flank. 'With Taranu, you'll have to be strong. Control him or you'll be thrown.'

I think of my mother and the times we went riding together. I rode a pony called Daisy, and it was the gentlest creature you could ever hope to meet. Mum and I would trot together through the woodlands and along country paths. They were magical, those Saturday mornings.

'I'm not sure this is such a good idea,' I say.

'You don't have a choice,' says Marc, resting his hand on Taranu's rear. 'When I'm teaching you, you do as I say. You're riding him, and that's final. So let's get you dressed.'

67

Taranu snorts and kicks his feet against the hard concrete behind the stables, and I watch him warily, thinking now would be a good time to change my mind.

Marc has fitted Taranu with a shiny brown saddle.

I'm wearing the beige riding trousers, fitted black polo neck and black boots from the boutique clothing store bag.

I'm shivering, both with cold and fear.

Come on, Sophia. Come on, you can do this.

'Ready?' Marc asks, holding the reins.

I nod, putting my foot in the metal stirrup before I have too much time to think about it. I put my hands on Taranu's soft coat, and he gives a little twitch that knocks me off balance.

I nearly fall, but Marc catches me. I try to ignore the electricity that zips through my body at Marc's touch, and plant my feet firmly on the ground.

'Easy. Easy, boy,' says Marc, giving Taranu's flank a pat. I notice Marc isn't looking at me and guess he feels the electricity too.

Sophia ... you've got to stop thinking like that.

'Okay.' I put my foot in the stirrup again, grab the glossy brown saddle and heave myself up and over.

Whoa.

I'm about five feet in the air. It's a *long* way to the ground.

I take the reins, trying to be cool and confident, but in truth, I'm sick with nerves.

Taranu takes a step forward, and I jolt back, then to the front.

'Oh! Wait. No. Stand still,' I say.

My nervous words aren't calming Taranu, and he trots a fast little circle on the concrete.

I freeze, holding tight to the reins, my whole body rigid. Every jolt sends my stiff body flying the wrong way, and I throw myself down against the saddle, clinging to Taranu with both hands.

'Sit up,' says Marc. 'Now. Take charge of him. Or he'll run away with you. *Now* Sophia. This isn't a game.'

Oh my god, he really is serious. 'Okay.' I struggle upright and pull the reins tighter.

Taranu responds by walking forward.

'Marc! Where's he going?'

'Wherever he likes right now. You'd better take charge of him.'

Oh my god.

Taranu heads towards an open field. He trots at first, but as soon as there's grass beneath his hooves, he begins to canter.

I'm still completely tense, my body bouncing up, down, up, down as Taranu goes from a canter to a gallop.

Oh my god.

I pull the reins tight, but it makes no difference. Wind pushes at my cheeks, and my eyes water. We're galloping now. Properly galloping, and I'm bouncing all over the place.

I can't hold on. Any minute now, I'm going to go flying off. I look down at the soft grass and see Taranu's thick hooves pounding into it. There's no way I want to fall at this speed.

I pull the reins again.

'Stop, Taranu. No.'

He doesn't slow at all, even though I'm tugging as hard as I can. I'm growing more and more terrified now. There's a fence up ahead, and if he tries to jump it, I'll fall. And he'll be loose in a neighbour's field.

Bump, bump, bump – I'm bouncing so hard that I'm flying up and down in the saddle. The fence is only metres away, and part of me wants to throw my hands to my face and brace myself for impact.

'Stop. *Stop.*' I pull at the reins with all my might, hearing Taranu snort and feeling him alter his footing, ready to jump the fence.

'Turn. NOW.' I've never heard that voice before, but it came from me alright – deep and guttural and from my very core. My hands slide further up the reins and tug. Not desperately. Not fearfully. But forcefully.

'TURN. No, you will *not* throw me. You will turn. You will turn.'

I pull the reins with all my might, pulling Taranu's neck to the side and ...

He turns.

Just in time.

I keep the reins completely taut in my hands, not letting them slip even a centimetre, although the leather is cutting me. We gallop back towards the stables, but this time at a slower pace. I pull tighter and tighter until he slows to a canter, then a trot.

'Easy boy.' I lean forward and stroke his strong neck, hearing him snort in approval. It's only when I see Marc by the stables that I realise how shaken I am.

I pull Taranu to a stop, then slide free of the saddle. My knees nearly give way as I hit the ground, and I have to lean against Taranu for support. My arms are shaking too, now they're not taut and tense.

'Good ride?' Marc takes Taranu's reins. The horse bows its head to him, nuzzling its nose against Marc's long fingers.

I glare at him, flinging my shaking arms to my hips. 'Are you crazy?' I shout. 'What on earth ... that horse was out of control. You let me ride a horse like that?'

'Out of control?' Marc raises an eyebrow. 'He was anything but. Because you took charge of him.'

'And what if I hadn't?' I say, angry tears in my eyes.

'I would have used this.' Marc slides a black whistle from his pocket.

'What's that?'

'A stop whistle. He's trained to come to a careful stop when he hears it.'

'But ... he was heading towards the fence ...'

'And he would have turned at this whistle and stopped. He's a well-trained horse. Despite appearances.'

'It didn't feel like he was about to turn.'

'Trust me. He would have done. But you turned him yourself. I was watching you. Extremely carefully. At the tiniest hint that you were losing your seat, I would have blown the whistle.'

I'm still glaring at him, my heart pounding, but my hands slide down from my hips. 'You mean ... I wasn't in charge of him at all?'

'You were in charge,' says Marc. 'But you had a safety net. You just didn't know it. How are you feeling?'

'Angry.'

'You look exhilarated.'

'Perhaps a little.' I put a hand to my pounding chest.

'You did well,' says Marc, cocking his head. 'Extremely well. Now. You have rehearsals to attend. Do you understand what that little exercise was all about?'

'I ... yes. I think so. I mean ... I see what you're doing. You forced me to take control. It's made me feel more confident. Like I can take charge of a situation that seems impossible.'

Marc drops the whistle in his pocket. 'I think it would do you good to attend Denise's lessons, too.'

'There's no time,' I say. 'My rehearsals last all day.'

'You didn't let me finish,' says Marc, frowning. 'I know how long your rehearsals last. So I've booked you some evening lectures with Denise.'

I look down at the concrete. 'I know I should train with Denise. But Marc ... when it comes to singing, maybe I'm just not good enough.'

'Utter nonsense,' Marc snaps. 'Believe you're not good enough, and you won't be. You'll attend evening lectures with Denise.'

'Marc -'

'No arguments. If you want my tuition, you follow my rules.'

I let Taranu's reins slip around in my fingers. 'Are we back here again?' I say. 'You instruct, I obey?'

'You said you wanted me to teach you.' Marc takes a step closer, his blue eyes clouded.

Oh good God. How can he still have this effect on me? I'd only just calmed down, and now once again my heart is pounding.

'Show me your hands.'

'My ...'

'Your hands. Now.' Marc lifts my hands from the reins, and turns them so he can see the palms. Red burn marks run across my left hand where the reins tore at my skin.

'You're hurt.' He frowns. 'Why didn't you tell me?'

'I ... they ... it's only a few little marks.'

'Those need to be cleaned up.'

'But Marc ... my rehearsals.'

'Wait in the back of the limo. I'll meet you there in five minutes.'

69

I'm barely in the car a minute when the door clicks open and Marc climbs in. He has bandages and antiseptic burn cream, and he's still frowning.

'It's okay,' I say. 'Really. You don't need to be worried.'

Marc squeezes a dab of antiseptic cream on cotton wool, then very carefully takes my left hand in his.

'This might sting a little,' he says, patting at the red lines on my palm. He's like an artist, painting something really delicate. He frowns. 'I never wanted you to get hurt.'

'It's fine. Really.' I watch him clean the wound. 'Marc. Can I ask you something?'

Marc keeps dabbing, concentration making cute little lines appear above his nose. 'What do you want to know?'

'When we were ... together. Did you like hurting me?'

Marc pauses, the cotton wool hovering near my fingers. 'I can't abide the thought of hurting you.'

'But ...'

'No.' Marc shakes his head. 'I was teaching you something pleasurable. Pain and pleasure are very closely linked. It happened to work for me because I need to be in charge.'

'You *need* to be in charge,' I say slowly. 'Not like. *Need*?'

'And you found it pleasurable,' says Marc, gently wrapping a bandage around my hand.

'Yes,' I say. 'The times we had ... they were ... I'll never forget a moment of it. They were the most amazing times ever. Do we ... is there any chance for us?'

Marc ties the bandage tight, then holds my hand gently in his. 'I still want you,' he says. 'This is torture for me. You do realise that, don't you? But my main priority is keeping you safe. And right now that means being apart.'

'I miss you, Marc. I wish we could still be together.'

Marc is still holding my hand, and I feel the electricity that comes from him, running up and down my arm. We're like two magnets fighting the current.

'You're the first woman who ever, *ever* got so close,' Marc says. 'Don't you know how much it hurts being apart from you? Do you think I'd do that without good reason? I want to protect you.'

'But don't you see?' I say, feeling the car begin to move. 'You're hurting me right now by staying away. I guess I always knew I'd get hurt. I should have known by our sex life.'

Marc's grip tightens on my hand. 'Did you ... think I was hurting you?' His forehead creases up. 'You thought I liked seeing you in pain?'

'Didn't you?'

Marc leans back. 'No. That wasn't what I liked. I liked taking charge of you. Of you yielding to me. Of dominating you and being in control of your pleasure.'

'Do you ... is that how it's always been with you? With women?'

'Are you saying I'm interested in men?' Marc's lips quirk up.

'I'm guessing no.'

Marc laughs. 'Good guess. And no ... that's not how it's always been. I used to be different. Younger, more afraid. Out of control.'

'You've been with women and not had to take charge?'

'That's correct.'

'But I wasn't the first. Right? The first woman you ... took charge of.'

'Before you, there were others. Women who ... I had that dynamic with. But things didn't start out that way. I wasn't always in charge.' Marc puts his hand to his forehead. 'Something ... some*one* happened.'

There's a long pause.

'Oh,' I say, to fill the silence. And then I can't help asking, 'Did you love her?'

Marc laughs. '*Him*. He was nothing more than a friend, and he showed me the way, in a manner of speaking.' Marc's watching me now, one eyebrow slightly raised, those amazing lips tilted up just a little. 'You really don't know, do you?'

'Know what?'

'He didn't tell you?'

'Tell me what?' I'm confused.

'The friend. The friend who showed me the way, for better or worse. You can't guess who he is?'

I stare at him, bewildered. 'I have no idea,' I say.

'The friend was Giles Getty.'

'*Giles Getty?*' I practically spit the words out.

Marc nods. 'He introduced me to the scene. A scene where women liked men to take charge.'

I feel sick. 'You're kidding me. Giles Getty?' Just saying his name makes my tongue feel slimy. 'He ... he said you were friends, but I thought ...'

'That he was exaggerating?' Marc's blue eyes are wider and clearer than I've ever seen them. 'No.'

Green turns to grey as we enter the outskirts of London.

'How?' I say, hearing utter confusion in my voice. 'When?'

'A long time ago. He wasn't quite the evil bastard he is now, but he was on his way. But I didn't see it. Until it was too late.'

Marc puts his head in his hands, and I see his pale fingers slip through his thick brown hair. I want to touch him. To hold him. To tell him it's all okay. But ... I don't know if everything is okay.

'What happened?' I ask.

Marc sighs into his hands.

'I was young and stupid and didn't realise what I was getting into until it was too late. When Getty introduced me to his scene ... the world he showed me, it awakened something. Who I really am, I guess you could say. Or at least, who I wanted to be. In charge. Cool and in control. And the pleasure I could bring by being that way. I guess Getty saw something in me that was ... similar to him.'

I shake my head. 'You're not similar.'

'We are,' says Marc. 'More than you know. Getty got

me into ... domination, shall we call it. Taking charge, sexually. He brought me to the clubs, introduced me to the women.'

I feel sick. Partly about the thought of him with other women, but mainly because Getty was involved in such an intimate part of Marc's life.

'When I hooked into that scene,' says Marc, 'all the bad feelings I carried around ... those worthless, frightened feelings that came from a life with my father ... they left. Just like that. The power I felt was tremendous.'

Somehow, our bodies have moved apart.

'The first night I was with a woman from one of Getty's clubs,' Marc continues, 'she asked me to tie her up. The more I restrained her and took charge, the more she liked it. And I felt alive. I felt like me. The real me.'

'So you and the woman ...'

Marc waves a dismissive hand. 'I have no idea what happened to her. She's not important. It wasn't about her. It was about me. I met many more women like her. I got good at reading the signs.'

'Did you read the signs in me?'

Marc doesn't miss a beat. 'Yes.'

'You knew I'd enjoy you hurting me?'

'Not *hurting* you. Taking charge of you. It's what you needed. It's what you still need.'

Marc stretches his legs out and puts an arm on the edge of the window.

'Getty was clever. He didn't show me exactly who *he* was at first. We visited clubs where women wanted men to be in charge, and I thought that was Getty's thing too. But Getty wanted more. He liked watching women get hurt. Women who weren't necessarily enjoying themselves. It excited him. And there are specialist places where you can watch that sort of thing. And take part.'

I swallow thickly, feeling sick.

'And ... did you take part in that?'

Marc shakes his head sharply. 'I already told you. It's not about pain for me. It's about bringing pleasure through taking control. Sometimes that control means pain. But I can't abide the thought of a woman getting hurt against her will. My mother and sister were both beaten by a man who was supposed to be taking care of them. The thought of hurting a woman who isn't consensual sickens me.'

'So what happened?' I ask. 'With you and Getty?'

'When I found out what he was in to, I told him that was the end of our acquaintance. And I reported his activities to the police. He responded by hounding my sister, and selling story after story on her.'

'Your poor sister.' I swallow, nausea stirring my stomach.

'It ruined her life,' Marc says, matter-of-factly.

The car is slowing now as it meets London traffic, and Marc turns to gaze out of the window. 'If it wasn't for those press stories, she could have turned her life around before now. But she never had a chance.'

The car drives on, and we sit in silence for a while. Then I say, 'Thank you. For telling me. I wish you'd told me sooner. Not that it matters now, I guess. But I'm glad I know.'

'I'm glad you know the truth, too. At least, part of it.' Marc's jaw becomes firmer, and he takes his Blackberry from his pocket, flicking his thumb over it. 'Back to business. You'll be seeing Denise tonight. And after your rehearsals for the rest of the week. Then we'll meet again. Okay?'

'Okay,' I say, my head in a whirl. I don't know what to think or what to feel.

I'm on time for the rehearsal, and predictably I perform better than I have in a long time. I don't know if it was riding the horse, Marc's praise or just being with Marc that made me more confident, but I waltz into the theatre like I own the place and act my heart out.

Davina's mouth opens and closes a few times, but it seems she can't think of much to criticise me about today.

I'm positively glowing when we finish that evening, and I trek across the college for my lesson with Denise.

I've been thinking about Marc all day, of course, and even more so now the rehearsals are finished. As I walk across the cold grounds, I think about all the pain Marc's had to deal with. How difficult his life has been. I understand that after a life like his, you could become a little addicted to being in charge.

It's bitterly cold now, and light puffs of snow swirl and flick around. The college looks so beautiful with snow floating around, especially now all the Christmas decorations have been hung. Fairy lights decorate the trees, making the college look even more magical and mysterious, and nets of twinkling stars have been thrown over the college roof tops.

When I reach Denise's classroom, I see candles flickering in the window and hear low, soft music. There are fake blue snowflakes stuck all over the windows, and I see Denise inside, sitting on a beanbag, flicking through *Stage* magazine.

I knock on the door.

'Sophia?' Denise calls.

Where the Ivy Grows

'Hi.' I creak the door open, and dust snow from my arms and hair.

Denise gets to her feet. 'Well, look at you. More beautiful than ever. And performing in the West End, no less. But ...' She puts a finger to her lips. 'What's on your mind, my love? Or should I say, *who*?'

I smile. 'The usual who.'

'Oh? Our Mr Blackwell?'

'Who else?'

'I've missed you in my classes,' says Denise.

'I'm so sorry.' I hang my coat over a plastic chair. 'I've missed you too. But the rehearsals are taking up so much time.'

'And how are they going?' Denise asks, bustling over to her kettle. 'Tea?'

'Yes, please.' I put my cold fingers against a radiator. 'They're ... going okay. Today they were okay. Before today, it's been awful.'

'Awful?'

I nod. 'Marc was right. I never should have taken this part. It was offered to me for all the wrong reasons, and now it's too late to back out.'

'Ah, the lovely Marc,' says Denise, pouring hot water into cups. 'I hear the two of you went horse riding this morning.'

'*I* did. He stood and watched.'

'How are the two of you? Still struggling?'

'That's one way of putting it.'

'So no hope for the star-crossed lovers?'

I sit heavily in an orange plastic chair. 'I don't think so. I wish there was. Marc's pretty determined.'

'I'm sorry to hear that.' Denise hands me a tea, and I smell cinnamon. 'Do you want a drop of brandy in it?' she asks. 'Christmas time, and all that?'

'Yes, please,' I say. 'I could use a drink right now.'

Denise takes a little bottle of toffee-coloured brandy from a cupboard and sloshes a good measure into my tea.

I take a sip. 'Mmm, delicious.' I taste cherry, spices and brown sugar.

'So you and Marc ... he's tutoring you again, is that the story?'

'Yes,' I say. 'And it's helping.'

'I can imagine,' says Denise. 'He really is an excellent teacher. Very strict, but he has such faith in his pupils. Such trust. It carries. When we feel someone's faith in us, we believe in ourselves.'

'Maybe that's why I have such a hard time with Davina,' I say. 'She doesn't have any faith in me.'

'Diva Davina? Don't let her get to you. She's well known in musical circles, and from what I've heard, she's nothing but a bully. A great director in some ways, but she takes her moods out on her performers.'

'She's fine with Leo.'

'Well, she would be. He's a Hollywood star. She knows what side her bread is buttered. She's going to keep him as sweet as possible. Connections.' Denise taps her nose.

'She has a point, though,' I say. 'I'm nowhere near as good as Leo. I'm an amateur.'

'An incredibly gifted amateur. Don't you forget that. Leo may have had years of practise, but he doesn't have your talent. You just need a little refining, that's all.'

I laugh. 'That's what Leo said.'

'And what does Marc say?'

'He says I need to take charge more.'

'A good point. Well, my dear. Shall we get started? Get you warmed up, and then get you belting out those *Beauty and the Beast* numbers?'

'Okay.'

72

The singing lesson with Denise is exactly what I need, and I leave her studio feeling lighter than I have done since Marc and I broke up.

It's late, but I'm liking being out in the dark, under swirling snow, lost in my thoughts.

There are no students around, and I half remember Tanya saying something about a test tomorrow. I guess everyone must be inside studying. But as I near the accommodation block, I hear a man's voice.

'You promised me access. This isn't access.'

Oh my god. I recognise that voice, and it makes me feel far chillier than the snow.

I flatten myself against the nearest wall, my heart pounding. Then I hear another voice – a female this time.

'How was I to know she wouldn't be there?'

And then the man again.

'You'd better not be playing games with me.'

Oh my god, oh my god, oh my god.

The man is Giles Getty.

73

My throat goes thick and hot, and my fingertips cling to the crumbly wall.

Every sense in my body tells me to run in the opposite direction, but if I move, he might see me.

Giles's quick, smart voice floats into the night air again.

'You've blown it. She must be with him. I'll have to come back another time.'

There's the smack of leather on concrete, and I realise someone is heading my way.

Pushing myself flat against the wall, I inch away from the voices. My feet are in a flower bed, and I winch as I realise the damage I'm doing to the winter pansies, but still I creep, creep along, towards a privet hedge near the edge of the building.

Giles turns the corner, just as I pull myself into the hedge and feel twigs poke and stab my face and hands.

He stops dead and looks right at the bush, but it must be too dark for him to see me because he walks straight past.

I hold my breath, feeling the agitation and anger in his movements. He is not a happy man. Not a peaceful man. I remember what Marc said about him liking to see women hurt, and feel sick to my stomach.

I'm still hidden, too scared to move, when I hear a sound that cuts right to my stomach.

It's the deep, haunting sound of sobbing, and every muscle in my body tenses. It's awful, that sound. Frighteningly. It seems to suck the joy from my very soul.

Tentatively, I step out from the bush, still feeling

afraid, but sad too, for whoever is sobbing. It's a crazy kind of crying. Unnatural.

I peer around the corner.

Oh my god.

It's ... Cecile.

She's leaning against the accommodation block, head in her hands, whole body shaking with grief. She was the woman Getty was speaking to.

Cecile lets out a long, piercing scream that makes me jump and wrap my arms around myself. Then she vanishes inside the accommodation block.

I stand there, open mouthed, shivering in the thickening snow.

74

When I get to my room, I turn on every single light, sit on the bed and pull the duvet around my shaking body.

Did Getty come here for me? What if he's still on campus and sees my lights on?

I leap up and turn all the lights off again. But I can't sit here in the dark. It's way too creepy. I bundle the duvet around myself and hurry down to Tanya's room.

Knock, knock.

No answer. I knock again, louder this time.

Still no answer.

It's cold out here in the hallway. And dark. I don't want to be out here alone. I call Tanya's number, but it goes straight through to answer phone.

What's going on? Where could she be? It's term time and a weekday.

I try her door one last time, then give up, letting my thumb run over my phone. I should call Marc. And not just because I want to talk to him. I should call him because I need someone to protect me right now. But no. He made his feelings clear today. He wants us to stay apart. We're teacher and student only.

Just as I'm about to call Tom, there's a bleeping sound and I see a new text message.

Tanya, I think. But the message is from Leo.

'Hey honey, has your singing lesson finished yet? Fancy a drink?'

I slam the phone to my ear and call Leo's number.

He answers on the third ring. 'Hey Sophia. I -'

'Leo!' I breathe. 'Something happened. Are you on campus?'

'Hey, hey. Slow down. What's going on?'

I look up and down the dark corridor.

'I can't talk here. Can I come meet you?'

'Sure you can. I'm in my room. Come right on over. Two zero three on the second floor. Are you okay? You sound out of breath.'

'No, just ... scared.' I hurry down the dark corridor to the stairwell.

75

Leo throws the door open before I have a chance to knock.

'Enchante,' he says, standing aside. 'Welcome to the pleasure palace.'

I hurry inside, pushing the door tightly closed with both hands.

'What's up?' Leo asks.

'He was ... someone was on campus,' I say, seeing a fireplace and antique wooden bed just like the ones in my room. Leo's space is bigger than mine, but it doesn't have the balcony or the views. Just a huge closet and bathroom, and enormous silver fridge.

'Whoa,' says Leo, going to the fridge and pulling out a Budweiser. 'Calm down and tell me what happened. You want one?' He waves the bottle at me.

'No right now,' I say.

Leo bangs the bottle on the mantelpiece so the lid goes shooting off. '*Who* was on campus?' He takes a swig of beer.

'Giles Getty.'

Leo chokes on his beer, coughing and wiping his mouth. 'You're kidding me. The pap guy?'

'I think Cecile let him in.'

'Who's Cecile?'

'You met her once. In the campus pub. Blonde hair.'

'Oh, sure. The director's friend. Spiky face. Had that look about her that nothing was ever good enough.'

'She's sold some stories on me, and I guess she and Getty must be planning to sell a few more.'

'So he was here? Actually on campus?'

I chew my thumbnail again. 'Yes. And I think ... maybe

he was trying to get a picture of me. Or something. But I was out. At my singing class. So my room was empty.'

'Are you sure about all this?' says Leo. 'You're not just getting paranoid? When the press start hounding you, it can send you boo loo for a while.'

He jumps onto the bed, crossing his legs and resting his beer in his lap. 'Tell me what happened *exactly*. Where did you see this Getty guy?'

'Right outside,' I say. 'Outside the accommodation block. He and Cecile were talking. They were saying something about 'she's not in', or something like that.'

'And you're sure it was Getty?'

'I saw him. It was really dark, but I think ... I'm pretty sure it was him. It was his voice I recognised, mainly. He's got this really manic way of talking. He says everything too fast.'

Leo takes a swig of beer. 'You've been working so hard. You must be pretty tired. Are you sure this wasn't ... you know, like one of those dreams you have when you're still awake?'

'I don't think so.'

'You seem jumpy,' says Leo. 'On edge. Maybe you just need a break for a few days. When I shot *Everlasting*, we had to do all this night filming on Hollywood Boulevard, and man, I just got so tired, I started seeing things. Weird things in the shadows.'

My phone rings, and I nearly jump out of my skin.

I pull it out of my pocket and see Tanya's name flashing on the screen.

'Are you going to answer that?' asks Leo. 'Or just stare at it?'

I blink and put the phone to my ear. 'Tanya?'

'Hey,' she croaks. 'What's up?' She sounds so sleepy. I can almost picture her, bleary eyed, red hair standing two inches above her head.

'I'm sorry to call so late,' I say. 'I just ... had a bit of a scare.'

There's a scuffling sound, and I hear a bang and '*shit*' floating down the phone.

'Are you okay?' I ask.

'Fine,' says Tanya. 'But *you* don't sound okay. What's up? It's not Marc, is it? Has he done something to you?'

'No, no, nothing like that.' There's another bang.

'Tanya? Where are you?'

A pause.

'Um ... in my room.' The words are sort of squashed and squeezed, and I get the feeling she's not telling the truth.

'But ... I knocked on your door not five minutes ago. You didn't answer.'

'Oh Jesus. I'm a terrible liar. Okay. Soph, I'm in Tom's room. And in answer to your next question, yes.'

'The two of you ...?'

'Yes. Hang on. Tom wants to say hello. I'll put you on speaker phone.'

There's a crackle.

'Soph!' calls a familiar, friendly voice. 'Are you okay?'

'Hi Tom.'

'Sorry about the deception. We didn't want to say anything, in case this is just ... you know, a stupid fling,' Tom continues. 'What's happening? You sound tense.'

'Something really weird's going on.'

'What is it, Soph?' asks Tanya.

I glance at Leo. 'Giles Getty was outside just now. At least, I think he was.'

'Who on earth let him in?' says Tanya. 'We should call security.'

'I think it was Cecile,' I say.

'Even more reason to phone security,' says Tanya.

'Let's grass her up and get her thrown out of college. Where's my dressing gown? It's freezing in here.'

'It's hanging on the door, my love,' I hear Tom say.

'There's something else,' I say. 'When Getty left, I heard Cecile crying.'

'And?' says Tanya.

'And it was ... I've never heard crying like that before. It was desperate. Absolutely desperate. Like someone badly in need of help.'

'We all know Cecile needs help,' says Tanya. 'Psychiatric help.'

'Do you think she let Getty into the college?' says Tom. 'Or do you think he forced his way in?'

'I think she let him in,' I say. 'I just ... got that feeling. They were talking like friends. I think she might even have let him in so he could get to me. But of course, I wasn't in my room.'

'That does it,' says Tanya. 'Next time I see her, she's going to get what's coming.'

'I felt sorry for her,' I admit. 'When I heard her crying like that, I just couldn't feel angry. She's in trouble. I just know she is.'

'Serves her right,' says Tanya. 'It's nothing she hasn't brought on herself. Bad things happen to bad people.'

'Sounds like she's made a deal with the devil and now he wants paying,' says Tom. 'Wasn't she at the GMQ newspaper offices with him? Didn't one of you two tell me that?'

'Will you please let me call security now?' says Tanya.

I chew a thumbnail. 'I should call Marc first.'

'Yes, call him,' says Tanya. 'He'll know security here better than anyone. Do you need us to come to your room?'

'No, it's okay.' I glance at Leo again.

'I'm ... I'm in Leo's room.'

'Ooo!' says Tom.

'No, it's not like that,' I say, turning red.

'Well, we're right here if you need us,' says Tanya. 'And listen. Soph. If you need anything. Anything at all, just call, okay? I'll set my phone to mega loud.'

'Thank you,' I say. 'And Tanya? I'm really happy for you and Tom.'

77

'So.' Leo interlaces his fingers around his beer bottle. 'Is Mr Marc Blackwell going to come charging along on his white horse?'

A smile pulls at my lips. 'He's not exactly the white horse type. More a dark Aston Martin.'

'But you're going to call him?'

I sit next to Leo on the bed. 'Yes.'

'Are you so sure you saw what you saw?'

'Pretty certain. I know I'm tired, but ... no, I'm certain. And Marc will want to know about this.'

'Well. You know best.'

I call Marc's number, my fingers scrunching up Leo's duvet.

Ring, ring.

Will he think I'm calling to get back with him? To talk things over?

Ring, ring.

Perhaps this is a bad idea. The thought of him picking up sends shivers through me. Good shivers. A little too good.

Ring, ring.

I'm losing my nerve now. I'm about to hang up, when –

'Sophia?'

His voice is so deep, so familiar, that all my senses wake up, and I feel like he's right here, sitting next to me. The hairs on my arms stand up, and my stomach goes soft.

'Hi. I ... I didn't expect you to pick up so late.' I know my words are shaky.

'Something's wrong. What is it?'

Panic and fear rush into my chest. 'Oh, Marc. Giles Getty was here. In the college.'

'*What?*'

'He was right by the accommodation block.'

'Do you know how he got in?'

I hesitate, knowing Tanya would kill me for not mentioning Cecile. But after hearing that awful crying, I can't drop Cecile in it just yet. I need to find out what's going on with her.

'I'm not sure.' It's the truth, just not the whole truth.

There's a pause, and I hear heavy breathing. 'Where are you now? Are you alone?'

'Still at the college. And no. I'm not alone.'

'Who are you with?'

I hesitate, gripping the phone tighter.

'Sophia?'

'I'm with ... Leo right now.'

I hear a low breath, almost like a growl. 'Fine. Stay where you are. I'll have extra security called in.'

'Marc, it's not what you think. I -'

But the line has already gone dead.

'Not what you think?' says Leo, flashing his perfect, white teeth. He downs his beer, then slam dunks the empty bottle into a wicker bin. 'You still have a thing for Mr Blackwell, don't you?'

'I didn't want him getting the wrong idea.'

'And why would he get the wrong idea?'

'It's late and I'm with you. That's enough to get anyone's mind working. I'd hate it if I called him and he was with a woman.'

'Really? You'd hate it?'

I nod, feeling sick at the thought, and suddenly wonder ... will I *ever* get over Marc? Will he have this hold over me for the rest of my life?

'Sounds like you've still got it bad,' says Leo. 'But hey – you're here with me now. The two of us. A double bed. How about you give some other guy a chance?'

He waggles his eyebrows, and I can't help smiling.

'Thanks for the offer, Leo. Very flattering.'

'Hey, I'm not joking. This is a totally serious offer. I will *happily* sleep with you tonight, and try to take your mind off Marc Blackwell. I will do my very best, scouts honour.'

'Very noble.'

'But something tells me you're not going to be so easy. Not a one night stand kind of girl, huh?'

'Not so far.' I slump down on the bed and stare at the ceiling. 'What an evening.'

Leo comes and lies next to me. 'Hey. Life can hurt sometimes.'

We both stare at the ceiling for a few minutes.

Then Leo says, 'You see that crack up there? It reminds

me of an ocean wave. What do you see?'

'A sapling,' I say.

'Do you need to stay here tonight?' says Leo, turning to stare at my cheek. 'I'll sleep on that couch over there. It's just I get the feeling you don't want to go back to your room.'

'I don't,' I admit. 'I'm too scared.'

'Hey, it'll be alright,' says Leo. 'You shouldn't think so much. Look at you – your face is all scrunched up.'

'Sorry.' I roll to face him. 'It's been a weird night.'

'That's better,' says Leo. 'Your eyes look much prettier when your forehead isn't all tense.' He kisses me on the cheek, then leaps up. 'See you in the morning, sleeping beauty. It's a big week for us. First rehearsal back at Tottenham Theatre.'

He takes bedding from the large built-in wardrobe and throws it on the sofa.

'Sweet dreams, Sophia.'

'Sweet dreams, Leo.'

The next morning, I wake to hear Leo snoring. He's lying on the couch, one large hand flung towards the ground, the other on his chest.

Soft blonde hair falls on his tanned forehead, and his pink lips are slightly open.

I feel hot and sticky, and realise I slept fully dressed in Leo's bed. Slipping out from under the duvet, I creep to the kitchen area for a glass of water, then head to the bathroom.

There are organic grooming products around the sink and shower, most of them open and leaking on porcelain. There's something called 'snake peel' that's dripped little black granules onto the sink, and a goat's milk moisturiser with a missing lid by the tap. I smile. Leo's messier than I am.

I wash my face with cold water, then clean my teeth with my finger and Leo's fennel-flavour toothpaste.

Leo's snoring floats through from the other room and I consider waking him, but ... there's something I need to do right now. It's making me nervous just thinking about it. I splash more cold water on my face, then head out the door.

Cecile's room is number 132. I know because I heard her complaining about it on my second day of college. She was waving her key at Wendy, shouting about windows that let through drafts.

As I creep along the first floor landing, I hear taps running and toilets flushing. I guess everyone must be waking up, and I'm hoping Cecile is awake too.

When I reach Cecile's door, I hesitate. Should I be doing this? I don't usually seek out confrontation, but sometimes needs must. And in a way, it's not so much a confrontation. Yes, I want to find out if she let Getty in last night. But I also want to know why she was crying.

Knock, knock.

I take a step back and chew my thumb. I'm sort of regretting not going back to my room first and changing the clothes I slept in, but it's too late now.

The door is yanked open.

Cecile stands before me, looking perfect. She's wearing a long, billowy nightgown, and a lace-trimmed eye mask sits above shiny blonde hair in a loose bun.

Without make-up, she looks younger and actually much prettier. But her eyes have the tired, crinkled look of someone who's spent the night crying. They widen when she sees me.

'Sophia!' The word is strangled and strange.

'We need to talk,' I say. 'I heard you last night. Talking to Getty.'

Cecile's forehead creases up, and her eyes dart frantically left and right. 'I don't know what you're talking about -'

I hold up a hand. 'We both know it was you. So. Can I come in?'

Cecile pokes her head out into the corridor, glancing up and down. Then she stands back. 'I suppose you'd better.'

Cecile's room is totally different from mine, which is funny considering all the rooms are sort of similar.

Her bed is made up with crisp white, lace-edged linen that looks incredibly hard to wash. Scattered between her white pillows are arty cushions with gold animals printed on them.

There's a Mercedes number plate hanging on the back of her door that says 'Cecile 1', and art house film posters decorate the walls. Everything is pin neat, not a speck of dust to be seen, and I feel like I've walked into a magazine photo shoot.

I stand awkwardly by the bed, not sure what to do with myself. There's a chaise longue near the window, but it looks far too clean and perfect to actually sit on.

'So?' Cecile straightens the duvet on her bed, then plumps the cushions. 'What do you want to talk about?'

'I know Getty was here last night.'

Cecile pauses, mid-plump, then carries on cushion bashing as if she hasn't heard.

'I'm guessing you let him in,' I continue.

'You can't prove anything,' says Cecile, her eyes fixed on a cushion printed with gold giraffes.

'I don't need to. If I tell Marc I heard you with Getty, that's all the proof he'll need.'

That gets her attention.

'You wouldn't!' She whirls around.

'I might,' I say. 'If you don't tell me what's going on.' It's hard to feel sorry for her right now, but I try to remember her crying last night and my shoulders soften a little. 'You sounded ... so upset.'

'It was nothing,' says Cecile, far too quickly.

I take a step towards her. 'Look, I know we're not friends. I know we'll probably never be friends. But if something's going on with you, something bad, tell me. Because if I don't know, the only option I have is to tell Marc that you let Getty in last night.'

Cecile goes to the window and stares out at the college grounds. She puts her hands on her tiny hips, and I see how frail she looks under her billowy nightgown. 'So you mean to blackmail me.'

'No.' I shake my head. 'Not at all. I mean to give you a chance.'

'You think I need chances from someone like you?'

'Right now, yes.' I find my hands going to my hips too. 'Look, this is getting ridiculous. I came here to let you share your side of things. If you don't want that, then no problem. I'll phone Marc and tell him -'

'No!' Cecile turns, her eyes wet with tears. '*Please*.' She's shaking her head. 'Don't tell. I ... if I get thrown out of college, my life is over.'

'So what's going on?' I ask. 'Did you let Getty in last night?'

She gives the tiniest, stiffest little nod.

'Why?'

'Oh, you know why.' She waves her perfect nails at me. 'So he could get pictures of you. But you were out.'

'Cecile, how well do you know Getty?'

'What does that mean?'

'Exactly what it sounds like.'

'My personal life is none of your business.'

I frown. 'Your personal life?'

Cecile puts a hand to her forehead. 'Forget I said that.

Look, I know him pretty well, okay? Too well.'

'Do you know ... I mean, he could be dangerous.'

'What do you need to worry about? You have Marc Blackwell to protect you.'

'I'm not thinking about me,' I say. 'I'm thinking about you. Do you know ... I mean, with women. He ... I heard that he likes seeing women get hurt.'

Cecile's pale little lips fall apart, and I see her tiny, neat white teeth. 'How do you know what he likes?'

'Cecile, has he hurt you?'

Cecile's eyes drop to her hands, and she takes one wrist between her thumb and forefinger. Around her wrist, I notice green and blue bruising.

'Did Getty do that?' I ask, quietly.

Cecile snatches her fingers away, like a guilty child caught in the cookie jar. Her shoulders start to shake, then her chest. She wraps her arms around herself and tears slide down her cheeks.

'Yes,' she whispers.

I cross the bedroom in a second and put my arms around her, letting her sobbing face rest on my shoulder. I feel the vibrations through my bones as she cries.

'It's okay,' I soothe. 'Really. It's okay.'

'No.' She shakes her head, sitting on her bed and swiping at tears. 'It's not okay. Everything's a mess. Such a terrible mess. You wouldn't understand. I'm so jealous of your life.'

'You? Jealous of me? I'd love to come from a wealthy family. Life would be an awful lot easier.'

'Are you kidding me?' Cecile's eyes widen. 'My family ... they control everything I do. My life is all about how it reflects on them.' She breaks into sobs again.

'Whatever's wrong, I'm sure it can be sorted out,' I say, stroking her hair. 'I'll help you.'

'No one can help me,' says Cecile, her eyes wide and nervous. 'I'm so sorry, Sophia. I never meant for things to go this far.'

'This far?'

'It's just such a mess.' Cecile buries her face in her hands.

I let her cry, knowing it's good to get the tears out. After a few minutes, she takes deep breaths into her hands, then lifts her face.

'So what's going on?' I ask softly.

'I'm pregnant,' says Cecile, her voice hoarse. 'Getty's the father.'

I don't mean to, but my hand flies to my mouth. 'Oh my god.'

Cecile looks at her lap. 'I was so stupid. He's pretty well known, so ... I was flattered when he asked me out. But all he really wanted was to get to you.' She puts her head in her hands. 'I can't be a single mother. I just can't.'

'It's okay,' I say. 'There's a lot of support out there. Plenty of girls go it alone.'

'Maybe where *you* come from, but in my family, it's just not done. My parents will never speak to me again if I have a baby out of marriage ...' She starts sobbing again. Deep, painful sobs that hurt me to hear.

'Does Giles know about the baby?' I ask.

'Yes.'

'What does he think about it?'

'He couldn't care less.' Cecile picks at the lace frills. 'Except that now he has a hold over me and a way to get to you.'

'A hold over you?'

'He says he'll marry me. A proper wedding. He'll do the right thing. But of course, that comes at a price.'

'Letting him into the college and selling stories on me,' I finish.

Cecile bites her lip. 'It didn't start out that way. I mean, at first it was my choice. I wanted to sell a story on you. It wasn't fair, the way you got Marc. I wanted to get you back. But then ... Giles and I ... he can be very charming. I had no idea what he was really like. Not at first.'

'And now?'

'Now I know.' She rubs her wrist again.

'Cecile, surely you don't want to marry a man like that?'

'What else can I do? If I don't, my family will disown me.'

'Are you completely sure about that?'

'Oh, I'm sure.' Cecile's lips pucker. 'I had a cousin once. Not anymore. She married an Indian man who the family didn't approve of, and now no one speaks to her. It's like she's been wiped out of history.' She throws her hands over her face. 'I'm trapped. Completely trapped. If I get rid of the baby, Giles says he'll run a newspaper story on the 'Ivy College abortion'. I'll be publicly shamed. My life will be over.' Her lip begins to wobble.

'There must be a way,' I say, feeling pity stir in my chest. Tom was right – she's done a deal with the devil, and now she's paying for it.

'Trust me, there isn't,' says Cecile. 'He's a monster. Christ, how could I have been so stupid?'

'Cecile, how are we going to work this out? You can't keep letting him in here. It's not safe. For either of us.'

'Tell security he was on campus, and he won't be able to get in again. But please, Sophia, don't tell Marc it was me who let him in. I'm so sorry. For everything. I've been such a bitch to you. I was so jealous. Crazy jealous.'

'I won't tell Marc,' I agree. 'But he already knows Getty was on campus. So he'll be tightening up security.'

'Okay, good.' Cecile nods.

We look at each other for a moment, and then Cecile does something I totally don't expect. She reaches out and takes my hand.

'I don't expect you to forgive me. But for what it's worth, I totally regret selling those stories. It was ...

beneath me. And I've got pay back, big time.' She squeezes my hand tighter. 'You have to be careful, Sophia. Getty is ... he'll stop at nothing. He's a monster.' Cecile hasn't let go of my hand. 'I *had* to let him on campus. He blackmailed me. I would never have done it otherwise, I swear. If he tells my parents ...'

'Cecile, they're going to find out eventually. One way or another.'

'But if we're married before they know -'

'Then you'll be married to a monster.'

Cecile closes her eyes for a long time. When she opens them, she says, 'Perhaps that's a sacrifice worth making.'

I feel more churned up than ever when I leave Cecile's room. The truth is, I much preferred disliking her than feeling sorry for her. It was easier. Now I have to face up to the fact that, in her own way, she's Getty's victim too.

I arrive at rehearsals a little bleary eyed, thoughts of Cecile and Getty racing through my head. But I perform well. My singing is stronger and clearer, and my acting is more confident.

Of course, every chance I get, I check my phone to see if Marc has called or messaged me about Getty and extra security. Leo teases me about it so much that I take to sneaking away to the toilets to check messages. But by the end of the day, there's nothing – no texts, no missed calls, no answer machine messages. I guess Marc must have taken care of things, but he doesn't see any reason to let me know.

After rehearsals, Leo asks me out for a drink.

'I can't,' I tell him. 'I have another coaching session with Denise.'

'How about afterwards?' he asks.

'Maybe. But I might be too tired.'

The session with Denise goes well, and I can feel my voice getting stronger and stronger. But Marc still hasn't called, so I decide to bite the bullet and call him. I want to find out when our next session will be. And, if I'm honest with myself, I want to make sure he knows there's nothing between Leo and I. Just in case there's still a chance for us.

As his phone rings, my heart beats faster and faster.

'Sophia.'

'Marc ... I ... I hope you don't mind me calling.'

'Not at all.'

'I wondered ... are we going to have any more tuition sessions?'

'Of course. But you'll be busy with Denise this week.

I didn't want to tire you out.'

'Oh. Right. Listen, Marc. I just wanted to say. About Leo and I. It's not what it looks like.'

'You thought I'd be jealous?' says Marc.

'Um ...'

'My feelings are irrelevant. I gave you my word that I'd help you. And I will. Get some rest over the weekend. I have some sessions planned for you next week.'

'But Marc, I'm not with Leo -'

'Sophia, what you do in your private life is up to you.'

The line goes dead.

I notice a text from Leo on the screen.

'Finished yet? Changed your mind about that drink?'

Oh, what the hell. Lord knows I could use some relaxation time, and Marc has made it pretty clear there's no chance for us.

I reply: 'Sure. Where are you?'

Leo replies straight away. 'Greens in Soho. See you there!'

When I arrive at Greens, the bar is heaving. Leo is surrounded by adoring fans, and I smile as I watch him sign autographs on beer mats.

I push through the crowd.

'Hey, Leo.'

'Oh, hey! Sophia! You want a drink?'

'Um ... sure. White wine, please.'

'Oh, come on. You can manage something stronger than that.' He taps the bar. 'Two vodka shots, a white wine and a jack and coke.'

He turns to me. 'So. Did the call come through from Mr Blackwell?'

'No. I ended up calling him, actually.'

'So are you guys back together?'

'Not at all. But he's helping me with my acting. Strictly on a teacher student basis.'

Leo nods slowly. 'I hear he's a pretty good teacher.'

'He is,' I say. 'But other than that, we're over.'

'You sure about that?'

'I'm sure.'

My phone bleeps, and Leo raises an eyebrow. 'Maybe that's him. On a strictly teacher student basis.'

I smile and shake my head, seeing Dad's home number on the screen. It's gone eleven. Why would Dad be calling now?

'Sorry, Leo, I have to take this.' I head out of the bar and stand on the cold pavement outside.

'Dad?'

'Sophia, you have to come home now!' It's not Dad - it's Genoveva.

'Genoveva? What's going on?' Samuel is screaming

in the background. I've never heard him scream like that, and it unnerves me. 'Is Sammy okay?'

'It's your father. He's ... had an accident.'

My blood runs cold. 'Oh my god. What happened?'

'I can't ... NO Samuel, not now. I can't cope with this! You have to come now!'

'Okay. Please, Genoveva. Calm down. Where are you? I'm coming right over.' I feel sick to my stomach. Samuel's screams get louder.

'At the *cottage*,' Genoveva screeches. 'You have to come *now*.'

'I'm on my way. What happened? Tell me what's going on. Where's Dad?'

'He's in the hospital,' Genoveva wails. 'I'm all alone. I can't cope.'

'Genoveva. What's happened to my dad?'

'He had an accident. In his taxi. He's in the local hospital. They say ... they say it could go either way.'

'I'm coming right now.'

'To us or the hospital?'

'The hospital. You and Samuel can meet me there.'

My head in a whirl, I run towards Oxford Street. There are a few stray paparazzi on the way, but I barely notice them. They must think it's their lucky day as I charge past, tears streaming down my face. What a picture. But I couldn't care less.

I flag down the first taxi I find.

83

By the time I reach the hospital, I'm a complete mess of tears and snot. I blather my dad's name to the receptionist, and she sends me up to the critical care ward.

Outside the ward, a nurse tells me to go to the visitor room and wait until the doctor is free to see me.

I feel like falling to my knees right there in the hospital corridor and bawling my eyes out, but I manage to hold it together.

'No, I can't,' I say, amazed that I'm stringing a sentence together. 'That would be torture. Please. I need to see him now. Or at least know what's wrong.'

The nurse is a chubby blonde lady with huge round glasses. 'You're Sophia Rose, aren't you?'

'Yes, I -'

'Thought so. I recognise you from the newspapers.' She folds her arms. 'He's been here for hours. You certainly took your time. Did you have a prior engagement?'

I open and close my mouth, feeling angry tears bubble under my eyes. 'No, I ... I only just found out.'

'Really?' She leaves the question hanging in the air.

'I love my dad very much,' I say. 'I'd do anything for him. Don't believe what you've read in the papers about me. I need to see him.'

'He's unconscious -'

'*Please.*' The word is somewhere between a cry and a shout.

'He's sleeping right now while we prepare him to travel.'

'Travel?'

'For a brain scan. We don't have the right equipment in this hospital. It would be better if he stayed put, but what with cut backs, we're just not set up to treat him.'

My throat burns. 'Can I see him while he's sleeping?'

The nurse sighs. 'Come this way.'

When we get to the ward, I see Dad, but I don't see him, if that makes sense. The sleeping man on the bed doesn't look like my dad. He looks much older and greyer.

My face and neck are damp with tears as I go to the bed and take his warm, limp hand.

'Dad, it's me. Soph. You're going to be okay, Dad. You're going to get through this. It's all going to be alright.'

I sob into the waffle blanket that covers his sleeping body. Sensing the nurse behind me, I turn to her.

'When will he come round?'

'It's impossible to say. Some people make a full recovery, but – it all depends on the brain scan. That'll tell us what his chances are. We don't know the damage done to his body yet. We've got him stable, but it's very much a waiting game. We need to get him ready now.'

I grip Dad's hand tighter. 'Just a few more minutes.'

'I'm sorry.' The nurse puts her hand on my shoulder. 'We've a special room for critical care visitors. Come this way.'

In the waiting room, I stare at the snack machine, wondering how anyone could eat in this place. I feel hollow. Empty. I've said so many prayers to God that I'm sure he's getting bored of me.

I try to ring Jen and Genoveva, but I have absolutely no signal here. I guess all the machines must be blocking my reception.

I'm considering buying a powdered drink from the coffee machine, when I hear clipped, male footsteps.

Finally. The doctor.
The waiting room door swings open.
I put a hand to my mouth.
Marc strolls into the room.

'Marc!'

I go to him. No, I don't. I run to him. Leap at him. Throw myself into his arms and bury my head against his warm black jumper. He doesn't say a word. He just holds me as I shake and cry and speak a load of gibberish about the awful nurse and how old my dad looks and how no one knows if he's going to come around or not.

Marc strokes my hair and locks his arms tight around my body. Somehow, I don't need him to say anything. Only hold me. Eventually, my words and tears run out, and I sag against him, breathing heavily, held in his arms.

Marc leads me to some plastic chairs, and we both sit down.

'I've been talking to the doctor,' says Marc. 'Finding out about your father's condition. There's hope, Sophia. I promise you that.'

'Thank you.' I breathe into the soft fabric of his jumper. I'm not surprised by anything – not Marc knowing I was at the hospital or him managing to talk to the doctors already. This is all just so ... Marc. And I love him for it. Truly, honestly love him. In a moment like this, no one else would do.

'They've decided he won't have to travel now,' says Marc, stroking my hair. His voice is deep and soothing. 'He's staying put.'

'How come? The nurse said they didn't have the equipment here.'

'Well. They do now. Do you need anything? Food? Hot chocolate?'

I shake my head. 'No, it's fine. I just ... will you stay with me? That's all I want right now.'

'Do you think I'd leave you at a time like this?'

'No.' I shake my head so fiercely that my hair flies around. 'Never.'

The night struggles on. I sit with Marc, watching the clock tick, tick, tick, and waiting for news. It's torture.

At 2am, a doctor in a white coat peers around the waiting room door. He has thick black glasses and is very short – almost child height.

'Sophia Rose?'

'Yes.' I stand up and Marc stands with me.

'I'm here to give you an update on your father. He's ... it's not looking good.'

My face crumples, and I feel myself leaning into Marc's chest.

Marc puts an arm around my shoulder. 'Could you clarify 'not looking good'?'

The doctor pushes his glasses up his nose. 'He's been unconscious for a long time. In these instances, it's wise to prepare for the worst.'

Marc glares at him. 'Prepare for the worst? That's not a medical term I'm familiar with. Hospitals are in the business of saving lives, are they not? If you've written him off before he's even had a brain scan, then we're in trouble.'

'I just thought I'd keep you updated -'

'And we appreciate that. But a little positivity wouldn't go amiss.'

'Yes, well ...' says the doctor meekly, leaving the waiting room.

Marc takes his phone from his pocket and dials a number.

'Who are you calling?' I ask.

'I'm bringing in some specialist medical assistance. The best people I can find. I have no doubt the people here are trying their best. But they're limited by their experiences. I'm going to find someone who's dealt with a case like your father's before.'

I slump onto a plastic chair. 'Preparing for the worst,' I murmur.

Marc frowns and puts a hand on my shoulder. 'Don't even start thinking that way. It won't help you or your father. You have to think positive. Something that doctor doesn't seem to understand. Damn it!' He looks at his phone. 'No reception. Sophia, are you okay if I head outside for a moment?'

I nod stiffly.

'I won't be long.' He takes my hand and kisses my fingers. 'I promise.'

Five minutes later, I see Marc pacing back and forth in the hospital car park, barking instructions into his phone.

I stare at the stars above him in the night sky, wishing, wishing that my dad will be okay.

I don't know how, but I manage to doze for a few hours against Marc's shoulder. When I wake, dawn is trailing its muddy grey fingers across the rising sun.

I turn to Marc. He's wide awake, bolt upright, watching me. If he's tired, he doesn't look it.

'Sophia. You're awake.'

'Did you sleep at all?' I murmur, my throat croaky with old tears.

He shakes his head. 'I can do without sleep. But I'm glad you got some rest. There's good news.'

'News?' I clamber up, my hands clinging to Marc's arms.

'Your father came around. The scan showed a blood clot that's now been removed. He's going to be okay.'

I jump from the seat.

'Oh my god. He's going to be okay? Really? He's awake?'

Marc smiles. 'He's talking a little, apparently. You can go see him.'

86

Dad is propped up in bed against four pillows, looking weirdly alert and fresh for someone in a hospital bed. I knew I'd break down when I saw him again, and I do.

'*Dad*,' I blubber, hurrying towards him.

'Hello, love.' His words are a little tired, but he still sounds like my dad, and the tears come even more fiercely.

When I reach the bed, I take his hands in mine. 'How are you feeling?'

'Like I got hit by a car,' says Dad, pulling a smile onto his face. The cover moves a little as he pulls himself up, and I see huge black bruises along his shoulder.

'Trust you to joke at a time like this,' I say, trying to return his smile. 'I was so worried. I still am.'

'Don't you worry, petal. Not about me. I'm fine. Absolutely fine and dandy. I need to thank that fella of yours, is he around?'

'Marc?' I turn to the doorway. 'He's in the waiting area.'

'Well. You tell him if it wasn't for him, I might not have made it. Tell him that. Without that equipment -'

'Equipment?'

'He donated a new scanner to the hospital. Didn't he tell you? Without that, things could have turned out very differently.'

I shake my head. 'No. He didn't tell me that.'

'Modest and generous. You don't get many men like that around.' Dad starts coughing, and grimaces in pain.

'Hey.' I squeeze his hands. 'You just rest, now.'

'I probably should have a sleep. Let the bruises heal.

You don't mind, do you?'

'Not at all.' I smile at him. 'You sleep. I'll try and track down Genoveva. Tell her you're okay.'

'She's not here?' Dad's face falls. 'What about Sam?'

'Not yet,' I say. 'I'm sure they're on their way. I'll leave you to sleep.'

Out in the hallway, Marc is waiting. 'Thank you,' I tell him. 'For everything. Without you ...'

'You have nothing to thank me for,' Marc interrupts.

'I'm so relieved,' I say, putting a hand to my chest. 'Just to see him ... awake and talking ... oh my god.' I take my phone from my pocket. 'I need to go to the car park and phone Genoveva.'

We both head outside.

To Genoveva's credit, she answers the phone on the first ring.

'He's come around,' I blurt out, without waiting for her to speak. 'I just spoke to him. He's going to be okay. They say he'll make a full recovery.'

'When will he be coming home?' Genoveva asks.

'I don't know.'

'I can't stand this!' Genoveva shouts. 'I'm here all alone with Samuel.'

I don't know if it's the lack of sleep or the trauma of what's just happened, but something inside me snaps.

'Genoveva,' I say, my voice measured. 'My father is in hospital right now. He could have died. Stop thinking of yourself for a change and think of him. Okay? He'd like to see you and Sam. So. If you haven't got anything better to do, get yourself in a taxi and get to the hospital. Right now.'

I hear something like a whimper, and then a very chastised Genoveva says, 'Alright. Yes, okay, I'm on my way.'

Genoveva arrives soon after my call and sobs on my shoulder while Dad sleeps.

When Dad wakes up, I warn her not to stress him about domestic stuff, and to my surprise, she doesn't. She asks him about the accident and how he's feeling, but never once talks about how she's going to cope.

Marc stays with me the whole time. He doesn't say much, but he's there. A rock of support. He even plays with Sam, taking him out in the hospital grounds and buying him a bag of jelly tots. It's so cute to see him with a little boy, and my mind starts to wander, thinking of Marc and me with our own baby to chase around.

No, Sophia. Stop dreaming.

Genoveva leaves at five o'clock to give Samuel his tea, and I see Dad again. He looks fresher than this morning. More awake. And the hospital staff are talking about discharging him tomorrow.

'You should go, love,' Dad says. 'You look exhausted. Everything's going to be fine now. Get some rest. I'd offer to drive you, but ...' He gestures to the bed, and we both laugh. 'Is that fella of yours still here?'

'Yes. But he's not my fella. Not anymore.'

'Shame.'

'I know.'

'Go on, love. Go home. I'll just be sleeping from now on. You can call if you need to – the nurse said so. Go on. Get some rest.'

I rub my eyes and realise he's right. I'm absolutely exhausted.

'Okay.' I kiss him on the forehead. 'I'll see you very soon, you hear?'

When I head back to the waiting room, I find Marc by the coffee machine, dropping pound coin after pound coin into the slot. Five beige cups of brown coffee stand on a nearby table.

I watch as another cup rattles down, followed by steaming water.

'Who's all the coffee for?' I ask.

Marc carries on inserting coins. 'The staff. I thought they could probably use a hot drink.'

'Very thoughtful.' I give a tired smile. 'Dad thinks I should head home. Get some rest.'

Marc turns to me. 'Yes, I think that's an excellent idea. You need to rest. I'll call Keith. Have him drop you off.'

'Thank you.'

Marc gives the tiniest of smiles. 'I'm glad you didn't argue about that.'

'I don't have the energy.'

It's raining when we reach the hospital car park.

When we reach the car, Marc turns to me. 'I'll stay with you if you need me to. You don't have to be alone.'

I feel rain splash on my nose and forehead as I look up at him. 'Will you? Will you stay with me?'

'As long as Leo wouldn't have anything to say about it.'

I shake my head. 'We're just friends.'

Marc smiles. 'Get in the car, Sophia, before you get drenched.'

The car feels safe and warm and achingly familiar. We've had some times in this car, Marc and I. They swirl around in my head as Marc slides onto the seat beside me.

'Put your seatbelt on.'

'Oh. Is it not on?'

'No.' Marc pulls the belt over me and clips it in place. Then he knocks on the glass between us and Keith. The plate slides aside.

'The townhouse, Keith,' Marc instructs.

'Right you are, Marc.' The glass slides closed.

'The townhouse?' I ask, rubbing cold, rain-soaked arms.

'I can take care of you there.'

'Okay.'

'Still too tired to argue?'

I nod.

'I'll have to remember the effect exhaustion has on you.'

We drive on in silence, me staring out at the city, my eyes glazed. In my head, I'm so relieved that Dad is okay, but the emotion of the last twenty-four hours, plus the lack of sleep, makes this all feel like a dream. Nothing seems real, especially not sitting next to Marc.

I fall asleep again during the drive, and the next thing I know, I'm being carried up Marc's wide staircase and placed carefully on his bed.

'I haven't been here for a while,' I murmur as a soft duvet is laid over me. 'Are there any strange guests I should know about this time?'

Marc smiles. 'No one. Annabel's still in clinic. She's

doing very well by all accounts. I'll stay with you. Until you fall asleep.'

'Is that a good idea?'

'That depends.'

'On?'

'On whether you'll forgive me.'

I prop myself onto my elbows. 'Forgive you?'

'I realised something today. I can never keep you totally safe. Life will always throw things that I'm not expecting. But I can keep you a damned sight safer if I'm by your side.'

My eyes widen. 'Marc? Are you saying what I think you're saying?'

He nods.

'But ... what about the press?'

'There'll always be obstacles. Dangers. I gave in to my fear before. I couldn't bear anything happening to you. But ... that fear didn't go away when we weren't together.'

'So you'll let me make my own decisions? Even if you think they're unsafe?'

'It will be tough to watch you out there in the big bad world, but nothing can be tougher than being away from you. I was wrong to try and make decisions for you. I gave in to my own fears. I have to let you make your own choices.'

Even though I'm tired, a smile spreads all the way across my face. 'We can ... are you saying there's a chance for us?'

'Yes.' He kisses my forehead. 'If you'll have me. But I don't want you making any decisions right now. You're tired. Emotional. You don't want to be making any rash choices right now.'

I look up at his handsome face.

We gaze at each other, and time stands still.

Before I know what I'm doing, I'm reaching up, pushing my fingers through his thick hair and pulling his head towards mine. His lips come closer and suddenly they touch my own.

My body reacts before I completely realise what's happening, and my mouth moves over his as I cling to him, warmth rushing around me.

Marc frowns. Then he responds, kissing me deeply, passionately, his mouth pushed softly against mine, his arms pulling me closer.

My skin tingles and the hairs on my arms stand up. I hear little sighs and murmurs, and realise they're coming from me.

Marc's chest is heaving, and his neck is red and thick.

'Stop me now,' he says, his voice low. 'Before I go too far. This isn't the right time.'

'I don't want you to stop,' I whisper, my hands clinging to his shoulders. He feels so good under my fingers. I reach a hand into his thick hair again, and my fingers tighten as I pull his head towards me.

He kisses me again, and I melt into the bed. His eyes tell me he's only just holding it together, and I know exactly how he feels.

'Make love to me Marc,' I whisper, wrapping my legs around him, pulling him close.

He lets out a moan and kisses me harder, scooping his hands around my buttocks and pulling me tight.

I feel him hard against my stomach, and my breathing quickens.

Marc pulls away from my mouth, shoulders rising and falling. He takes in a few long, deep breaths. 'No.'

I can tell by the crumple on his forehead that this is painful for him.

'Marc?'

'We can't do this. Not now. Not like this. You're not thinking straight. I'd be taking advantage.'

'No. You wouldn't. I know my own mind and I want you.'

'You're emotional. It wouldn't be right to do things this way.'

'Please,' I whisper.

Marc sits on the bed. 'I ... can't. I won't be able to control myself. And that wouldn't be right. Not after what you've just been through. I should go.'

'Don't leave.' I shake my head, tears appearing.

'I have to.' He kisses my forehead. 'Don't worry. You won't be alone. I'll take care of that.'

'What? You're leaving the *house*? Where are you going?'

'Just ... somewhere.' Marc rubs his hand over his forehead. 'Let's just say I have something to do that will help me be the person you want.'

'The person I want would stay here.'

'I can't right now. Just ... trust me.' Marc looks away. He stands. 'I need to leave. You won't be alone. Rodney is here, and I'll have Jen driven over to keep you company.'

'Where are you *going*?'

'There's something I need to do.'

'And you can't tell me what it is?'

'There's nothing to tell right now.' He puts on his shirt and does up the buttons. 'I'll have Jen picked up. I have her number and address.'

'You have Jen's *number* and *address*?'

That quirky smile. 'I like to keep certain details that might be important in locating your whereabouts and keeping you safe.'

I shake my head in disbelief. 'How did you get those *certain* details?'

Marc opens the wardrobe and throws on a suit jacket. 'Don't ask me too many questions, Sophia. Especially not right now.'

He stalks out of the room, and I'm left sitting there in my underwear. I half want to stick my tongue out at the closed door, but that would make me feel even more like a chastised child.

So here we are again. Close for a moment, then something pulls us apart.

Half an hour later, I get a call from Jen.

'What's going on Soph? Is everything okay?'

I hear traffic noises and guess she's in a car. Probably the limo with Keith.

Just hearing her voice makes me start blubbing, and I sniff and snuffle down the phone. 'It's ... been a tough few days.'

'I'm on my way to you. Marc called.'

'He actually called you?'

'He actually called me. And said he needed me to look after you. That it was urgent. So what's going on?'

I gulp. 'Dad had an accident. But it's okay now.'

'Your dad?' Jen's voice goes shaky. 'Christ, Soph. I'm so sorry. Is he alright?'

'He ... was in an accident. A car accident. It was a rough night, but he came around and they say he'll make a full recovery.'

'Oh my god. Oh my *god*. Soph, I had no idea. Why didn't you call me?'

'I did, but in the hospital there was hardly any reception. And then ... Marc and I went back to his.'

'Wait. Was Marc at the hospital with you?'

'Yes. He ... without him, I don't know how things would have been. He donated scanning equipment so Dad didn't have to switch hospitals.'

'Wow. Well ... good. I'm glad.'

'But he's gone now.'

'You sound sad about that.'

'We got close again. He was saying all the right things. But ... then he just vanished without a word. I have no idea where he's gone, and I feel like he's keeping something from me.'

'Wait.' I hear a rustle. 'We're driving into Richmond. Does Marc live in Richmond? He said you were at his house.'

'Yes,' I say. 'You must be close.'

'Hold on. We're slowing down. Is Marc's place like four storeys high? A townhouse?'

'Yes.'

'The gates are opening. I'm here.'

The line begins to crackle.

'We're going underground,' says Jen incredulously. 'Wow, is this a -'

The line goes dead, and I leap off the bed and run down the big wide stairs. When I reach the hallway, I hear Jen talking to Keith through the garage door.

'Thanks. I'm shit with steps.'

'No problem at all. My pleasure.'

The next moment, the door opens and there's Jen, looking magazine perfect as always, her shiny blonde hair swinging straight down her back. She's working her casual look, which is still pretty smart – skinny black jeans, black boots and a designer off-the-shoulder sweatshirt.

'Babes!' She flings her arms around me, and I'm covered in kisses and perfume. 'What a place. You could get lost in here.'

'I know,' I reply. 'I nearly have a few times.'

'Where's the kitchen? I'll make you a coffee.'

When we reach the kitchen, I smell fresh coffee and see a drip filter jug filled with steaming black liquid. Two large blue and white striped mugs sit by the machine, next to a carton of cream and a bowl of brown sugar.

'Is this house psychic?' asks Jen.

'In a way.' I smile. 'There's a housekeeper here. Rodney. He's got a sort of sixth sense about what you might need. And he knows when to keep out of the way. He must be around somewhere, but I guess he's making himself scarce.'

Jen pours coffee into the two mugs and adds cream and sugar to mine. She leaves hers black, meaning she's on yet another diet, and plonks herself on a kitchen stool.

'Your poor dad,' she says. 'And more than that, poor you. It must have been so stressful.'

'It was,' I say. 'The worst night of my life.'

'I wish I'd been there.'

'It's fine,' I say. 'Honestly. Marc was amazing.'

'Makes me see him in a new light,' says Jen. 'I mean, don't get me wrong. I never disliked him. If he was the total heartless bastard the press make him out to be, you wouldn't be with him. I know that. But still. He's not exactly the warmest guy.'

'I know,' I say. 'I felt so close to him at the hospital. And just now. But then he closed right down. He's vanished and I feel like we're miles apart. I have no idea where he went ...'

'He didn't tell you where he was going?' Jen frowns, and I know there's something on her mind.

'No. Why. Do you know something?'

'Maybe. Well. I *could* know something, put it that way. I spoke to Ben at my firm before I called you. There's a rumour that Marc's on his way to East London.'

'East London?'

'That's what the paps are saying. A couple followed him earlier.'

I take a sip of sweet coffee, trying to get my head around this new development. 'I love him, Jen.'

'I know.'

'There could be a chance for us. But not if he keeps closing down.'

'Why not call him?'

I do, but the call goes straight through to an answer machine. I hold the phone to my chest. 'I need to find him. He says there's a chance for us, but how can there be if he's still hiding things from me?'

Jen lays her fashionable slate grey fingernails over my hand. 'Do you want me to phone Ben again, find out if there's any update on Marc's location?'

I nod.

'I'll say one thing for paps,' says Jen. 'They have their uses. They're the best tracker dogs when it comes to celebrities.' She opens up her diamante clamshell phone and puts it to her ear. 'Hello? Ben? I need a favour. Marc Blackwell. Do you have his location? *Really*? Great.'

She digs a hand in her patent leather handbag and pulls out a tiny pink notepad. Scribbling an address, she hands me the pad. 'Thanks, Ben. I owe you one. You too. See you soon.' She snaps the phone closed.

I stare at the note. Jen has scribbled a street address in East London.

'So what's next?' Jen says, glancing at the pad. 'Shall we go there?'

'I should,' I say.

'Alone. I'm not getting you mixed up in this.'

'Oh no.' Jen shakes her head. 'You're not going on your own. I'm coming with you.'

'I can't let you do that, Jen. What about work?'

'What about it? This is a family emergency. They'll understand.'

'If I'm going to stand any chance of Marc opening up to me, I should go alone. Please Jen. Look. I'll turn my phone sat nav on so you can track me.'

Jen sighs. 'Okay.'

'Maybe Keith is still in the garage. He can drive me there.'

'Let's go see.'

92

Down in the gloomy garage, Jen and I discover that Keith has left already. We stand surveying Marc's ultra-shiny top-of-the-range cars, me biting my thumb, Jen opening and closing her clamshell phone.

Then I notice something.

'Jen. It's gone.'

'What's gone?'

'Marc's father's car.' I stare at the black parking space where the spiky yellow car sat earlier on. 'He ... I guess he must have taken it.'

'So?'

'It's not a car he ever drives.'

'And yet he's driving it right now.'

'I guess he must be.'

'Is that a bad thing?'

'I don't know.'

Jen surveys the rest of Marc's vehicle collection. 'These cars must go really fast.'

'I know.'

'Are you thinking what I'm thinking?'

'Probably.'

'Will he be mad if you take one of his cars?'

'I don't think so. He doesn't care about possessions. Despite appearances. But we need to find the keys.'

'I think I know where they are,' says Jen, going to a red metal box on the wall. 'My dad has a box just like this.' She opens the lid and peers inside. 'Aston Martin, anyone?'

She holds out a fat gold key with a black fob.

I chew my thumbnail. 'Okay. Quick, give me the key. Before I change my mind.'

As I climb onto the leather seat, I start to giggle.

'What is it?' Jen asks, leaning against the roof.

I put my hand to my mouth, but the giggling won't stop. 'Sorry,' I manage to say. 'I think I'm a bit in shock. But ... I just remembered that time we drove your dad's car.'

Jen starts giggling too. 'And we got lost and thought we'd have to phone him and admit we'd taken it.'

We laugh and laugh, bending over, holding our sides, tears running down our faces. 'Why is it always the times you shouldn't laugh that you do?' I splutter.

'Okay, enough of this,' says Jen, clearing her throat. 'Come on, Evel Knieval. You need to get going. Good luck.' She slams the door shut.

I start up the engine, and the car shunts forward towards the wall. 'Oh!' I slam on the breaks and notice the car is already in gear.

I see Jen smiling and shaking her head through the windscreen. 'Your driving,' she mouths.

'I'll be fine,' I mouth back, putting the car in reverse and gently touching the accelerator.

'Mind the wall!' I hear Jen shout, and I slam on the brakes again.

Whoops.

I manage to manoeuvre the car around and towards the garage door, which to my relief opens automatically as I approach.

That's one obstacle out of the way.

The gate opens automatically too, and I ease the car forward onto the pavement.

As the black bonnet creeps towards the road, two

paparazzi fling their cameras at the car window and start snapping away.

I'm flustered, but also furious. This is not the time. I swerve the car so it pushes into them, just a little. A warning. And I beep the horn for good measure. It does the trick. The paps back away, and I pull out onto the road and put my foot down.

I realise this is definitely not an incognito car as I power along London's traffic-jammed streets. I'm kind of scared by the car's speed, so I'm doing under thirty, but this seems to irritate the other motorists. I guess if you're driving a car like this, you're expected to go fast.

As I get nearer to the address, I start to feel more and more nervous.

I'm heading into a rough neighbourhood, I realise, as grimy tower blocks and kebab shops shoot past. The streets and buildings around here kind of remind me of that TV programme, *Shameless*.

Sickly nerves work their way into my stomach as I get closer. Maybe this is a bad idea. Maybe I should turn back. But curiosity gets the better of me. What is Marc doing somewhere like this? Is it to do with a woman? I have to know.

I drive on, and the nerves in my stomach start running around in circles. The streets around here look grey. Sad. And the people on the street look restless and angry. They hold Special Brew cans and inhale cigarettes like oxygen.

Red graffiti on a crumbling wall says: *Skag heads forever*.

I grew up poor, so I'm not scared of people with no money. But this isn't just a place with no money. It's a drug place, and drugs can turn the nicest people into the nastiest people.

Just as I decide I should definitely turn back, I see the bright yellow shell of Marc's dad's car parked with two wheels on the pavement. It's outside a little terraced house with a stained mattress pushed up against the window.

Two paps sit on the crumbling wall out front, so this must be the place. They're shivering like they've been there a while.

I pull up behind the yellow car, letting out a long breath. My fingers feel for the car door handle, and I climb out.

The two paps leap up when they see me.

Snap, snap, snap.

'Can't you guys get real jobs?' I mutter, stalking past them.

I head towards the house. The front door is made of that pressed cardboard stuff that lets in water, and there are bubbles of damp all over it.

God, I'm nervous now. Maybe this was a bad idea. But no. *No.* I need to know what's going on.

I reach up and knock loudly on the door. Behind me, the photographers go crazy.

I duck down and open the rusty letter box. The smell of mould floats out.

'Marc?' I call.

There's a scuffling sound, and then the hard knock of someone jogging down wooden stairs.

Dirty trainers come into view, and I take a step back. It's not Marc. My heart catches in my mouth.

The front door is wrenched open and a grey-haired man stands before me. I stare at him in shock.

He has dark eyes, but other than that, there's no colour in him at all. He's washed out grey like an old shirt.

The bones of his shoulders stick up through his loose white vest, and his dark trousers hang off him. He looks dishevelled and dirty, and shields his eyes from the winter sunshine.

'Who the hell are you?' The man's eyes dart to the photographers behind us. Then he looks at me.

'Oh. Sorry.' I take a step back. 'I think I've got the wrong place. I was looking for Marc.'

The man rubs his greasy forehead. 'Who the fuck

wants to know about Marc?'

A shadow looms at the top of the stairs.

'Sophia?' Marc thunders down the staircase in his black shirt and trousers. He looks paler than ever, and not at all happy to see me.

Marc shoulders past the man, who vanishes back into the house.

'How did you get here?' Marc asks, his eyes wide with concern.

'What's going on, Marc?'

Marc runs a hand through his hair. His eyes focus on the Aston Martin over my shoulder. 'You drove here?'

I bite my lip and look sheepish. 'Yes.'

Marc's lips part, and I can't work out if he's angry or not. He stares at me for a moment, then snaps his mouth closed. 'Sophia, this is a dangerous part of town. You need to go.' He takes my arm and leads me down the front path. The paps have the good sense to take a step back and let us pass.

'No.' I shake my arm free. 'Tell me what's going on.'

'This is my mess. I don't want you having anything to do with this.' He glances back at the house. 'I never, ever want you to see inside that house. You'd ... see me differently.'

'I love you,' I say. 'Do you think that will ever change?'

'Yes. If you saw ... look, you shouldn't be here. I'm fixing things, so you never need to see this.'

'You're wrong,' I say. 'The more I know about you, the more I love you. Who was that man?'

Marc closes his eyes and tilts his head up to the white sky. 'Nobody important. Sophia, this isn't the place for you.' His glances over my shoulder. 'You drove the car okay?'

'Yes.'

'Then get back in it. Right now. And go back to the townhouse. I'll meet you there.'

'No, Marc.'

'Sophia, I don't want you to be any part of this mess.'

'Marc.' I shake my head. 'Whatever's going on, I want to be part of it. I want to be part of you. Of your life.'

'No.' Marc says the words sternly. 'Not this part of my life.'

'Every part of your life,' I insist. 'Relationships aren't about editing out the messy parts. If you won't tell me what's going on, I'll find out for myself.'

I charge past him into the house.

'Sophia!' I hear him shout, but I'm already in the hallway, nearly losing my footing on bare, wobbly floorboards.

I charge up the stairs two at a time and see three open doors and one closed one. There's a stained toilet in one room, and sagging double beds in two others.

I face the fourth room – the closed one – and pull the door open.

I don't know what I expect to find in the room, but ... I'm just so confused.

The man who answered the door is in here, sitting on a stained mattress, his legs splayed out in front of him. But there's no one else. I notice empty vodka bottles lined up on the window sill and a half empty one by the bed.

It's a dirty, squalid room, and I don't get what Marc has to do with this place.

The man's head snaps up when I enter.

'Sophia.' Marc appears behind me and puts his hands on my shoulders.

The man pushes himself up on the mattress. 'Who's the girl?'

'She's none of your business,' Marc growls, pushing me behind him.

'That's no way to talk to your old man.'

My mouth drops open. 'Your ... Marc, he's your ... he's your *father*?'

Marc's silence tells me everything I need to know.

'You said your father was dead.'

'I know.'

'What's going on, Marc?'

'My father isn't dead. I lied. He's still alive and drinking himself to death. I haven't seen him in years. But I needed to come back today.'

'Why?'

'To return the car. And say my goodbyes.'

'I don't understand.'

'I'm making my peace. Trying to forgive. He's just a sad old man now, and I have to let my anger go. Because

Where the Ivy Grows 275

otherwise, I'll never move forward.'

'Why didn't you tell me your father was still alive?'

'I never wanted you to meet him. I never wanted you to see ... who I came from.'

I slip my hand into Marc's and feel his fingers tighten around mine.

'This is your old family home?' I ask, staring at the bare boards and peeling wallpaper.

'Not anymore. Only when mum was here. There's nothing left now. Only him. After I stopped paying his bills in the States, he came back here. And ... well, you can see the sort of lifestyle. He's all alone.'

'Are you ashamed of your old family home?'

'No,' says Marc, glancing at his father. 'I'm not ashamed of where I came from. I'm ashamed of *who* I came from.'

'You shouldn't be ashamed,' says Marc's father. 'I made you who you are.'

I look at the bitter, broken figure of Marc's father, swigging vodka on the dirty mattress. I can feel the ugliness coming from him. The hatred towards his son and the jealousy. They have the same nose, the two men, but nothing else about them is similar at all.

'And I don't need your forgiveness,' Marc's father adds.

'Well you have it, anyway. Come on.' Marc takes my hand. 'I've done what I came here to do. For better or worse.' He leads me into the hall.

'You thought I'd see you differently if I met your father?' I ask. 'That I'd love you less?'

'I thought ... perhaps ...' His eyes search my face, and I see a desperate vulnerability in his eyes. They're so clear today, it's astounding.

'Well, you were wrong. I love you more the more I know about you.'

'We should go.'

I feel Marc's eyes on me all the way down the stairs. When we get to the front door, he reaches out a hand to stop me opening it.

'Wait. Let me go out first. I want to keep the wolves at bay.'

I step aside and let him march out, glaring at photographers. Predictably, they back off.

I follow, and then Marc takes my hand and leads me to the car.

'I'll drive,' he says.

'You're leaving your father's car here?' I ask.

'Yes. It's staying with him. He can do what he likes with it. Sell it for drink. I don't care. I'm letting that part of my life go.'

I squeeze his hand. 'Marc. I'm so proud of you.'

'It's all down to you,' says Marc. 'The student taught the teacher.' He raises his eyebrow and gives me a little smile.

'I guess she did.'

On the drive home, Marc and I sit in silence. I sense Marc needs some thinking time, and so do I.

When we arrive back at the townhouse, I glance at Marc in the dark garage and his face is... sort of softer. A little tired perhaps, but there's a glow in his eyes. A peace I've never seen before.

He jumps out of the car and opens the passenger door for me, then pulls me out into his arms, pushing his face into my hair and bringing me tight to his chest.

I rock forward to meet his body.

'God, I missed you. Christ. For you still to accept me ... to love me ... after meeting him ... it's just beyond anything I could ever imagine.'

Marc picks me up and carries me up the stairs. Soon, we're inside the house and taking the big wide stairs up to the second floor. He doesn't take his eyes from mine, even when we reach the bedroom.

Slowly and carefully, he lays me on the bed and undresses me. His movements are tender and loving, but urgent too. He kisses my neck and breasts with an abandon I've never felt before. He's not trying to hold it together. He's not trying to stop himself or take charge of me.

He flips me over and runs his lips from the nape of my neck all the way down my spine to my buttocks, lips pressed so passionately against my skin that I feel he's eating me up.

I'm so used to Marc needing to dominate that I'm kind of expecting a little slap on my buttocks, and my legs twitch in anticipation.

'I won't spank you,' Marc says, running his hand

around. 'Today isn't about me being in charge. It's about letting go.'

'I'm happy with that,' I murmur.

Marc turns me over again and slides himself inside me, his face inches from mine as he moves back and forth. His lips are a little open, and there's a softness to his eyes that, little by little, tells me he's giving way to me.

'Wait,' he says suddenly.

'No, Marc -'

'It's not what you think.'

Marc doesn't leave the room or take some sex toy from a drawer or shelf. Instead, he reaches up and finds a pillow, which he props under my buttocks.

'I think you'll enjoy things more this way.'

He's right. With my hips tilted up against the pillow, Marc rubs against me in all the right ways, outside and inside, and a dull bruisy pleasure builds up.

We watch each other as Marc moves back and forth, and I don't think I've ever been so in love with him.

Eventually, soft pleasure takes over me, and I moan and groan, moving under Marc, tilting my hips up to meet his.

Marc comes too, with a gentle murmur, and rests his cheek against mine.

'I love you, Sophia,' he whispers.

'I love you too.'

'You look like you're in a world of your own,' says Keith as we shunt along in London traffic.

'Oh. Yeah. Sorry, Keith.'

'Are you nervous then?' Keith glances at me, then back at the road. 'About dress rehearsals?'

'A little bit. But ... Marc has taught me so much. He's been tutoring me all week. To help me with my confidence.'

'Like when he took you to the farm?'

I nod. 'Riding that horse was so scary. But ... Marc was right. It brought out the best in me. And I've been growing ever since. I'll miss the college, though. It was nice rehearsing in Queen's Theatre. I felt safe there.'

'Don't you worry about safety,' said Keith. 'Marc has got the whole place rigged for security. How was your trip to East London?'

'You heard about that?'

Keith nods at the road. 'Rodney mentioned it.'

'It was ... enlightening,' I say. 'And it's brought Marc and me closer. Much closer.'

'Glad to hear that. Any plans for Christmas?'

I smile. 'I really don't know yet. Marc and I haven't spoken about it. It's come up so fast. It's next week, isn't it?'

'Same every year. You blink and it's on you. I haven't bought any presents yet.'

'Me neither.'

'Do you know where you're going to be?'

I shake my head. 'Usually we spend Christmas at my dad's cottage. But this year ... I don't know. I don't know what Marc has planned. All I know is that I'll be performing before and after Christmas Day, so I'll have to stay near London.'

I see the theatre up ahead, and it's surrounded by a black swarm of paparazzi.

'I've got orders to go the back way,' says Keith, swinging the car around and heading down a narrow side road. 'So. You nervous about opening night? It's getting pretty close, isn't it? And right before Christmas.'

'I should be petrified,' I say. 'But for now, I'm just focusing on the dress rehearsal. That's enough to be nervous about.'

Keith pulls to a stop by the stage door, and I'm relieved to see a tall security guard with a thick brown beard. He's wearing the navy blue and yellow baseball cap that tells me he's with Marc's firm, and he looks tall and tough.

'Well. Don't break a leg,' says Keith as I climb out of the car.

'I'll try not to.'

As Keith drives away, I knock on the bright red stage door and wait. The security guard is doing a good impression of a statue, so we politely ignore each other while I wait for the door to be opened.

But there's no reply.

I knock louder, biting a thumbnail.

Come on, come on.

I don't like being out here alone when there are paparazzi nearby, and something about the silent security guard is making me uneasy.

I raise my fist to knock a third time, but before I can make contact with the door, the security guard's hand darts forward and clamps itself around my wrist.

'Nice to see you, Sophia.'

I recognise that voice.

It belongs to Giles Getty.

I turn to the guard, fear creeping up my throat. The thick beard covers almost all of his face, and the baseball cap puts his eyes in shadow. The beard – it's a fake. Of course it is. No one grows a beard that large.

'Getty,' I stammer, shaking my wrist away.

'You took your time.' Giles Getty steps forward. 'I was getting worried about you. I thought you might not make it.'

'How did you ... What are you doing here?'

'Why, waiting for you, of course.' How did I not notice it was Getty? His jaw is as jittery as ever, and he can hardly stand still.

We're in a blind alley, and he's blocking my route to the road. I turn to the stage door, but it's tight shut.

Getty takes a step closer. He reaches forward and strokes my hair.

I smack his hand away. 'Don't touch me.'

The busy street is a long way away, and London traffic makes my voice small and lost.

Getty's eyes glow with excitement. 'I like the way you say that.'

He reaches forward and I step back, but I stumble and he grabs my wrist again.

'Where are you going, Sophia?'

'Get out of my way.'

'You owe me a story,' says Getty. His grip tightens on my wrist. It hurts, and my eyes water.

'Let go,' I breathe. 'I'm not kidding.' I try to wrench my arm around, but he tightens his grip.

'I thought you liked being held down,' Getty whispers.

'If you're Marc's girlfriend, I thought that was a prerequisite. Or have his tastes changed since I knew him?'

'You don't know him at all.' I'm getting a Chinese burn from twisting my wrist around in his hand. 'Let me -'

It happens before my brain can work out what's going on. Getty's fist comes towards my jaw, and my head spins fast around. Then everything goes black.

100

When I wake up, it's completely dark, and my knees and elbows ache. I realise I'm curled up into a ball, and there are shooting pains at my wrists.

I can hear a car running, and I feel vibrations bumping me around.

Oh my god.

My wrists are bound. *My wrists are bound.*

Getty's fist comes back to me in a flash, and I begin to struggle and kick. My legs strike metal. I see a long line of white light, and I realise with horror where I am.

In the trunk of a moving car.

Bile floods into my mouth, and I swallow it down.

'Help,' I shout, shocked to hear how weak and broken my voice sounds. 'Someone help me.' The left side of my jaw aches, and so do all my molars. I feel like I've had a tooth taken out.

Abruptly, the car comes to a stop and I hold my breath, my heart flying into my mouth. A car door thunks closed and my body stiffens. He's coming.

Inside the trunk, I see a shadow fall across the line of white light, and then hear a click as the trunk opens.

I squint up at Getty, who stands over me – the beard and baseball cap disguise now dispensed with.

'Well, well, Sophia. I hope you enjoyed yourself in there. Marc only likes to play act, but the real thing is so much *better,* don't you think?'

'Please. Let me go. You can stop this now. Before it goes too far.'

'Too far?' Getty hauls me out of the trunk by my shoulders, and I stumble onto tarmac. 'Oh, we've got a long way to go yet. Like I say. You owe me a story.'

'Where are we?' I see we're on a driveway, and there's a two-storey red-brick house up ahead. Its windows are completely dark, so I'm guessing no one's home. I don't see London skyscrapers, only black sky.

'I'm surprised Marc hasn't taken you anywhere like this before,' says Getty, pulling me along by my wrists. 'We're going to have a lot of fun here.'

I stumble, struggling the whole way up the path to the house, but Getty holds me firm.

He slips a key into the front door and pulls me into the hallway.

'Is this your house?' I ask, struggling to keep my balance.

Getty laughs. 'You think I'd set something like this up at my own place? Then everyone would know the pictures weren't real.' He moves his face close to mine. 'Of course, the pictures might *become* real. If you start to enjoy yourself.'

'Please,' I say, my wrists burning. Some cruel part of my brain reminds me of the last time my wrists burned – with Marc – and I begin praying for him to find me. But how can he? No one even knows I'm missing. 'Let me go. I don't know what you think happens between Marc and me, but you've got it all wrong.'

Getty laughs again, and his voice is high pitched and manic. 'Like I told you, I've known Marc a long time. I know *exactly* what he's into. And a man like that doesn't change.'

He leads me towards a narrow set of steps leading downwards. I can tell by the damp smell that there's some sort of basement down there.

'No,' I scream. 'Please. Stop. Let me go.'

'Sophia,' says Getty, stroking my cheek, his voice sickly calm. 'All I want is some pictures. That's all. And who knows? You might even enjoy the experience.'

'What experience? What are you going to do?'

He grips my wrists tighter and hisses, 'You know exactly what. Don't play games with me.'

He pulls me downstairs, and I stumble and trip, trying desperately to keep my balance. When we reach the bottom, my chest turns to ice.

I scream and struggle back towards the stairs, but Getty holds me firm.

My vision clouds over as I take in everything I'm seeing. I'm going to faint. Truly, I'm going to faint.

I'm in a basement room full of torture equipment.

In this room, Getty looks more manic than ever. No, manic isn't the right word. Insane. He looks insane. His jaw is working, working, working, like he has ten pieces of chewing gum in his mouth, and his eyes are wide and crazed.

There are manacles on the wall, like some sort of medieval prison, and a wooden rack in the corner.

There's a black leather bench in the centre of the room, a little like a beautician's table, if it weren't for the chains hanging off.

Various different instruments hang from nails on the wall.

My eyes flick over a curled black whip, a cutlass, a crowbar and a large Stanley knife.

'Let me go,' I scream.

Getty's eyes narrow. 'Pose for the pictures, and then I'll let you go.'

I see white light at the top of the staircase and will myself towards it.

'You ... just want me to pose? That's all? And then you'll let me go?'

'Exactly right.'

'O ... okay.'

'Good girl. I have an outfit for you.' He goes to a black metal cupboard, like a school locker, and opens it. There are various red and black garments hanging inside, and he takes out a rubber corset with an eye-wateringly small waist.

'Painful to get into,' he says, his eyes shining. 'But you must be used to that by now.'

'Marc and I ... it's not like that,' I say. 'He doesn't like hurting women who don't want to be hurt.'

'So he used to say.' Getty runs his knuckles down the corset. 'But ask yourself, what normal man likes seeing women restrained? Spanked? Gagged? There's something in him that wants to hurt you. You're just in denial.'

'No. He loves me.' I bite my lip so hard it bleeds, and Getty's thumb instantly goes to my mouth, pressing at the blood.

'You bleed so easily,' he breathes.

I turn my head away, but he pulls my chin back. 'I think you're going to look pretty good in these pictures. Good enough for my personal collection.'

I'm shaking now, pulling against the silver masking tape that binds my wrists.

'I like blood.'

'Don't hurt me.'

'Sophia, hurting you is the whole *point*.'

Oh my god.

Getty takes the Stanley knife from the wall, and I try to run to the stairs, but I trip and fall, bruising my cheek on the concrete floor.

'Nice of you to assume the position,' says Getty, standing over me.

'No. Please.' I try to wiggle away, but he grabs my sweatshirt and pushes up the Stanley blade.

Oh my god. He's going to cut me.

'NO!'

Getty stabs the blade through my sweatshirt, and I scream as he runs it up towards my neck. But it's not touching my skin, just my clothes. He's cutting me out of my clothes.

My jeans and vest are slashed next, until I'm lying shivering in my white underwear. Getty kneels over me, breathing heavily.

'Looking good,' he says.

I try to squirm away from him, but he puts his hot hand on my naked rib cage and I shudder.

He holds the Stanley knife up and levers it under my bra strap.

I swallow and close my eyes.

When I open them again, he's cutting at the fabric.

'I like to see you afraid,' says Getty. 'It makes your eyes even more beautiful.'

I put my chin up and lay perfectly still as he cuts at my bra. I know he's getting off on this and it sickens me, but he could do a lot worse than cut off my underwear, and we both know it.

I bring my bound hands up to my chest as my bra comes free, trying to cover myself.

Getty pulls my hands away and roughly fits the rubber corset over my head and around my middle, pulling the strings tight. I wince as the waist gets tighter and tighter, but I try not to make a sound. I know if I look or sound in pain, Getty will enjoy it.

Getty lifts me onto the black bench, and I try to look calm. Dignified.

'I'm going to enjoy wiping that look off your face,' says Getty, lowering me onto the cool black leather.

'Just take your pictures and let me go,' I say.

'Tut tut,' says Getty. 'Is that how you speak to Marc? Young ladies who talk to me that way get punished.'

I suck in my breath as he goes to the wall of instruments.

'Now,' says Getty, fingering the whip. 'What shall we begin with?'

'Please don't use that on me,' I say. 'I'm dressed how you want. You don't need anything else.'

'You're not *behaving* how I want,' says Getty, taking down the long black barbed whip, and pressing his fingers against the barbs.

'Did Cecile behave the way you wanted?' I blurt out,

trying to keep him talking.

Getty's jaw twitches. 'That stuck up bitch. She was on her back before the first meal out. Did anything I wanted. No satisfaction at all. All I needed her for was to get to you. But she couldn't even get that right.'

'But what about the baby?' I ask.

Getty frowns. 'Oh, she told you about that, did she? Not a bad family to be connected to. And she's pretty desperate for me to make that connection. I might make a decent woman of her if she's lucky, who knows? But then again, she wasn't much use to me in getting pictures of you. So ... we'll see.'

'You don't need to do this,' I say, my voice getting very tight.

'I like hearing you beg.'

I push my lips together, realising talking isn't helping.

Getty unfurls the whip. 'This is one of my favourites,' he says. 'We'll get you nice and bloody. I like to take women when they're bloody and begging me to stop.'

'*Take*?' The word shivers on my lips.

Getty smiles horribly, showing his bottom teeth. 'You didn't think I'd just take pictures of you in costume did you? What a waste.'

'But you said -'

'You trust people too easily, Sophia. Now, I want you to scream for me.' He raises the whip.

Even though every fibre in my being wants to scream the walls down, I bite my teeth together and hold it inside. I won't give him the satisfaction. I won't do it.

'If you won't scream, then I'll make you scream.'

'I won't. No matter what you do to me.'

Getty moves his face so it's inches from mine. 'You stubborn bitch.' I can feel the agitation in him. It's leaping around under his skin, making his eyebrows twitch and his fingers grip and release the whip. He needs this. It's his release.

I meet his eyes, trying not to waver or show even a glimmer of weakness. I've figured out his secret. This isn't about anything he does to me. It's all about my reaction. My fear and pain. Without that, he has nothing.

'Let me go,' I say calmly.

He glares at me. 'You'll stay here until I'm finished with you.'

'I won't scream,' I say. 'Or show fear. You won't get any satisfaction from me. Take as many pictures as you like, but I won't be afraid for you.'

He throws the whip to the floor, and upends the bench so I go crashing to the concrete floor shoulder first.

Ouch.

I stay completely still, my body tense. Getty stands over me, his fists clenched, and I know what's coming. If he can't make me scream and get his satisfaction that way, he's going to work out his frustration through his fists.

I wince, bracing myself for the punches.

103

There's a crack and I expect to feel pain, but ... nothing. I turn my head up and hear another crack – this time from a few metres away.

I blink in surprise.

Getty has been flung backwards into his wall of instruments, and I see a length of chain unwind from a wall nail and fall to the floor with a clink, clink, clink.

I struggle around and see Marc striding towards Getty, his fists clenched.

Marc.

Oh my god, oh my god.

Warm relief runs around my body.

Whack! Marc's fist connects with Getty's jaw again, and Getty slumps to the floor.

Marc stands over him, fists clenched. He turns to me.

'Sophia. What did that bastard do to you?'

'Marc,' I croak, feeling tears rush down my face.

Marc comes to me, kneeling and taking me in his arms.

'He was outside the theatre,' I say through the sobs. 'He knocked me out and then ... we were here.'

'Did he -?'

I shake my head. 'No.'

'If he had of done ...' I feel Marc's fists ball up against my back.

'But he didn't.'

Marc lets out a long breath.

'Will you help me out of this?' I say, looking down at the corset.

Marc picks up the Stanley knife and slashes the corset strings. My body falls free. He peels off his black cashmere jumper and fits it over my head. I thread my arms into the long sleeves, smelling Marc in every inch of the wool.

He lifts me into his arms and carries me up the stairs.

'How did you know I was here?' I croak, shivering as we meet the cool air upstairs.

'Someone inside the theatre was supposed to report when you arrived. But they didn't. So I put two and two together. I know what Getty's capable of.'

Marc kicks open the front door, and I see his Aston Martin parked outside.

'But ... in this house. How did you know I was in this house?'

Marc carries me across the driveway. 'I didn't. I went to three other places first. This was a lucky guess. A place I remember from the time I knew him.' He opens the passenger door and lowers me onto the warm leather seat. Then he slams the door closed and jogs around to the driver's side.

When he slides into the driver's seat, I say, 'Did you ... have you been here before, then? In that basement?'

'No.' Marc's jaw hardens and he starts the car. 'Never. But I've been in the house before. A long time ago. I'll have someone come over to take care of Getty. An old friend from Baz Smith days.'

'Someone to ... *take care* of him?'

Marc puts the car in drive and pulls out onto the empty road. He doesn't look at me.

'Marc? What does that mean, take care of him?'

'Use your imagination.'

'You're not going to ... is someone going to hurt him? Kill him?'

Marc turns the wheel, keeping his gaze on the road.

'Please, Marc, no.'

Marc stops the car at a junction, one hand on the

steering wheel, the other resting on the handbrake. 'Why the hell not?'

'I don't want him hurt. Or killed. I just want him to be stopped from hurting anyone else.'

'You really are remarkable. You know that? After what you've just been though ... I don't know, Sophia. I don't know if I can let him get away with this.'

'Please, Marc.' I put my hand over his on the handbrake. 'Just ... let's just go to the police.'

'Is that what you really want?'

'That's what I really want.'

He sighs. 'Okay. I know a few people on the force. I'll arrange someone to come to the townhouse. I don't want you going to a police station. Not after what you've just been through. Are you sure you want to do this?'

'I'm sure.'

104

Two hours later, I'm sitting in Marc's lounge with a hot chocolate when there's a crackle, and I hear voices over the intercom. Marc leaps up and heads into the hallway.

'Who is it?' I call out.

'The police,' Marc calls back.

I hear the front door open, then voices. Marc returns with two female police officers and shows them into the lounge.

'Sophia. These are police officers Bridges and Dale. They're here to take your statement.'

One of the women is large and blonde – sort of big boned, like an Olympic swimmer. The other is smaller, with mousy brown hair and glasses.

'Good to meet you, Sophia,' says the blonde officer, reaching out to shake my hand. 'I'm Officer Bridges. We don't usually take statements in people's homes, but ... in this case, we've been able to make an exception.'

I glance at Marc and know he must have pulled a few strings.

'I'd like to be with Sophia while she makes her statement,' says Marc.

'No.' I turn to him. 'Please, Marc. I'd rather do it alone. I don't want you having to hear all the details.'

Marc raises an eyebrow. 'Sophia -'

'Please.'

'Okay. I'll have Rodney bring in some coffee.'

He vanishes into the hallway.

I turn to the police officers. 'Let's get this over with.'

105

It takes nearly two hours to give my statement. The officers have so many detailed questions, and I can't answer all of them, but I try my best. I'm surprised by how calm I sound, because inside there's a storm going on. Thunder claps of fear. Lightning flashes of panic. Right now, I never want to leave Marc's side again.

The officers take a DNA sample from my cheek before they leave, and snap pictures of my bruised cheek and wrist. They tell me to call them if I remember anything else.

Letting out a long breath, I relax back into the sofa, trying to let the images of what we've just spoken about slip away from me.

I feel Marc before I see him.

'I'm proud of you, Sophia.'

He's behind me, and I feel his arms come over my shoulders and around my chest.

'It's done now.' I feel tears coming. 'Over with.'

Marc's arms tighten. 'I can hardly live with myself for not protecting you.'

'But you did,' I say. 'You saved me.'

'I should have been cleverer than Getty. It kills me to think what could have happened to you.'

'But it didn't.' I turn to him, slipping around in his arms. His eyes are cloudy. Sad.

'I'm doubling security,' says Marc. 'And I'll stay with you during your dress rehearsals and performances at the theatre. The whole time. I won't let you out of my sight.'

'Marc, I don't think ... the play. I don't think I can do it. After what just happened. I'm just too afraid. You were right. I should never have taken the part. I wasn't ready for all this ...'

My gaze is on the carpet. Marc puts a finger under my chin and very gently lifts my face so I'm looking into cloudy blue.

'You should play the part.' His eyes are soft, and I see the love in them.

'Marc, I don't know.'

'You were born to play that part. It's perfect for you. I was wrong to stop you taking it. I should have helped you from the start, but ... I was afraid.'

'You? Afraid?'

Marc smiles. 'Terrified. Of losing you. Of losing control of you.'

'And look what happened.'

We both smile.

'Don't let Getty ruin this for you. You've worked so hard, fought so hard. Your audience are waiting. I'll help you. We have one more week. I'll work with you. Help you get your confidence back.' He pulls me into his chest. 'And I'll protect you, Sophia. Always.'

106

The next week is both the longest and the shortest of my life.

It's long because Marc makes me do all sorts of training exercises with him, and arranges sessions with hypnotists and psychotherapists.

It's short because, before I know it, opening night is here.

I find the hypnotist really helpful. She gets me to work through the logic of what happened – and how unlikely it is that it will ever happen again. And she gives me techniques to help me focus on the present moment and reduce my anxiety.

Whenever I feel anxious, I squeeze my thumb and forefinger together, and it helps me calm down. It works. Kind of.

Marc arranges for me to see my family and Jen, too. He's so clever – he knows they're part of what I need for my recovery. He has Jen come and hang out at the townhouse, and even arranges a family meal in an Italian restaurant for Dad, Genoveva, Jen, Samuel and me. Marc comes too, of course, and it's great to see him play with Sam and chat with Jen and my dad.

I'm so relieved to see Dad up and well. He's positively glowing with health, and the doctors say he's in great shape.

Although we're closer than ever after what happened with Getty, Marc and I still haven't made love since the incident. Marc treats me like a fragile little doll. He lifts me carefully into bed at night, kisses me tenderly on the forehead, then folds me in his arms and watches me until I fall asleep. But he doesn't try to make love to me, and soon I begin to ache for that connection.

I love him so much, and I know he loves me, but until we're together properly, I know I'm not healed. Things aren't right.

Anyway. Opening night is here already. And I'm scared. The thumb and forefinger is working a little, but not a lot.

Marc drives me to the theatre and parks up by the stage entrance.

'You can do this,' he says, pulling up the handbrake.

I nod, staring at the red stage door. There are two security guards outside, and my heart beats fast at the sight of them. I grab Marc's hand.

'I don't know if I can.'

Marc turns to me, his expression serious. 'You can. Believe me. You can. Wait there.' He jumps out of the car and marches towards the security guards. Once he's checked their IDs, he opens the passenger door.

My legs are shaking as my feet hit the tarmac.

I take Marc's hand and pull him close to me.

'It's okay,' he says. 'I promise. You'll be okay.'

I wait in the wings, my heart beating hard in my throat. I'm holding Marc's hand so tight that I'm pretty sure I'm leaving nail marks in his palm.

I can hear the audience murmuring behind the heavy red curtain.

Oh my god. This is really it. This is really happening. I'm about to perform in a West End musical in front of thousands of people.

I don't know if I can do this.

I glance down at my free hand and see that it's shaking. My knees feel so weak that I'm amazed I'm still standing.

Boom boom!

The music starts and the big, swishing red curtain begins to rise.

Oh my god, oh my god. No. I can't do it. I can't.

I watch the shadowy grey audience appear as the curtain goes up, up, up.

Oh Christ.

The auditorium is packed. It's a full house.

Marc loosens his grip on my hand. 'Time for your debut,' he whispers.

I should be walking on stage, but I'm frozen. Completely frozen.

The curtain tune finishes, and I hear the first notes of *One True Love*, Belle's opening number.

I try to make my legs move, but they won't.

Breathe. Breathe.

Oh my god.

'Sophia.' The word is a whisper, but it sends rushes through my stomach. 'You can do this.'

I feel Marc's heat, and turn to see his handsome profile.

'I have stage fright.'

'Everyone gets stage fright.' Marc squeezes my hand. 'The actor's job is to overcome it. No matter what challenges they've faced.'

My eyes drift back to the audience. I bet some of them would be really happy if I choked and didn't make it on stage. What a great story for the newspapers.

The newspapers. I think of Getty. We still can't get an update on what's happening with him. We're not even allowed to know if he was taken into custody, but Marc's working on it.

No, I won't let Getty ruin this for me. Marc's right. I won't let him win.

I hold my chin up and stand tall. 'Yes,' I say, meeting Marc's eye. 'I can do this.'

'I know you can.'

I suck in a deep breath. The music is building up, and the audience are starting to mutter. I can imagine what they're saying.

'Shouldn't someone be on stage by now?'

'Has something gone wrong?'

One foot in front of the other. Here I go. Step. Step. I concentrate on my feet. One more step. Then another. And another. Suddenly, I'm there. On stage. On a real life West End stage in front of thousands of people.

I turn to the audience.

There's complete silence.

The music has passed the point where I should have started singing, and I race through my mind, trying to remember the second and third verses.

Okay. Okay. Here comes verse two. I try for the first line.

They call me beauty, but what is beauty anyway?

I open my mouth, but the words don't come out. It's like someone has iced up my vocal chords.

Come on, Sophia. Come on.

I turn and see Marc in the wings. I expect him to be frowning, but he's not. He's looking at me like he loves me. And suddenly the ice in my throat melts.

I sing the second line: '*Just a word, a silly thing that people say.*'

The line sounds croaky and thin, but I manage it. And from there, I manage the rest of the verse too. As the song goes on, my voice gets clearer and stronger. I put all my heart and soul into it, singing for all I'm worth, and bringing all the emotion I can to the words.

When the song finishes, I'm flushed and elated. I don't think I've won the audience over just yet, but I haven't lost them either. They haven't written me off.

I perform the 'lost in the woods' scene, and then Leo comes on stage.

The chemistry between us is good. We bounce off each other, and the audience laughs and gasps at the right points. When we sing together, it sounds good too.

By the end of the first act, I'm in my element, loving performing, loving the reaction of the audience. I can tell I'm connecting with them emotionally, and that makes me happy.

The curtain swishes down to mark the interval, and Leo and I wait for it to reach the ground before leaving the stage.

Before the curtain touches the wooden floor, I swear I see Cecile in the audience, two rows back. Seeing her unnerves me. She looks ... I don't know. Angry. But. Maybe I'm wrong. It's probably someone else. After all, why would she be at my opening night? I know we had a moment together, but we're far from friends.

I head for Marc.

'You were astonishing,' he tells me, putting his arms around me and pulling me to his chest. 'I didn't think I could love you more, but seeing you go on stage like that, after everything you've been through ...'

I let myself melt into him.

'You're due an outfit change,' he says.

'Yes.' I nod into his chest.

'I'll take you to your dressing room.'

108

In the dressing room, a beautiful blue dress covered in glass beads hangs over the mirror. It's Belle's dress for the second act, and I love the way it makes me feel – like a heroine from a historic romance.

'I'll leave you to dress,' says Marc. 'I'll be right here. By the door.'

'No.' I shake my head. 'Come in with me. This dress has so many buttons. I always struggle with them.'

I go to the mirror and scoop up my hair.

Marc comes into the dressing room and closes the door. He stands behind me and begins to unfasten my dress. I watch him in the mirror, and with every twist of his thumb, a little flash of desire grows in my stomach.

As Marc slips the dress down from my shoulders, I turn to him, the dress pooled around my ankles. I'm wearing the fairy tale underwear he bought me when we flew to his private island.

'We haven't made love since that day with Getty.' I put my hands around his neck, and my hair drops onto my shoulders.

Marc slips his fingers into my hair, and strokes and twists. 'Sophia -'

'I know what I want, Marc. I need to move on. Help me move on.'

'Here?'

'Yes, here. I want you, Marc. Don't you want me?'

Marc laughs. 'God, if you knew how much I want you.' He scoops me up and sits me on the dressing room table, his eyes devouring me. 'Are you sure you want this? Here? After everything that happened?'

'I'm sure. I want this more than anything.'

I pull Marc between my legs and feel how hard he is. He's throbbing against me, and I'm heating up too, my legs tightening against his hips.

'Wait.' Marc breathes, one hand falling flat against the mirror. 'This should be ... slow. I want to take my time with you. To show you how much I love you. I don't just want to fuck you in the dressing room.'

'Mr Blackwell.' I take his hand and slip it inside my panties. 'Being fucked in the dressing room is *exactly* what I want.'

Marc's hand stiffens. 'Oh God, why did you have to do that?'

'Show me you love me,' I whisper, rubbing his hand back and forth. I roll my head back and give a little sigh as his fingers move where I want them.

Marc's eyes close in that pained way that tells me he's losing control.

I moan as his fingers work me open, sliding back and forth.

'Oh Marc,' I murmur, my head lolling around my shoulders.

'God. I can't stop myself.' Marc pulls my panties aside and frees himself from his trousers.

He moves between my legs, and the most amazing shudder goes through me. I bite my lip as he pushes me open, little by little, working his way inside. And now he's all the way in, filling me up.

'Marc,' I moan.

'This is what you want?' he asks.

'This is what I want.'

Marc begins to move. Slow at first, then faster as he begins to lose it. The dressing table shakes as he thrusts deeper, and my head and back knock the mirror. I hear things roll from the table to the floor, but I don't care. This feels so, so good.

Marc groans, thrusting deep between my legs with such power and strength that my whole body moves where he moves.

'I love you,' I murmur. 'I love to feel you ... lose yourself.'

'I'm lost,' Marc says, his voice thick and deep. 'Trust me.' He keeps on thrusting. 'So, so lost. In the best possible way.'

I wrap my legs around him, pulling him closer, and his thrusts get deeper and deeper until all I can feel is him inside me. The dressing table rocks, my eyes close and pleasure builds up and up until ...

'Oh God. Oh Marc.'

My body explodes around him, and I cling to his shirt with my fingers, my legs weakening their grip.

Marc's eyes are forceful and his jaw hard. He pushes forward in one big huge thrust.

'Sophia,' he moans, collapsing against me, panting, pulling me close, winding my hair around his hand.

We cling to each other for a moment. Then Marc pulls back and strokes hair from my face, lifting me carefully off the dresser.

'I love you,' he says as my feet find the ground. 'God, I love you.'

I smile at him, feeling flushed. Happy. Exhilarated. I catch a glimpse of myself and see my cheeks are glowing.

'On with the show, Miss Rose.'

The second act goes perfectly. I deliver my lines smoothly, sing flawlessly and laugh joyously when Beast turns into a handsome prince.

Leo and I finish to a thunderous round of applause, and I even hear a few feet stamping. I'm guessing those feet belong to Jen and my dad.

I leave the stage happy. Elated. Marc is waiting for me in the wings, the tiniest of smiles on his face.

'They loved you,' he says.

'I wasn't perfect, but we've got thirty more shows to do.'

'No, you were perfect,' say Marc. 'I've arranged for Jen and your dad to meet us backstage. I've been told there's a get together in Leo's dressing room, and I thought you'd want to be part of it.'

I smile. 'Yes. I'd like that. Marc? What's wrong?'

He looks ... thoughtful.

'There's something I want to show you first. Come with me. To your dressing room.' He leads me down the backstage steps, me giggling like a schoolgirl.

'Marc? What is it?'

'You'll see.'

At my dressing room, I push open the door a little cautiously and peer inside.

'Oh *Marc*.'

Huge bouquets of ivy and red roses cover the dressing table, sofa and floor. There's hardly a part of the room that isn't decorated with gorgeous green leaves and red petals. The bouquets fill the space with colour and fragrance, and I stand there, grinning like an idiot, breathing in the gorgeous smell.

'This is just beautiful,' I say.

'Come inside.' Marc leads me in among the ivy leaves and soft roses, and clicks the door closed behind us.

'How did you manage this?' I smile at him teasingly. 'You were in the wings the whole time.'

'Let's just say I've learned the art of delegation via text message.'

I laugh. 'These bouquets are beautiful. So, so beautiful.'

'Just like you.' Marc takes my hands.

'So.'

'So.'

'I have something to ask you, Miss Rose.'

'And what is that, Mr Blackwell?'

Marc drops one of my hands and lowers himself onto one knee.

He takes a crushed velvet box from his pocket and holds it up to me. It's a gorgeous vibrant green colour and decorated with an embossed ivy leaf.

'Marc?'

Marc opens the box, and inside is a ring. An antique, I think – the gold band is thin and very yellow, and the diamond is a perfect pear shape. It's gorgeous. Just the sort of thing I like. Unusual, but pretty.

My hands begin to shake.

I look into Marc's eyes and he looks up into mine.

'Sophia Rose,' he says. 'Will you marry me?'

Want to hear what happens next to Sophia and Marc?

The third and final part of the Ivy trilogy, **'Bound By Ivy'** will be released in **July/August 2013**.

If you've already been in touch with me, then I'll

email you the exact date as soon as I know it. If you haven't emailed me before, get your free secret scene below and you'll be automatically added to my mailing list. Su xx

FREE SECRET SCENE FOR ALL READERS!

For a **free secret scene from 'Where the Ivy Grows'?**

Follow this link: http://eepurl.com/xytXj

Thank you for reading!
Dear Reader,

I'm the author of the Ivy Lessons, and want to thank you from the bottom of my heart for purchasing this book. Welcome to the devoted family – there are thousands of us now, and I love each and every one you, and hope you keep on reading.

If you enjoyed it, please help your friends discover a good read by tweeting and sharing. I pay attention to tweeters and sharers and will often seek you out and give you free, exclusive reads. Xx

Printed in Great Britain
by Amazon